About

Sebastian was born in 1984 in ...., ..., Essex. He has lived in Hert-fordshire his entire life and now resides in a small village with his wife and two young daughters, two cats and three chickens.

Having children of his own has dampened his fascination with the idea of testing himself in a post-apocalyptic scenario – so what better way to explore such worlds than through the telling of a story? *Axiom* is that story.

AXIOM

AXIOM

SEBASTIAN IVES

Unbound Digital

This edition first published in 2018

Unbound

6th Floor Mutual House, 70 Conduit Street, London W1S 2GF

www.unbound.com

ISBN (eBook): 978-1-912618-61-3

ISBN (Paperback): 978-1-912618-60-6

Design by Mecob

Printed and bound in Great Britain by Clays Ltd, Elcograf S.p.A.

For Anna, Beatrix and Primrose – Team Ives; all ways, always.

Special thanks and recognition reserved for James Hutchinson; without his incredibly generous support this book could never have happened – I owe you a pint, mate!

Dear Reader,

The book you are holding came about in a rather different way to most others. It was funded directly by readers through a new website: Unbound.

Unbound is the creation of three writers. We started the company because we believed there had to be a better deal for both writers and readers. On the Unbound website, authors share the ideas for the books they want to write directly with readers. If enough of you support the book by pledging for it in advance, we produce a beautifully bound special subscribers' edition and distribute a regular edition and e-book wherever books are sold, in shops and online.

This new way of publishing is actually a very old idea (Samuel Johnson funded his dictionary this way). We're just using the internet to build each writer a network of patrons. Here, at the back of this book, you'll find the names of all the people who made it happen.

Publishing in this way means readers are no longer just passive consumers of the books they buy, and authors are free to write the books they really want. They get a much fairer return too – half the profits their books generate, rather than a tiny percentage of the cover price.

If you're not yet a subscriber, we hope that you'll want to join our publishing revolution and have your name listed in one of our books in the future. To get you started, here is a £5 discount on your first pledge. Just visit unbound.com, make your pledge and type AXIOM19 in the promo code box when you check out.

Thank you for your support,

Dan, Justin and John
Founders, Unbound

Super Patrons

Sophie Gardiner
Sara Garrett
Damian Giaouris
Ricky Gibson
Gemma Hadley
Rachel Hann
Emily Harris
Jo Hodson
Mark Hollis
David Houssein
James Howe
Olexander Hryb
Len Hulley
James Rajesh Hutchison
Jay Ives
Les Ives
Sheila Ives
Lyndon Ives
Puck Jackson
Peter Jay
Daniel Jones
Jamie Kellett
Dan Kieran
Cliff Lineker
Maya Linhares-marx
Chloe Llewellyn
César López Esteban
Jim Lucas
Lee Mackley
Alex Macleod
Rebecca Maloy
Riad Mannan
Isabella Mascarenhas
Guy Mason
Paul Matthews
Deborah McKenzie

Mark Mcloughlin
Barry Mingard
Alex Mitchell
John Mitchinson
Sarah Morris
Kimberley Munns
Jan Munt
Carlo Navato
Jacquie Newby
John Newsome
Mike Newsome
Katie Nye
Tom O'Neill
Alison Orde
Nick Pajger
Ruslan Pashov
Justin Pollard
Jamie Pratt
Lisy Reading
Ann Rees
Reece Richardson
Sara Rogers
Vincent Roy Bannister
Veena Saha Gupta
Lynne Salisbury
Julian Schwarzenbach
Phil Seale
Sarah Sennett
Philip Shaw-Stewart
Lloyd Shepherd
Andy Shipp
Louie Somerville
Tanya Spencer
Quentin Spender
Michael Spraggs
Amy Stokes

Dani Strickland
Nat Sullivan
Matt Taylor
Alex Taylor
Chee Pinp Teoh
Vladimir Terzija
Julia Thacker
Charlie Thomason
Rowan Thompson
Simon Timmis
Peter Vosper
Daniel Waller
Suzie Waller
Tim Waller
Ching Yee Wan
Aled Williams
Sam Wright
Danielle Wyatt
Jinlei Xing
Rob Yates
Helen Yates

Axiom: *A premise or starting point of reasoning; an idea, a suggestion so evident as to be accepted as true without controversy or challenge.*

Part One

JOINT VENTURE AGREEMENT

THIS AGREEMENT is made this 23rd day June 2034 by and between the PARTIES: SolarTech Corporation and Yarlung Zambo Limited... the Parties are each willing to invest capital to finance the conduct, construction, maintenance and eventual total joint leadership of the business (herein referred to as Solacity Biome) due for completion and occupant ready by June 2035...

Article 1: Administration and Governance.

1.1 Obligations of the Parties – The Parties agree to work together to accomplish the objectives of Solacity Biome by performing construction directly, and strictly without the use of knowing subcontractors...

1.2 *Only* the agreed members of the aforementioned Leadership Committee shall be privy to the true nature of the Project...

... 1.7 Future Governance. Parties' Owners, CEOs and predetermined Executive Directors shall form the basis of the Leadership Committee. The Leadership Committee of Solacity Biome shall remain that of pure blood and direct decendants are to be appointed only.

Chapter 1

He lay awake, flat on his back atop a soft bed, his head sunk into a plump pillow. It was warm in the bedroom and it smelt of clean linen. A soft yellow sunlight came through a crack in the curtain and fell across his toes, which were peeking out of the end of the blanket. Across his bare upper body, her slight weight lying on him was a comfort. Her fingers were entwined in his chest hair and her head was nuzzled into the nape of his neck, her hair in his face not an irritation, but a wonderful concoction of honey and chocolate tones in both scent and colour. He felt he could lie here like this forever, listening to her gentle breathing. She shifted ever so slightly.

'Good morning, did you sleep well?' Bevan asked, and he genuinely wanted to know; he cared.

'Perfectly. I've never slept any other way but perfectly with you.'

'Let's just lie here all day. It's a graduation day, the Jurisdiction will be so quiet and I switched my shift with Teddy... and I made sure you'd not be needed at the generator.' He could feel it in his neck as a smile spread across her face. 'Mycroft Shuster is happy to cover for you.'

'Then we can stay here all day,' said Evelyn as she leant up on her elbow and shifted to face him. 'I love you, Bevan,' she said, her deep red brown hair falling away from her face, and for a fleeting second he saw her one imperfection – oddly the feature of her appearance he most liked – a small mole on her left collarbone. He looked into her beautiful face, her pale porcelain skin, unblemished and soft, her deep, caring eyes a wash of hazel and green, her full pink lips framing her perfect white teeth to create the most stunning of smiles. His heart leapt as he marvelled at this wonderful woman – she was the epitome of beauty and kindness and she was his, his wife, Evelyn Hughes.

He looked at her again now as he had done during their very first encounter. His love for her had never diminished; every second with her was better than the last. He smiled at the memory of their first meeting, and she leant forward to kiss him and softly whispered in his ear, 'Filakes...'

His confusion at the peculiar, nonsense word that she had whispered so seductively in his ear could not break the spell of happiness this moment had over him, but in the next second her face was changing. Her mouth gaping, her cracked lips pencil-thin, teeth razor-sharp, a lumpy brown slug of a tongue, her eyes completely black and frenzied, her '17' tattoo returning harsh and ugly against the white skin of her cheek. She was being torn away from him by an unseen force into a blackness that had formed behind her. She was screaming and struggling against it and she was smoke, she was blood, and she was gone.

He woke, eyes shooting open but his body frozen with fear, his jaw clenched painfully tight. He was covered in sweat; the sheet was damp with it. His breath was rapid and he could see it in the cold air in the room. His bed wasn't comfortable – it never had been – and his pillow was flat. No sun – it was winter and the sun was far too low for a month or so yet to crest the horizon and shed light on the city. Plus it had been years since he left the curtains just slightly open through the sleeping hours to help warm the bed; he kept the world well and truly shut out. The only light came from a small oil lamp in the room.

He'd been having this same nightmare for near on six years now, since shortly after she was taken. The whiplash of emotions he felt during the dream was still no less vivid, the happiness no less comforting, the horror equally terrifying. It still completely duped him every time. He was so sure of its reality; not even the absurd luxury of their surroundings or the perfectly unrealistic way in which they spoke to one another were a giveaway. That was until the terrible realisation, the awful transformation and the frantic awakening.

They had been together for three years and married for two of them. He recalled their first meeting vividly. At the time, Bevan had been gaining something of a reputation amongst the electrical engineers of J17. His team leader had decided he would test his skills and sent him to deal with a case of salt erosion on the generator's transformers. He'd felt confident of completing the task and arrived on site early and eager to please. He knew also that if he could get the job done before the generator supervisor arrived he would score some serious marks for intuition and application – who knew, maybe even a coveted day off?

The job could be dangerous, especially if conducted alone. It involved spraying a high-pressure jet of water onto live electrical equipment to blast off the salt. He'd changed into the rubber suit, an awkward unwieldy outfit that even in the eternal cold of Axiom soon became unbearably hot and sweaty. His clumpy thick-soled boots, like two bricks, made a dull thud which reverberated inside his helmet as he stepped up onto the rubber-based trolley. Bevan had clumsily picked up the hose. With the big thick black rubber gloves on, handling the leaky slippery hose was like wrestling an anaconda from a swamp. He'd flicked on the pump and the water spewed forth. Raising the nozzle, he aimed the jet at the nearest transformer and the clumps of salt splintered away from the metal. *Easy*, thought Bevan. *Who needs a supervisor?* He had been young and overly confident; looking back now he knew that he was just complacent, that it was just when he was most comfortable in a task that his concentration would dip and problems would arise. For no sooner had the thought of finding the job easy crossed his mind than an almighty spark exploded from the transformer. The electrical current rushed down the highly conductive water, and in the blink of an eye it had reached the steel hose cap; it couldn't reach the earth though, so the surge had erupted in Bevan's hands. The hose dropped from his grasp and he was hurled through the air some twelve feet, landing on his back in the dust with a crash. He recalled a blinding flash of white followed by the most complete dark.

The next thing he remembered he would never forget. Before he'd seen anything, he'd heard her counting, 'One, two, three, four, five,' a gentle, reassuring, determined voice that was like an angel whispering in his ears.

'One, two, three, four, five.' He felt a rhythmic pressure on his chest, a firm touch, small but skilled hands massaging his heart back to life.

'One, two, three, four, five.' Then he felt her lips on his, warm and soft. Her life-giving breath filling his lungs as he spluttered back to life like an old engine turning over. He opened his eyes and saw a curtain of dark hair moving away from his face, the angle of a neck and shoulder covered in a light sheen of perspiration, the patch of pale skin flawless but for a brown blemish on the collarbone. His gaze followed the line up her neck and he looked into those striking eyes.

'You may wish I hadn't just saved you,' she said. 'That piece of kit is ruined. The bosses will be pissed!' Her words were ominous but her tone was kind and her smile gave her away – she liked what she saw and she was pleased she had a chance to speak with him. 'Let's just say it was a freak gust of the wind that took the water some place it shouldn't,' she said.

'Thank you,' he croaked, offering a handshake, 'I'm Bevan.'

'You'll have to do better than that, Bevan,' she said taking his hand and winking at him, 'I'm Evelyn.'

From that moment on he did everything he could to please her, to thank her, and quicker than he ever thought possible, he came to know that he loved her completely. He would seek out gifts – legally or, if necessary, illegally – to make her smile. He would perform overly romantic gestures that made her friends envious and his friends mock (but secretly feel bad for their own inadequacies, he was sure). They spent all of their time outside of their shifts together. Evelyn moved into Bevan's home after just a matter of weeks and they made one another utterly happy. As the weeks turned to months he thought of her constantly, always wondering how she might react in given situations, what she might say to a question posed, what observation she might make, all the while knowing that he would no doubt act and speak in precisely the same way, such was the similarity between them. As the months added up and their time together came to be termed in years, Bevan proposed, she accepted and they married on one of the last days before the long dark winter, as the sun was setting for the first time since they'd met.

Since the day Evelyn was taken he'd never quite been the same.

For months afterwards he was just a shell of a man. He'd mope about the Jurisdiction when not on shift, hood up, hands stuffed in pockets, his eyes glazed over, unable to speak more than two words to anyone. He barely ate. While on shift, he went about his work with no emotion, no great thought – indeed it was a wonder he didn't electrocute himself during this time. He had even on several occasions found his hand hovering over a live wire, daring himself to take hold of it, to feel its searing heat fuse the skin of his palm to the metal, for the volts to surge through his flesh, blood and bone, and burn and char it all. At home he'd cried openly for hours on end, sat on the edge of *their* bed staring through bleary eyes at the walls. They said time was a healer. Bevan found that in fact time was just a nullifier. It just gave you the chance to work out coping mechanisms, to build unseen barriers within yourself to keep out the darker thoughts. There was nothing anyone could say to make him move on from Evelyn, there was nothing he could do to forget her. He never once accepted that she was dead. She was out there, beyond the walls of Axiom, and when he returned home after his shift, instead of tears he would sit or lie and think of her out there. On good days he'd think of her being OK, leading a life that was… OK. In his mind, on the bad days… she was not OK.

His alarm began to sound – every J17 home was fitted with one, and it would ring for five consecutive minutes after which those with a shift would have 40 minutes to report for the start of it. He rose to a sitting position from his cold and sweat-soaked bed, picked up the cup containing the last of yesterday's ration of water and threw it into his face. Pulling his jumper, made from human hair, on over his head did the job of drying his face. He'd slept in his best trousers and so now he stood up and shuffled his already sock-clad feet into his boots and grabbed his overcoat, gloves and hat.

He cracked the curtains and peered out into the gloom. Up and down the street, others were rising and readying for the day ahead. Drawing back from the cold glass he saw his own reflection, a sight he usually tried to avoid.

Bevan Hughes was twenty-nine years old, but the face staring back at him looked older. An only child who had his father's looks – blue eyes, a full crop of blond hair, a square chin that was always covered in rusty blond stubble. In a strange way he actually quite liked how the '17' tattoo stood out against his olive skin and made his eyes seem even bluer. Evelyn had always said he carried an air of charisma, that he was effortlessly magnetic to others, and he supposed it did seem like people enjoyed being around him, sought him out for conversation or company. She always told him that just as he was adept with manipulating and handling machines and electrical currents, so he had a knack of saying the right thing. When he'd laughed this off as nonsense, she'd said that probably his greatest charm, of course, was that he was completely oblivious to these facts.

He closed the curtains, making sure there was no gap between them, and made his way to the kitchen.

His home was a combination of sheet metal, simple brickwork and a layer of insulation – the same as all the other homes in J17 and ninety per cent of those in the other Jurisdictions of Axiom. It was a single–storey property comprising three rooms – a living space which doubled as a bedroom, a kitchen and a toilet. He skirted around his bed and crossed the bedroom-cum-living-area to his kitchen. He stood momentarily in the doorway and let out the smallest, saddest of laughs to himself as he recalled how Evelyn would always just call it the 'food prep room': she always said that 'to call it a kitchen would be to call a brick shithouse an en suite bathroom'. He wiggled free a knife he'd left buried in a chopping board and carved himself off a slice of bread for breakfast. It was stale and dry, and the glass of water he washed it down with tasted of the dust which had settled on its surface. He moved to the small closet 'room' which housed his toilet and nothing else. (Since water was too precious, all Residents used the communal showers and baths, the Powers-That-Be – specifically Eleanor De Sanctis, Axiom's resident dictator – having decided that they could not be trusted with their own supply.) He let out a long stream of urine acompanied by a sigh of relief.

Within his home there was no colour; everything was a shade of grey, black, sludgy green or brown. Everything was hard too; the bedding, a single towel and his limited supply of clothes were the only soft things in the house. Bevan's possessions, the contents of his home, consisted of the bare essentials, just one of what he needed and no more; after Evelyn was taken, for example, he'd even traded her set of cutlery for a pair of fingerless gloves. In fact he had hardly kept any of her belongings. The sight of her hairbrush, the smell of her pillow beside him at night, even the touch of her clothes would send him back to those dark days. It was better they were traded away.

There was one difference betwen Bevan's home and the other Residents' however. He was a resourceful, creative and curious man. The panelling on the dividing wall of the living room and the toilet – it required the sharpest of senses to see it, but it was false. Before he left the house for the day he had to collect a couple of items secreted away in the false walls. He pushed the uppermost corner gently and the spring–activated latch released the door which swung open on well–oiled hinges. A storage space of five shelves from floor to ceiling were revealed, each shelf approximately ten inches deep and all full of electrical items from a time long forgotten. A beard trimmer, a food processor, a halogen lamp, a mini–refrigerator, an electric carving knife, a kettle, a toaster, a convection heater, a soldering iron, a hairdryer (this was Evelyn's), a small device with a cable with ear plugs attached that opened to reveal a space for a thin circular item to sit in – an item that Bevan had never been able to find, a small shredding machine, an electric toothbrush, a power drill, a fan, an iron and a grilling machine. There was a small tool box full of wire cutters and strippers, spark plugs, nuts, bolts and screws and a coil of solder. They were of course all illegal, and he risked being Farmed if caught with them. More risky than ownership of this treasure trove though, and a hundred times more likely to land him in the deepest of trouble, was the fact that he had rewired and rigged his home so that he had access to a constant electricity supply at the flick of a switch, also concealed in the wall cavity. Electricity was very much a rationed luxury. The only items that had been used more than two or three times were the heater and the soldering iron. In truth, Bevan neither needed nor cared for the tasks they performed. It was more about his love for electricity, the power it provided and the complexity of the devices themselves. He loved to acquire them in poor condition, disassemble them and spend months seeking out the parts to repair them, and he revelled in the accomplishment of their whirring, buzzing, humming and blinking back into life again.

He stood before his precious contraband and ran his fingers lightly over all the devices in front of him. He felt cold smooth plastic and metal, the worn edges of the various dials and buttons, until his hand settled on his most prized possession. He carefully lifted it from the shelf. It was not a large device, no bigger than a book and much thinner. He'd traded it for a large plastic bowl a month ago down in the Merchants' Quarter. The stall owner had roared with laughter as he made the exchange and turned for home – Bevan had heard him exclaim to another how some mad man had just traded in a good, useful bowl for a useless piece of junk. Bevan was intrigued though. He'd immediately spotted a port along the base of the device and was quite sure that back home, amongst his collection of cables, he had one that would fit this thing, the likes of which he'd never seen before. It had a hard rubber back and the front was toughened glass from edge to edge and top to bottom. It had a button on the top and two more along the left side and along the bottom there were two small ports. He caught a glimpse of himself again in its dark reflective surface and instinctively swept his hand through his great cow's lick of a side-parted quiff. He gently removed the charging cable – it and the fridge were the only items he always left plugged in but the fridge had come second. This special piece of kit was the main reason for taking the decision to hardwire his home into the power grid. Prior to its discovery he had been quite happy to only play with his toys during the allocated times. Its screen burst into light, and an image Bevan had looked at every morning and night since he'd acquired it filled the screen. He'd been right about having the correct cable but since that first exciting day when he'd plugged it in and it satisfyingly pinged into life after a full charge he had never been able to get it to do anything more than display this same image. It was broken; it was frozen and unresponsive. Seared into its screen was something that had more than piqued Bevan's interest. He knew that he was well and truly obsessed with knowing more, with trying to learn whether there was any truth to the words he knew off by heart by now but still stood and reread for the umpteenth time. The text which fascinated him so was flanked on either sides by images. There was one offering fancy-looking shoes, which promised a special discount just for the reader. Another showed a delicious meal of perfectly cooked meat, potatoes and a vegetable the likes of which Bevan had never seen all coated in a deep red sauce; according to the accompanying text you could dine on such a feast at 'Olivia's Ristorante di Carne'. Sometimes Bevan would stare at Olivia's meal and just salivate. More tantilising still though was the main body of text. Across the top of the passage there was a banner that read 'The Solacity Daily Chronicle', and the date was marked across the bottom – '22 July 2147'.

Travelling with the speed of light – The new cell that could mobilise us again!

NO LONGER HELD captive by our own salvation, we could be on the move again. In an exclusive reveal, The Daily Chronicle can confirm that a new prototype solar cell battery technology could prove the turning point in mobilising our populace once more.

'SolarMotive', a niche subsidiary business of our city's founding company and majority representatives on the leadership committee, 'SolarTech Corporation', have been working exclusively on a revolutionary solar powered cell. The Mark 17 CellBatt can capture, store and manipulate the energy of the sun in such a way that it might be able to literally power and move an entire biome.

As all good citizens know, our current biomes' membranes very effectively and efficiently capture and store enough solar energy to power Our Great Sanctuary. But like all good citizens know, power remains at a premium and has to be strictly governed. 'Our new Cell-Batts can absorb and utilise solar power like never before' says Managing Director and Chief Engineer, Efran Mourdorant. 'The Mark 17 is able to take this energy and convert it into drive-train motion at precisely the same time that it is gathering more.' And, if Mourdorant and his team are to be believed, it can do this at alarming and impressive rates.

Our current biomes work because The Founders saw fit to capture and store energy over a period of years prior to tidal lock and mass population of Our Great Sanctuary. At current rates of usage we merely use and top up the originally stored energy reserves. A report from the Leadership Committee six years ago following the grand opening of Biome4 stated that 'should the plans for expansion of Our Great Sanctuary be finalised and carried out, Biome5 would be required to collect and store energy for a full two years before it could be occupied and the power utilised by citizens. Immediate use would cause power leaching from the established biomes and consumption surpassing the collection and storage rate.'

There is no such issue with SolarMotive's revolutionary technology. 'It's like filling a bucket with a hole in the bottom with water at precisely the same rate at which it is leaking. The bucket will always be full but you're getting something useful out the other end,' Mourdorant explained in our exclusive interview. 'We've been able to power a drive train that we predict could propel a small village along at a rate of 30mph while sustaining a comfortable level of lifestyle for say fifty to sixty people without a problem! We could move, actually *move* location – a previously unheard of proposal. The intense heat provides us with life but it also keeps us in place – what more is out there?'

These are bold and exciting claims but are still to be tested. Mourdorant is due to meet with the Leadership Committee in the coming weeks to gain permission to develop what he calls a 'test village' comprising a Mark17 CellBatt biome membrane and fifteen semi-permanent structures mimicking housing and manufacturing sheds. All of which will sit atop a specially designed drivable, manoeuvrable rig. The aim would be to venture away from the city for some 30 miles at the predicted 30mph speed and return, without stopping to store energy, undepleted.

It is perhaps on this point that some might have concerns. Carter LeShay, CEO of UltraViolet Securities, the city's chief supplier to the enforcement police, questions the desire and need to be mobile. 'Why venture away from this blessed haven? Why would any man want to leave the borders of Our Great Sanctuary? We have everything we need here. What would stop investors building their own mobile biome villages, leaving Solacity and starting up mini-dictatorships all around us? They'll strip the land of resources then look enviously towards us, and likely act violently. I'd sooner see this kind of kit used for increased surveillance and security measures.' It is a strong counter–argument and perhaps one that will be shared by the Leadership Committee who have always wished to remove competition beyond our borders and keep all that we have inside the biomes.

It remains to be seen how SolarMotive's new technology will be utilised; it is bound to divide opinion amongst citizens, investors and the Leadership Committee alike, but it could have the real potential to change the way we consume our solar power permanently.

Bevan tapped the button on the top of his tablet and the screen went dark. He touched it again and the familiar yet mysterious news story reappeared. It was all it had ever shown him but it seemed likely that it should do a whole lot more. He'd thought it through and his best guess was that another device could be plugged into one of its ports and he could then control it in some way, perhaps move the images around and read more. He chewed the inside of his cheek as he contemplated all it could mean – could this other place exist? Was Solacity out there still? Had this Efran guy been successful with his fantastical – but not impossible, Bevan knew – technology? Most of all though he wondered if, and had hope that, maybe Evelyn could have found sanctuary there. He was certain it wasn't fiction. It was not just a story but rather a piece of news – it was fact and opinion woven together to tell real people about a real event. It had awoken an urge in him to know more, a thirst for more knowledge about what it could all mean. He knew that in the old world everything had been mass-produced. There had to be more of these devices and if he could just find one perhaps it would hold some more answers or offer up some more clues. He pushed the button a final time and the screen went black. He plugged it back in and set it back down upon the shelf.

On the way out of the house he quickly removed a package from the mini-refrigerator, stuffing it into his coat pocket. Before leaving the house for his shift he made sure to carefully replace the wall panelling.

Chapter 2

General Curtis Stricken could see the cattle's breath in the freezing air of winter, chilled even further by two weeks of bitter easterlies and unrelenting cloud cover. Though it had been risen for some weeks now, the sun was still not quite high enough to get above the city walls. It wouldn't be long before it crested the walls and spring would have officially arrived. So they had huddled together for warmth in a corner on the far side of the compound, heads bowed against the wind blowing in from the icy wastes to the east, in a circle of dim light afforded by one of the overhanging lamps.

The Farm, or Jurisdiction 13, was roughly a square mile of cattle sheds, free–range paddocks and feeding stations, encircled and sectioned off into smaller pens to segregate the herds by twelve–foot–tall electric fencing atop of which sat coils of barbed wire. It housed around six–and–a–half thousand head of cattle, was lit by oil burning lamps and was overlooked by armed guard towers – the meat was one of the most precious commodities in all the city, it was strong trading currency in the black market, a delicacy enjoyed by only a select few high–ranking officials regularly and the average Resident just once a year at a graduation ceremony.

Others might have been uncomfortable in his role, given the exact nature of the *cattle*, but not him. Stricken knew himself to be a blunt instrument, a tool of the system used to bludgeon the populace to ensure order was kept. He enjoyed his role and allowed most thoughts outside of his orders to pass him by. It was this way, it always had been.

His lofty position in the hierarchy of the ruling regime meant that he knew things of the past, so he knew of course that before the history he'd been taught, before Axiom existed and its society conducted itself in the way that he fully accepted, there had been something and somewhere completely different. It meant nothing to him though; that world had been erased as if it never was. *All* the other Residents of the nine Jurisdictions of Axiom were taught, and so felt they knew categorically, that there was nothing and nowhere else. It was the centre of the earth, their entire world and the only beacon of civilisation situated on a thin strip of the Earth that was habitable. An island in a sea of nothing. A fully functioning society held within a walled city, Axiom sat in a bleak wilderness of tall pine trees, among canyons of razor-sharp rock and jagged cliff faces deeper than the eye could gauge, wedged between relentless sunlight and endless dark.

Stricken had been out beyond the walls, had travelled east into a wasteland of frozen open tundra, of snow-covered mountains with flaming, smoking, lava-filled caps, where temperatures plummeted to incomprehensible levels below minus, until eventually, just as his Tutor had taught him as a young boy, he'd reached a wall, almost a mile high, of impenetrable solid ice. Nearly half of all the world's oceans and seas held in one ice shelf of titanic proportions, he'd been taught. West revealed an opposite world of searing heat, ash and rock, as desolate as the surface of Mars. Here not a drop of water could be found and anything that would burn was long gone. One could not travel far westward before the intense sun began to blister and scorch the skin. It had not been since before forever that any intrepid explorers had travelled to properly map out the world, longer still that anyone had heard or uttered rumour of another settlement, and no–one had ever arrived at the gates of Axiom to tell them they weren't alone. Alone here in this little patch of civilisation sat within the thin sliver of twilight zone between the dayside and nightside hemispheres of an Earth that had been 'tidal-locked', as his Tutor called it, for as long as anyone remembered.

It was this way, it always had been.

The De Sanctis family had always ruled over the city. Had always been Stricken's 'employers', masters and authority. The laws and rules that governed this society – those of trade, education, occupation, life and death, the food and supply chains – he and all Residents accepted, as established and engrained. There was no other reference point for the Residents; after all, one could only question How Things Are if there was a tangible alternative.

From his current vantage point, Stricken could see the Central Bastion, occupied by Eleanor De Sanctis, in its own secure area, standing proud and imposing over the rest of Axiom. He could trace out the divisions of the Jurisdictions' borders. The Bastion was surrounded by two concentric zones, each partitioned by radial walls into even sections, three in the inner zone – J1, 3 and 5 – and six in the outer zone – J7, 9, 11, 13, 15 and 17. The Residents were born in their Jurisdiction, lived in their Jurisdiction and died in their Jurisdiction. While Curtis had free rein, the average Resident only crossed to another area of the city to perform specific tasks, scheduled and supervised, or during strictly monitored slots in the day for trade only. They were given a tattoo under their right eye to mark them with their corresponding number; there could never be any misunderstanding of where they were from and the role they were born to carry out.

On the date of their third birthday, children were taken to J5, or the 'Jurisdiction of the Corruptible', where they remained until their graduation ceremony on their twelfth year. They wouldn't see their parents again until they rejoined the general populace. During this time they learned the ways of Axiom, and of their future responsibilities, their role in the community. There was nothing else they were told or taught, no external factors to sway their opinions – no tangible alternative. If by their twelfth year they were not proficient in their roles, they were Farmed. *Axiom carries no passengers* was an established piece of De Sanctis doctrine.

J1 was Curtis Stricken's private playground: no women lived there, no children were born there; its only permanent inhabitants were the General himself and his elite unit, the Shrouded. J1 was a law unto itself, and Stricken loved it there. He and his men regularly threw debauched parties, the epitome of excess – an orgy of food, alcohol, gambling and sex. Murders occurred on a whim. Some may have seen the reasoning for these killings as seemingly insignificant 'offences', but Stricken was a pedant for the rules. It housed the only brewery in the city, a great factory that churned out gallons of poli. The potent alcohol was only (legally) consumed here and Stricken was a big fan of the potent local tipple. J1 Residents demanded goods and services; they did not trade for them.

Young Residents of Jurisdictions 7, 9 and 11 discovered, amongst other things, what it took to drill for and extract, refine and utilise oil.

They mastered the skills of processing foods and of growing crops in the UV houses, learned how to manufacture furniture and clothing, developed expertise in construction, ice gathering and water purification. These were the cogs of Axiom; they were the knowledge and labour base of all that was required to make the city function. They were provided with food and water, occasional electrical power and all that they required to lead simple lives. Goods and services were traded; there were no other forms of currency.

Those born in military J3 were given combat, espionage, physical, weapons and survival training. Stricken found he spent a large portion of his time here – he enjoyed the sport of challenging (and always beating) the upcoming stars of the Jurisdiction. These young Residents had the laws of the society engrained in them, so they would be capable of enforcing them as second nature, without question. They were to become the police, the guards and the army. Like all other Jurisdictions, those who were not physically or emotionally capable of the tasks of their birthright were given to the Farms; they went on to serve Axiom in another way.

J17 was the smallest section of Axiom. Its Residents were male and were responsible for generating, transmitting and distributing safe electrical power. Supply was provided twenty-four seven to the Central Bastion and J1, and for the hours immediately prior to and after the designated working hours to the other Jurisdictions. They also maintained and monitored the UV houses for power supply, the electrical fences for the Farm and the city gates.

J15 was a dead zone, abandoned after the ground had been found to be unstable some seventy-odd years ago. Two hundred and seventeen Residents had lost their lives when several of the old factories collapsed into a deep sinkhole. It was nothing but a derelict section of the city left to wrack and ruin, attacked by the elements, the cold, the wet and the ice. The only people who ventured into J15 were Click addicts and those willing to risk being sent to the Farm for dealing in illegal goods and services. If the Shrouded or J3 were not deployed beyond the walls to hunt and exterminate Ferals, they were often to be found flushing out the lawless in J15 – each of which was another of Stricken's favourite pastimes.

Stricken had seen at first-hand, and had made it abundantly clear to all, that the world beyond Axiom's walls was not a better place, the grass was most certainly not greener. He would send out the Shrouded and have them whisper in ears, shout in public, sow seeds of doubt in the minds of the common Resident – Axiom was the best they could hope for. If the environment didn't take them some wild creature certainly could, and should they somehow manage to survive those two, then there was also the enemy from without to contend with. These small groups of people the Residents of Axiom called 'Ferals' were scattered, divided and leaderless; still the Ferals clung to life – through raiding the city mostly, when opportunity arose. They would take any useful resources and people (ideally women). They were vilified and feared. They survived by hunting one another and the wild creatures left in the world and gathering the scant edible plant life that remained.

In its thin band of twilight encircling the tide-locked Earth, meanwhile, Axiom received just enough heat not to freeze over and just enough cold not to be scorched. It sat within a relatively short journey of the frozen water and was built over a vast underground lake of oil. So every Resident was reminded of the sheer level of luck their descendants had when the world changed and they found themselves in the perfect location for continuing life. Quite simply, Axiom was the very best one could hope for. Toe the line and it would provide you with all you needed.

Of course there are always winners and losers; some were not so lucky.

Curtis Stricken held his position at the smart end of his rifle. Keeping one hand on the trigger, he released his grasp on the support grip and swept the light snow that had begun to drift slowly down from his well-groomed dark buzz-cut hair which, just like his thick beard, was flecked with grey; he knew that the herd could see him up on the gangway and that his tall, broad shoulders and muscular physique would make for an imposing figure above them, backlit by the gloomy sky. The slaughter of cattle was best conducted from the towers; it was not always safe to venture into the pens – one could be quickly overrun by a herd. So the animals were guarded from the outside by guns and kept in by the electric fencing. No-one got in, none left alive. Slaughtering them wasn't part of his remit, but quite simply Curtis Stricken took great delight in the pursuit, persecution and more often than not, the execution of prey. Over the years he had proven himself to be as much a lethal weapon as the one currently braced against his shoulder. Covered in the scars of combat, including a sickle-shaped one that bracketed his right eye and a grisly puncture wound that sat just at the point where jaw met throat, he was a living legend, he knew – but not the good kind. He was, to most in the city, a walking demon, a monster with authority. He held not a hint of mercy or remorse for the malicious and vicious acts he often carried out. He'd headed up the security force that imposed Axiom's laws and regulations for over twenty-five seasons, right-hand man to Eleanor De Sanctis.

His upper body was heavily inked. His three vices were: killing, women and tattoos. The only man he had ever feared and the predecessor to his role, his father, had insisted he receive the obligatory tattoo of his Jurisdiction, like all other Residents of Axiom, directly under this right eye. It was his first and, like all his others, it held significant meaning to him – they were symbols of achievements, of milestones and actions. Some were abstract, others realistic depictions of those he had fought and killed, others of those he had respected, places he had been and things he had seen.

The largest tattoo and the one of which he was most proud adorned his entire back – a stag's head of incredible detail. Individual hairs, eyelashes and mottling of the skin around the nostrils, the delicate patterning in the irises of its eyes, were all intricately etched into his skin. Its velvety antlers spread out from its crown and snaked their way across and over the General's shoulders and partially down his triceps – the left one was snapped at its furthestmost tine. It stared out from between Stricken's shoulder blades, deep with emotion and a sternness that showed it was ready to rut – and rut it had.

In addition to the usual ceremony, Curtis' father, General Magnus Stricken, a man as hard and cruel as any had known (prior to Curtis), had devised a separate rite of passage for his son and eventual successor on top of the standard ceremony. It was to be a day of firsts for

Stricken junior, which had begun with his father taking him and a small unit of the Shrouded out beyond the walls of Axiom. A well-armed intimidating force, they went unchallenged as they journeyed a short way through the Barrier forest until they reached a makeshift enclosure within which the test had taken place. Curtis recalled that, as he stood before the enclosure and a sense of what awaited him became clear, he simply thought that there would be meat for a mighty feast for celebration or mourning – the outcome of his test would determine which.

Into the enclosure Magnus had placed a dominant male red deer. This mighty stag had been captured at the peak of his powers, a proud owner of a large harem of hinds. He then had young Curtis brought out to the Farm.

'Take my hunting knife, son,' Magnus had said, offering out the handle while holding the dull edge of the blade. Curtis had taken it without hesitation. In truth, it had looked a little absurd, like a toddler with a broadsword. It felt heavy in his small hands, but a good kind of heavy, he had thought, not so much so that it might be restrictive, but rather that when swung or thrust correctly it would cause some serious damage. The blade had been paper-thin and incredibly sharp. 'I expect to be dining on venison this evening,' said his father, swinging open the enclosure's gate. Curtis strode through the opening and in with the beast. The gate rattled shut behind him.

His heart was racing but he was not afraid. It was, as he saw it, a glorious opportunity to show his father and all those he would one day command that he was worthy of the name and their respect. The stag was full of testosterone and it was agitated. It bellowed at the boy, puffed out its chest and stood tall and proud, its deep red coat the colour of pooled blood. It began to walk parallel to its challenger, sizing up the competition, Curtis did likewise and so they began to circle one another. The deer grew frustrated; to its mind this was clearly a lesser animal – its physical stature was inferior, its weapons so small in comparison to its own great rack of antlers and yet the boy would not back down, but stood defiant. The boy would not be intimidated. The boy insisted on a fight. The stag ceased its circling; it had had enough.

It stamped its front hoof in the dirt, the partially frozen earth cracking and squelching at the impact. It lowered its head and charged.

The space between them was covered in a flash; the boy could not avoid the impact. He parried as best he could with the knife, the metal connecting with the antler made a sound like a wooden bat perfectly striking a hard ball, and a large piece of the tine splintered away. The beast was undeterred though, and ploughed Curtis's young body into the fencing. He was entangled in a web of bone; he heard and felt the cracking of several of his own ribs. The wind well and truly knocked out of him, he slumped forward, his full weight supported by the animal's head. The stag did not welcome this; it snorted loudly and violently thrashed its head in an attempt to dislodge the boy. He was lifted off his feet, smashed harder into the chain link fence, and as he dropped back down his only meaningful contribution to the contest, the snapped antler, stabbed through his lower jaw.

He was impaled. Blood gushed from the wound but the antler had miraculously missed both his artery and windpipe. Feeling bettered by a superior foe, knowing he would be left in the dirt to bleed to death, Curtis was not scared, but instead he was furious at the defeat and just as he was moving in his mind to accept his fate he heard his father tut. A sound not more than a split second in length, but it said a thousand things that Curtis would not abide, did not agree with and was suddenly determined to show were falsely and too promptly assumed.

He recalled the knife in his hand and as the stag took a step back ready to thrash again, the boy raised his head and slid himself free from the sheared antler – the pain was exquisite. He reached out with his empty hand, grabbed at the nearest antler and twisted the surprised animal's head to the side, exposing its throat. He plunged the knife deep into the soft flesh, twisted and slid the blade free. The stag grunted and exhaled its final breath. The beast slumped down dead; the boy slumped down exhausted. The adversaries lay face to face on the ground and Curtis Stricken gurgled out a triumphant and defiant laugh.

Stricken scratched the old wound under his chin and gave a wry smile. Perhaps next time he'd simply enter the pen below him with a knife in hand and slaughter his chosen target just like he had that

stag all those years ago. Through the scope there was still no movement; this small herd had not shifted position for over half an hour or
more. Stricken's joints were seizing up in the cold as he stood with
his legs braced shoulder distance apart. The muzzle of the rifle was
resting on the rail of the guard tower's adjoining walkway. He was
used to this waiting game and he knew the cattle would need to move
soon or they'd freeze to death. A snowflake drifted down and landed
on the scope's lens and briefly distracted him. Without shifting position or removing his ghostly-pale blue eye from the piece, Stricken
reached forward and with the thumb of his left hand rubbed it away.
As his hand returned to the weapon, the animal he had been focusing
on shifted its head to glance across the compound, and in a heartbeat
he squeezed the trigger. The crack of a single round being discharged
rung out, with an echo that would be heard all across Axiom.

Below him in the dirt, Stricken was pleased to see that his intended
target was dead, just another slaughtered bull. It was a seventeen-
year-old boy; its face was gone, removed by his bullet. By the looks of
things it had been born to the Farm, a prime specimen. Lean defined
muscles from a life of physical exertion and regular feeds from the
farmhands. He would be the centrepiece to this evening's party dinner. His offal the base ingredient for cattle feed, his long blond hair
sent to the cloth manufacturers of Jurisdiction 9 and his fat processed
to make soap. To Stricken's annoyance though, the bullet had rico-
cheted off the skull and not come out clean. Instead it had changed
trajectory and continued its deadly journey straight through the chest
of another member of the herd. The bullet's final resting place was in
the lung of a scrawny fifty-seven-year-old female. She wouldn't go
to waste though; there was always demand for low-grade burgers or
sausages in the hedonistic clubs of Jurisdiction 1.

Chapter 3

Stepping out into the street, Bevan looked up to the sky while buttoning up his coat and putting up his hood. It was perhaps slightly lighter outside than it had been for months – *slightly*, since it was always a dim half-light, but it had also felt marginally warmer the last few days, maybe just a degree or two. Winter was coming to an end – spring would come soon and then summer would be following on its heels. The sun would climb just a short way but it would be enough to breach the top of the city wall and cast light down upon them.

Still, there was a wind blowing up the street now, and he knew it was going to be a long day working up on the gangways with that wind causing everything to sway and shake. None of Axiom was picturesque or pretty, but J17 was outright drab, desperately so. Along Bevan's street there was a single grey stone road that was so infrequently used by the handful of Resident-owned vehicles that it was almost indistinguishable from the pavements flanking it. Dotted in amongst the houses were power substations, and electrical cabling ran in vast bunches from the simple timber pylons out over the top of all the buildings, snaking away from J17 to the rest of Axiom. The air audibly hummed with electrical current, and all around there was an aroma – ozone. The electricity itself, of course, had no smell, but the combination of gases produced by sparks created this mild sulphur-like scent that clung to everything in J17. It coated the buildings and even the people and all they owned.

It was just a short walk across to the Farms so there would be time for a quick detour before the shift started. His co-workers were also emerging from their homes and were all heading off to complete their shifts. There were always repairs to the grid to be made, projects going on to increase or add power to existing and new buildings, generators to be manned, substations, converters, circuit breakers and transformers to be maintained, updated and developed. It was the Residents of J17's collective task to ensure that the power never went out throughout the city of Axiom; of the utmost priority were the central bastion, J1 and the Farm's fences. For some time now, Bevan had been assigned to work at the J13 Farms, checking, rechecking, testing, maintaining and repairing the fences along the high gangways that linked all the guard towers – the cattle could never get loose.

He cut across the street, head bowed against the wind and his hands in his pockets. All about him his fellow electrical engineers were stirring from their own sleep and making their ways to work.

'Morning, Bev,' came a yell. 'Quick pit stop before work?'. It was Teddy. Bevan looked up to see him stepping out of the side alley that led through to the home he shared with his family. He trotted over, one thumb up, one thumb down, gesturing to him, yes or no? Bevan took his left hand out of his pocket and raised it high, thumbs up.

Teddy Smithers was big. Big, not fat – there were just a handful in Axiom who you could ever say were overweight. He was tall, broad and stocky, his torso a steel drum, his arms twice that of Bevan's, and his hands were like shovels. He had to barter harder and trade more items to get his clothes since they were made of considerably more material than the average Resident's. He had a great mohawk which he sported like some kind of giant crested bird. His skin was so dark it was difficult to see his black '17' tattoo. For all his physical size, his kindness and his generosity were just as big, and he always seemed unshakeably cheerful. It was not often that one might see him without his huge beaming smile.

Together, nowadays, Bevan and Teddy were an odd couple, one more often than not brooding and lost in his thoughts, the other eternally content and positive.

An oversized teddy bear wasn't a bad way to describe Teddy, and amongst his colleagues on the construction team he was known as 'Grizzly'. Teddy was married and had two children, a son and a daughter – currently an extremely rare family set-up in Axiom since they were in the midst of a one-child policy enforced upon their generation – thirty years in which women were only given legal licence to birth one child. In this way Axiom's population remained relatively static. People had their places and their roles. The Authority-to-Resident ratio was maintained and the resources managed. The boy, Teddy Jnr or 'Lil Ted' was in J5, learning the ways of oil refinement.

He was the spitting image of his father, tall for his age but proudly sporting a huge perfectly round afro instead of Teddy's Mohican. Everyone knew that Lil Ted was destined for a high ranking position, he was bright, forthright and fearless. He was the pride of the Smithers family.

Lil Ted's sister and Grizzly's daughter was the elder of the two. Grace had graduated five freezes ago and was working an unusual mixed job as an electrical engineer on the systems that controlled the city's single vast security gate but, since it was only opened perhaps three times a year, she also doubled as a (very) low-ranking J3 security guard. Grace was also not technically Teddy's daughter, but his niece. Grace had never been told that her birth parents were killed in a fertiliser tank explosion just days after her birth, but she suspected that she was different – after all, why had her parents been given special dispensation to have a second child? Teddy and Monika loved her completely, as if she were their own – no more nor less than they did Lil Ted. Grace, though, was not without her difficulties: she was headstrong, fiery and stubbornly uncooperative.

Teddy and Bevan had been fast friends from their first days in J5. In a pattern that had continued throughout their adult lives, it had been a five-year-old Bevan, curious as ever, who had snuck off to wonder at and meddle with the electronic combination lock to their dormitory. It wasn't through a desire to escape but rather to play with and investigate the only remotely interesting thing in the entire block. Its bright red illuminated numbers and the 'dit, dit, dit' sound it had made when Tutor had sealed them in before bedtime had been a temptation to his curiosity.

Bevan had lain there just staring at the red glow on the far side of the dorm. He could not resist. He'd hopped out of his bed, and when his small bare feet touched the cold concrete floor, it had taken his breath away and his knees began to tremble from the excitement – or was it shivering from the cold? He'd wrapped his blankets around his shoulders and stealthily padded over to the door. Reached out to touch the number '1'.

'Hey, psst, no, you'll get in trouble' – a voice in the dark. Bevan had swivelled on his heels, shocked and worried. He'd peered back into the gloom across a row of tiny beds. All the blankets were gently rising and falling rhythmically with the breathing of the tiny bodies sleeping beneath them. There though, he saw, sat in the bed beneath the barred window in a shaft of dim moonlight, the covers pulled up to his chin, was the big kid all the others, including the Tutor, had called 'Bear'.

'No Bear, come look it,' junior Bevan had whispered back.

'Shhh, get in your bed. They'll hear.' Teddy was the voice of caution and reason even back then during their first adventure together.

'No… come-play-Bear,' Bevan said as he tapped a button with each syllable that he spoke. A 'dit-bleep-bleep' echoed through the silent room.

Bear hesitated. Then curiosity on his part too swept aside his reservations, and he said back in hushed tones, 'Erm… OK,' and lowered his blanket as a smile spread across his face and he made his way over to the door and this noisy little boy.

'Hello, my name's Bevan, Bevan Hughes.'

'Hi, Be-van Hughes' Bear said, pushing the buttons to match his words too, 'I'm Ted-dy Smith-ers.' They both began to giggle.

'Op-en Se-sa-me –' dit, bleep, dit, dit, bleep.

'Op-en Says-me,' Teddy said chuckling, hitting 1, 7, 1, 7.

To their surprise and dismay, the door had actually slid open. Sat on the other side were two guards playing cards. Both the two young boys had stood in the doorway of their dorm stunned, mouths gaping open, their smiles gone. They were in trouble. The room behind them was flooded with light from the guards' table lamp, and as the guards sprung to their feet and approached the two naughty youngsters, their shadows grew and danced huge and menacingly over all the other sleeping children. The Tutor had not been impressed. They'd each received four lashes of his cane and spent the weekend in the Dark Room together. Their friendship was forged though, and they'd been thick as thieves throughout their time in J5's education system and ever since. Teddy had kept Bevan going after Evelyn was snatched.

'Morning, mate, Monika OK?' Bevan asked, his intention pleasant, his tone glum.

'Blimey! Cheer up, mate, it may never happen!'

'It *did* happen… and my dreams won't let me forget.'

'I'm sorry. You had another one then last night?' They walked as they talked as all around them others were emerging from their homes. Their boots left footprints in the snow, and as more workers joined them in the commute it turned to a slippery sludge.

'Yep. They always feel so real, always trick me. Everything's like it was before, I mean feelings-wise, contentment, love… I don't know why I'm fooled – my bed has never been comfortable!' Bevan's mouth forced itself into the suggestion of a smile at that. 'But then she's being dragged away from me, and there's nothing I can do! There was something else though this time, a word whispered just before it all went bad. Does "Filakes" mean anything to you?'

'Nope, sorry man, never heard that before. What does it mean?'

'Your guess is as good as mine, but I've never heard anything like it before. I mean never in the dreams or otherwise. I don't think it's a word of Axiom. I… I wonder if it means something outside?'

Teddy stopped walking and looked all around for anyone that might be listening, prodded one huge finger into his friend's chest, 'Shhh, stop it man, that's the sort of talk that leads to the Farms. We both know full well there's nothing out there but Ferals and snow!'

Bevan's shoulders momentarily sagged and he let out a sigh.

'OK, look,' said Teddy. 'I'll ask around and see if anyone knows anything, if anyone has heard that word before. I seriously doubt it and frankly it's the sort of shit you should just be dismissing as non-sense from a dream.'

Bevan lifted his head, put on a brave face and started again. 'Morning, mate, Monika OK?' Bevan asked, his intention to deflect, his tone cheerful.

Teddy smiled and played along, 'She is, thanks, pal. Junior will be returning from J5 in a couple of months and she's busy fixing things ready for him.' He put his arm round Bevan's shoulder pulled him in closer and said more quietly, 'She's got me building another room off the back, I need to speak to Vulture about getting some more corrugated panels. I'll be living in a four-roomed palace, my friend – gotta love this city, eh?'

'Erm No. No, you don't. But hey, you enjoy the illusion of your mansion!' Bevan said back with a cheerful, playful enough tone but underneath there was the bitterness that Teddy had been working so hard to get his friend to give up. 'Right, so you're up for a pit stop first, yeah? Let's just go to Vulture's quickly now, I know I'll not want to after the shift and I've some good produce I want to get traded myself.' Bevan finished in a hushed tone.

They set off at a jog.

Vulture's was this side of J17, right on the border with J15, but they would then have to get back across to the other side and the Farms of J13 in under thirty–four minutes. They cut through the next alleyway on the left side of the street, past a row of larger houses occupied by some of J17's shift leaders and squeezed by a set of cabling collection columns that were sandwiched in between two of said houses, rising up high above the properties around them before trailing off in all directions to send power to the furthest points of the whole city. After a swift trudge through the snow up the adjacent street and skirting down another alleyway, the two of them emerged just a few buildings up from their intended destination.

This was the most run-down street in the entire Jurisdiction. It directly bordered the derelict J15 and as such was not a desirable place to live. It was as if the decrepit state of the neighbouring Jurisdiction was taking over and spreading its state of neglect and disrepair to all it touched, like one piece of rotting fruit in a bowl. The entire street of some thirty plus buildings had just a handful of Residents. The most notorious of them was Vulture.

There was no telling which of the abandoned houses he might be in, so Teddy stepped into the debris-covered road and yelled, 'Vulture, where you at? Vulture, we've literally two minutes and we gotta dash. You ain't gonna want to miss out on this produce, man!' They waited for thirty seconds or so, but all was quiet, just the sound of the wind tossing pieces of rubbish up and down the street and the continuous hum of electricity. No movement from any of the homes.

Teddy huffed, 'Sod this! Let's get going. He's too unreliable. I'll speak to McCourt after shift instead, he can usually get good stuff too.'

He raised his voice so that anyone listening would hear, 'Vulture's Feral spawn, man, let's go.' He turned to leave, but Bevan caught his sleeve and tugged him back.

'Ignore him, Vulture. He's having an off day, slept badly and has a nagging woman, you know how it is.' He then said more quietly for Teddy's ears only, 'At least pretend to be his mate, nobody's going to trade with someone they don't like. Vulture always has the best stuff and the best rates; Earl McCourt is full of empty overpriced promises and bullshit. Just need to appeal to his ego a bit!' He raised his voice again 'Vulture, I've derriere steaks and I've set one aside for my best supplier.'

There was a creaking sound up the street as a corrugated sheet covering a window eased ajar. A single whistle, less than a second long, came from the opening before the metal sheet pinged back into place with a clatter. They began walking over to the front door. 'Think it's probably best I do the talking eh, you ol' grump,' Bevan said with a wink.

'Me the grump? You can talk! I'll get a genuine smile out of you one of these days!' Teddy said, grinning.

The front door was already open just a crack and they let themselves in, pushing the door open on its rusted hinges. Inside was dark; it smelt of stale air and damp plaster. It was cold (but then everywhere was cold!) and they decided against removing their gloves, scarves or hoods. A corridor led directly off in front of them with three doors on the right–hand side. The first obviously led to the room with the corrugated–metal–sealed window; the door was wide open and there was nothing inside but ancient packaging, old paper and mouldy clothes scattered all over the floor. The furthest door, a clearly new and solid one, was shut and locked with four slide bolts that were padlocked – this seemed particularly odd to Bevan. Why would a room need sealing shut from the outside? The second door was open and the unmistakable dim glow of an oil lamp spilled out into the corridor. From inside came the rasping cough of Vulture.

They closed the front door behind them and walked up the hallway towards door number two to trade with Axiom's most notorious dealer of illegal merchandise. Inside there was very little of anything;

Bevan couldn't help but think it made his living space look plush and homely. In the far right corner there was a small table with two rickety chairs tucked up to it. Upon it there sat a bowl of some green-yellow gruel, with a spoon stood almost upright in it. Taking up most of the floor space there was a huge muddy, tatty rug. Bevan guessed that at some point it would have been quite an expensive piece of furnishing. In the far left corner, the simple metal frame and flimsy mattress of a bed were topped with a sleeping bag. In the sleeping bag, hood pulled up over his head and toggles pulled in tight to his chin, lay Vulture. He had one arm poking out through the broken zip and was coughing into a stained rag.

Vulture was nicknamed (Bevan suspected not even he recalled his real name) not just for his scavenging habits but also because of his appearance. His skin was veiny and red, a remnant of his old Click addiction, his bald head was sparsely populated by just a few wisps of hair, his nose was long and sat so irregularly close to his top lip it was as though he had a beak and his eyes were small and set close together. Under his right eye was a horrible-looking scar where almost his entire cheek had been sliced away. No-one knew what his original Jurisdiction was, but rumour had it he'd removed the tattoo himself while Clicking. He had been slinking about in J17 for near on twenty freezes.

'Hey, Vulture, sorry 'bout the Feral remark, man,' said Teddy.

'Fuck you, big man, what do you want, huh? Why have you come here?' he snapped back.

'Woah, ease up, Vulture, he didn't mean anything by it,' Bevan cut in. 'Like I said, his wife has been on at him about buil –'

'Building a new section to their lovely family home!' Vulture mockingly sneered, 'I know, I've seen him.' He switched to address Teddy directly. 'So big and strong and clever building a house, isn't you just, boy! Wowee! But that's very naughty, big man, don't let them Shrouded catch you, tsk tsk indeed. Size of you, you'd make quite the banquet centrepiece boy, a big roasted bear!' He spluttered out a cackle at that. 'There you'd be, an apple stuffed in your loud mouth and a spit up ya jacksie, just spinning and roasting and dripping those tasty fats, eh boy?' He waited for a reaction, grinning slightly and wheezing a little from his last laugh, his yellow teeth standing out against his raw, red skin. 'Say, you got on that nice jumper I seen you wearing under that coat, big man?' he asked Teddy directly.

'What if I am?' he replied folding his huge arms across his chest.

'Well, see, now I know you *is* wearing it boy. Leave it in the front room on your way out, and you come to this street tomorrow morning same time and you'll find the sheet metal you need in house number 71, OK?'

Teddy stood, clearly weighing up his options, and Bevan wondered how Vulture knew a) what his friend was wearing and b) what he had come to trade for. Teddy put on his best grin, feigning appreciation and admitting defeat. 'Fair trade's a trade made and I thank ya.' He muttered the words begrudgingly. 'Bev, I'm gonna wait outside in the fresh air. This place stinks like a rotting carcass!' He shot this parting remark and walked out. Bevan heard Teddy undoing the zipper on his coat and then something being tossed into the adjoining room, the front door scraping open, the wind momentarily whistling in and then it slamming shut.

'You cut a hard bargain,' Bevan said. 'He'll be frozen stiff working today.'

'Hey, I'm working boy, do I look toasty warm to you?'

'Yea, fair point.' He smiled and took a chair from the table, swivelled it, pulled it closer to the bed and sat down, leaning forward, elbows on his knees. A little too close for comfort. Teddy was not wrong; Vulture stunk just as bad as he looked.

Bevan smiled and hid his revulsion. He spoke in pleasant but hushed tones; he knew the importance of keeping Vulture onside. 'Listen, I'm leaving you one of these steaks regardless, OK? I know I owe you and we all know that a fair trade is a trade made, but I've another four... if you've any goodies for me?' Vulture stared back making a clicking sound with his tongue against his lower lip while he mulled it over. He stopped clicking and swallowed down a mouthful of saliva. Bevan knew he had him; he was literally salivating at the prospect of the meat. 'You know, that toothbrush you got me is amazing, man,' said Bevan, ramping up his 'I'm your friend' act. 'I can't use it too often though – people will talk, they'll be like, "There goes Mr Snow Smile, he must think he's from the Central Bastion."'

Vulture cackled, which promptly turned into an outburst of coughing. 'Well, Mr Snow Smile, your lucky day, I'd say, since I may have one or two things that'll tickle your fancy, boy.'

'Tickle away then, Vulture, tickle away… though keep ya talons to yourself,' Bevan said with a chuckle as he stood up and pushed the chair back under the table. He took the package of rump steaks out of his pocket and dropped them onto the table. In turn, Vulture wriggled out of his sleeping bag with a cough and a spluttering laugh. Standing up it was clear he was wearing at least four jumpers, yet oddly just a pair of shorts and his big clunky oversized boots, no socks. The vulture similarities didn't stop with his face, thought Bevan as he saw his scrawny, red–skinned, scabby legs. He was also surprised that they had the strength to kick back the heavy rug, revealing the trap door beneath. Even more surprising were the nimbleness and strength he demonstrated in bending down to unlock and heave open the heavy door and leap down inside. He landed with a puff of dust in the dry bottom and spread his arms out and looked up to Bevan, proudly showing off his wares.

Inside the six–foot–square hole were three electrical items – a lamp, (useless, Bevan knew, since a working light bulb was incredibly rare), a circular saw (which would be a fun toy but also way too loud to be able to ever use) and… the third device was something he'd never seen before. He'd seen something similar but not the same; this was different.

This looked a hell of a lot like his own mysterious device with the even more mysterious news bulletin frozen on its screen.

Curiosity gripped him, his palms became sweaty and his heart rate picked up. He asked Vulture to pass it to him for a closer look. It was about seven inches wide and ten high; a couple of inches bigger than his own device and incredibly even thinner. Its front was bordered with a shiny black plastic, and in the centre it was glass (which unfortunately was cracked in the shape of a 'Y'). It was, Bevan mused, much like a window in a frame. He decided that was just what he would call it – the Window. It had a single button at the base, on the top a button and a socket which he knew was for a headphone jack, two more buttons on the side and on the bottom a socket for something to plug in. This was the power port and he thought he might just have the right cable for it at home. On the back, it was a silvery colour and had an odd round symbol in the middle. He picked it up and tested all the buttons – nothing, no sound, no whirring, no flashing lights. This would either power straight up or take some serious work to make it do whatever it was supposed to do, but he had to know if he could use it to find out more about Solacity, about Efran Mourdorant, about the world outside Axiom. If he knew more about that then he might even be able to piece together the whereabouts and fate of Evelyn.

'Hmm. Not a whole lot of value in this lot, is there, but I suppose I'll take this,' he said, attempting to appear nonchalant.

'Pleasure doing business with ya as always, boy. Fair trade's a trade made and I thank ya,' he replied, leaping out and slamming shut the trapdoor. 'Now you better run on. Your big mate will be freezing his bollocks off out there with just a coat and no jumper on!'

Chapter 4

Bevan and Teddy had barely made it on time; they both checked in with the guard on duty and went off to their separate stations. They would meet up in ten hours' time at the end of shift to accompany one another on the walk back home. Under his clothes, strapped to his back with his belt, Bevan had secured his traded electrical good; he knew all day he'd work with it there teasing him, its contact a constant reminder of the deep curiosity he felt towards it.

While it did feel a little warmer than normal today, he thought, up on the gangways it was certainly anything but. The wind was biting cold and it made the platforms sway and shake – it was just as well Bevan had always had a good head for heights. The device at his back seemed to be a magnet for the cold and was like ice against his bare skin.

A few days prior one of the cattle had thrown itself against the electrical fencing in an attempt to test the current, to break free. As a result, a section had been tripping on and off intermittently for a couple of days. The animal in question had mistaken a lull in the humming sound from the fence for a power cut; it was however just a dip in current and the voltage was still ample to incapacitate and badly burn her. She was promptly slaughtered by the guards as she lay in the dirt, slightly charred but still alive and moaning in pain. The J13 farmhands had then rehoused this section's herd and called in the J17 boys. It was in fact this very animal's meat that Bevan had traded with Vulture before his shift.

Teddy Smithers and a few others worked below him digging out new holes for fence posts and earthing columns while connecting the new fencing back into the power grid, which itself had required a whole new stretch of mesh and cabling. Bevan meanwhile was working alone, connecting the barbed wire atop the fencing onto the overhead cables and insulating the metal gangway railings and footways. He paused for just a moment, standing up from his uncomfortable crouched position, and arched backwards to stretch, his vertebrae popping a contented drum line as he let out a long groan of satisfac-

tion at the feeling. As he came back upright, he twirled his wire cutters around his index finger and holstered them in his trouser pocket.
Grinning to himself, pleased with his little trick, he glanced across the
compound to a neighbouring section. A herd had grouped together
in one corner beneath one of the large hanging oil lamps. In their
bedraggled, tatty clothes, they huddled against the cold. Their heads
were bowed and they were rubbing their hands together. Many were
occasionally making little stamps to attempt to warm their frozen feet,
and puffs of their breath escaped upwards and were quickly dispelled
by the wind swirling all around them. Up on the opposite gangway
there stood the unmistakable figure of General Stricken. A rifle bal-
anced on the railing and braced against his shoulder. 'Sadistic bastard,'
Bevan muttered under his breath. 'Who kills animals for fun?'

He'd met Stricken just once previously. The day after Evelyn was
taken he'd gone to the Bastion to request that a scouting party of the
Shrouded sweep the surrounding areas of the city in the hope they'd
find her and her captors, kill them all and return her to him. He knew
before he even left his house to make the request that it was folly. At
best he'd be laughed at, at worst Farmed, but he had to try. Even sac-
rificing his life, to be sent to the Farm would be worth it for her safe
return. As he sat outside the office waiting for an audience with the
ranking J1 on duty, just working out what the hell he was going to
say, his eyes red from crying, Stricken arrived.

'What business do you have here, sparky?' he'd asked, standing over
Bevan, so close he would not have been able to stand up if he tried.
The butt of his sidearm in its holster was just an inch away from his
nose. He could smell gunpowder. It had recently been fired.

'I have a request of the Bastion, sir... ' Bevan replied glancing up
but immediately looking back down at his own hands. An involun-
tary shiver had run through him as he'd met those ghostly eyes.

'What's your name?' Stricken asked, his tone calm and seemingly
interested.

'Hughes, sir, Bevan Hughes... My wife, sir, she has been...'

'She's been what?' he barked, interrupting: a complete change of
tack.

'Taken, sir, Ferals took her, I need to get her back.' Bevan was beginning to get a little frantic now, confused by Stricken's constantly switching demeanour. He shifted in his seat to attempt to stand up. 'I need to leave the city and get her back. I need –'

Stricken's elbow came down hard and fast, cracking into the back of Bevan's skull as he tried to rise; he crashed to the floor, and the chair he had been sitting on clattered away from them. He was seeing nothing but white spots and stars, felt himself being swung upwards by his collar and slammed against the wall. He was utterly disorientated and confused and his head felt like bruised fruit.

'Will your wife's absence stop the electrical power?' he yelled into Bevan's face.

'What?' Bevan asked genuinely confused. The head-butt that answered his question was even more unexpected than the elbow and made a complete mess of his nose.

'Will the power go out anywhere in the city because of the loss of one J17?'

'Sir, the grid is fine. It's my wife, sir. I need… ' His eyes were streaming and blood ran down over his mouth and chin. Its metallic taste made him feel sick.

Stricken pulled him close and hissed, 'Then no–one here cares and neither should you! You carry the mark of your Jurisdiction; your only concerns are for the power grid. Did you learn nothing in J5? Get back to your shithole section of the city and don't ever come bothering the leadership of this city with your trivial bullshit again, Hughes.' He'd finished, sounding more exasperated than angry, let Bevan go as though dropping a piece of litter, smoothed down his shirt, then turned and sauntered down the corridor towards the private quarters of Eleanor De Sanctis.

A gunshot rang out, dragging Bevan back from his memory and into the present. The herd had scattered in the compound below him and two of the animals lay in the dirt. One, a young buck, was certainly dead; it was lying in a pool of blood that was spilling out from where the face once was. The other, an old female, was not going to survive and would be left there till she stopped writhing on her back and her rasping breathing ceased. The rest of the herd were regrouping, hoping for safety in numbers, their eyes wide with fear, whimpers of despair from some, muted acceptance and mumblings from others.

Looking back up to the opposite gangway Bevan could see Stricken smiling. He turned away from the compound and tossed the rifle to a section guard who'd come running up to him – with a message, it seemed. They had to raise their voices above the wind and Bevan heard their brief exchange quite clearly.

'I want the best cuts from the male, and I want them for tonight! Break down and mince the female. Straggly old thing, she'll be good for nothing but graduation grub.'

'Sir, yes, of course, sir. Sir, I've been told to inform you that there is a situation that requires your attention in J5.'

'Well of course there fucking is.' Stricken sounded exasperated and angry, and with this he turned and strode off back down the gangway, boots clanging loudly on the metal. Bevan hated the man and felt a wave of fury rush through him. Yet it subsided as he sensed an opportunity.

'Guys, I gotta piss,' he yelled down to the others working on the fence below and jogged off down the gangway. *I gotta take the piss* he thought, a grin on his face, knowing he'd easily be able to talk his way into securing some of the bangers or patties they'd make from the recently slaughtered old female. He was certain he'd need to visit Vulture again and he'd need some more meat to barter with. His new gadget was going to be a tricky project and he relished the challenge.

'You have just two weeks until your graduation, Benedict! This simply will not do!'

'I am trying, Tutor. I is, I promise, yes!'

'You is? You *are*! And you *are* trying my patience and you *are* as good as twelve years old. A grown man of Axiom! So tell me, what is the 17th Principle?'

'But it's boring, Tutor. They make my mind hurt, I doesn't like tests, uh ah, no way, no!'

'It is not just you who'll be in a whole world of trouble if you fail! I'll literally be mincemeat! A De Sanctis has never failed to graduate with anything but flying colours! Concentrate, *dammit!* The 17th Principle, now!'

Benedict's lip began to quiver and his eyes welled up. He wasn't upset, by the look of him; he was frustrated, refusing to let a tear slip free from his eyes. The Tutor stood up from the table, visibly infuriated by the boy's lack of effort. 'You shall not leave this room until you can recite that page off by heart and error-free,' he wailed, prodding a finger at the paper sat on the table. He turned away from the boy and marched towards the door, but stopped at the large mirror on the adjacent wall, to straighten his hat. 'How can you possibly be expected to succeed if you are not familiar with the Principles of Power? You know, Benedict, here in this classroom I am the De Sanctis. I am in charge, and you are just a student who... ' his voice lowered and he finished with a hint of defeat '... who I may have to give up on.'

The angry scowl remained on Benedict's face and he muttered, 'Principle 17 – annihilate your enemies, no less than total annihilation... yes,' and stuck out his tongue. 'So ner, yes,' he said with a swift nod of the head as he picked up the piece of paper and stuffed it into his mouth. The Tutor looked appalled, frozen on the spot in shock at this flagrant disregard for respect and the rules of the Jurisdiction of the Corruptibles. While chewing the paper the boy suddenly set about smashing the small table and two chairs (the only items in the bleak room) to pieces. All the while he cried and wailed incomprehensible babble in an attempt to clear his sense of frustration. The Tutor recoiled, his back making contact with the mirror.

From the other side of the one-way glass, Curtis Stricken witnessed the whole exchange. He found himself oddly amused: the old fool was afraid of his pupil. The Tutor stood in his ridiculous uniform of heavy robes, a pair of daft slippers poking out the bottom and a stupid-looking tall hat perched on his head, which signified his role as the highest ranked Resident in all of J5. A powerful man but old and weak, and scared of a young boy. Even his '5T' tattoo was fading and its definition warped by his wrinkled skin.

Stricken knew the boy well. Benedict De Sanctis was an only child, the only son and heir to Eleanor De Sanctis, and the future ruler of

Axiom. Just like all of those of his blood line who Stricken knew to have come before him, he was a naturally well-built young man with broad shoulders and a muscular physique. He was tall for his age, he had a good square chin, a crop of dark shoulder-length hair and deep hazel eyes. Also like those before him – and the trait the General most admired – he had an aggressive, unpredictable streak. On more than one occasion, while at J5, Stricken had stood this side of the one-way glass and watched as the Tutor had had to have Benedict restrained until he calmed down. He'd give trained guards twice his age a damn good wrestle.

The concern for all who had a stake in the boy's development was his mental aptitude. The problems in his head, his mind... this was fundamentally where he differed from his predecessors. Ben (which no-one but his parents called him) was academically poor, failed to grasp simple arithmetic, was at the lowest grade for literacy and, perhaps most worryingly for a future leader, his social skills were appalling. He could hold a simple conversation of sorts with those he came to know well. Yet those he did not know or trust were greeted with simple nods or shakes of the head – his shyness was painful. Love and affection were for the most part alien concepts to him. Physical contact he could not abide.

Benedict's love was for things that blinked and whirred, things that flashed and chimed, that moved and buzzed, electrical devices that he only saw on his weekly visits to his mother. Such things mesmerised him, it seemed; he would stare at them for hours, take in the sounds they made and the movements of their parts. Furthermore, despite his learning difficulties he had an uncanny knack and natural ability to logically disassemble and rebuild them faultlessly; he could understand their faults and repair them. On more than one occasion Stricken had personally called for Benedict to be given leave from J5 to come over to J1 to fix some broken mechanical device.

In the classroom, Benedict was wearing himself out and finally sat down on the cold hard floor. He picked up a piece of the broken chair and began to carve a drawing into the splintered table top; it looked like a picture of a washing machine. His crying had subsided to the occasional sniff and sob, and mixed in with these were the sounds of him bleeping an impression of a cycle being set and mimicking the drone of a spinning drum. His frustration was melting away, the argument with his Tutor forgotten. He withdrew into his own little world and appeared to be happy. The Tutor let out a deep sigh and left the room. Stricken shook his head. He felt concern for the future of Axiom but there was also an overriding sense of disappointment. It was an emotion that didn't sit well with him, and he clenched his jaw and fists as anger rose to the surface. He left the viewing room and went to arrange a solution.

He followed the Tutor at a decent distance such that he was not noticed as they travelled up a sparsely lit corridor, but close enough that he could overhear the old man's mutterings. 'What the hell am I going to do? Never in my tenure have I encountered such a child. He cannot be taught – he's too simple to be broken… simply cannot undertake what is required of one destined for such a role,' said the Tutor as he nervously wrung his hands together. His feet scuffed a soft echoing symphony on the polished floor. 'But she knows, she knows it's not my fault! The boy is hopeless. I'll go to her, explain he can't be instructed, can't absorb the information… '

He'd been promoted to the position of Tutor from Head of Teachers twenty two winters ago, and it was a post Stricken begrudgingly had to admit the man had certainly made his own. It was testament to his leadership of J5 that productivity and efficiency throughout Axiom had steadily risen in this time, such was the level of excellence attained by graduating pupils under his tutelage. He opened the door to his office and stepped inside, but stopped short. As Stricken came up behind him, the cause became visible: sat directly in front of him, behind his huge wooden desk, was a man some fifteen years his junior, also dressed in the garb of the J5 Tutor and with a fresh '5T' tattoo under his right eye – the ink was jet black and the skin around it still red and sore from the procedure.

'Shut the door, Tutor,' instructed Stricken, and the Tutor visibly jumped with surprise. When thinking up his plan, Stricken had hoped that at this point the old Tutor would be unsettled, incensed even; he knew the man and strongly suspected that he'd be thinking, *How dare this upstart wear the outfit reserved only for me?*

He span around. 'General, a pleasant surprise.' The Tutor was attempting to sound unfazed but, like all prey Stricken pursued, in his chest his heart would be beginning to hammer against his rib cage like a captive animal frantic for an escape route. Stricken stepped into the room and closed the door behind him. He was reminded of the feeling he had when his father had sealed him in with that stag all those years ago. Death in a cage.

'I'll be taking the boy with me when I leave. He shan't be graduating,' Stricken continued.

The Tutor's shoulders relaxed and he exhaled, 'Thank you, General, I'm glad Madame De Sanctis has realised the child's deficiencies.'

Stricken smiled. 'Yes, some creatures just cannot be tamed it seems. You are relieved of his care.' The Tutor beamed, clearly elated – he'd not have to find a way to excuse his lack of progress with Benedict. The animal in his chest would be settling back down to its usual pacing. Stricken was revelling in toying with his own former teacher's emotions. 'It is not just the boy Eleanor has noticed deficiencies in, Tutor,' Stricken said walking around him and casually perching on the edge of the desk.

The Tutor's smile promptly vanished and he took a step backwards, bumping into the door. 'It's the boy, sir. He is impossible, he is –'

'No excuses, now.' Stricken's tone was calm, '*He is* your downfall and your undoing. Sat before you is your replacement.' The man behind the desk folded his arms, and a smile spread across his face.

'This is preposterous!' blurted out the Tutor. In his dismay at losing his position, it seemed he'd quite forgot whom he was addressing. 'The child is an abnormality! He is broken!... he is a *freak!*'

In a flash, Stricken drew his pistol, raised it and fired one round through his throat. The bullet tore through skin, cartilage and bone and finished up embedded in the door behind, a spray of blood that ran down the wood as the 'retired' Tutor staggered backwards and slumped into a seated position. There he sat, legs sprawled out in front of him, clutching at the hole in his neck and taking short, sharp, gargled breaths.

'That should silence your whining excuses,' said the General, standing up, casually holstering his weapon and flattening out his shirt, which had ruffled up slightly. He yanked on the door, opening it inwards and in turn pushing the old Tutor behind it and out of sight. 'Feel free to make this office your own, Tutor,' he said, addressing the man sat behind the desk. 'I'll send a guard down to take that away,' he continued, pointing at the door and what lay dying behind it.

He returned to the classroom. As Stricken stepped in from the dark corridor into the light of the overhanging oil lamp, the boy looked up from his artwork.

'Get up, Ben. Your mother wants to see you.'

'But it's not the right day to go, uh ah, no way, still fifty–three hours and thirty–seven minutes till I see her, yes,' he said with confusion.

'You are leaving with me now, you'll not need to graduate, and you'll be living with your mother till the day you die.'

'No, but Tutor said I had to stay till I could learn my work, yes.' His tone was matter of fact and carried no hint of genuine resistance but rather confusion.

'Get up, Ben!' Stricken raised his voice.

Benedict nodded and stood up. He stared straight back at Stricken, his fists clenched at his sides, he gritted his teeth, visibly agitated. 'It's not time though, no!' He continued to stand this way, glaring at the General for a few seconds before relenting. 'OK, yes, but will I get to play with my gadgets, yes?'

'You'll do precisely what your mother tells you to do.'

'Yes, I'll do what *she* tells me to do, what Mum tells me to do, yes,' he replied, implying he didn't much care for Stricken's orders. Benedict's momentary defiance waned. 'We go now then, yes?' he asked.

'Yes, right now.' Stricken held out a hand to the open door, signalling for the boy to lead on. He gave nothing away but inside he felt what most would describe as a feeling of pride. He despised the boy's weaknesses but he admired his nerve. After all, only his own son would dare to stand so boldly and brazenly in front of him.

Chapter 5

'Bevan Hughes!' A banging at the door, a voice he didn't recognise. As quick as a flash, he was on his feet, snatching up the new Window and his old charging cable, striding across the room and sliding open the secret wall space. He placed the device carefully on the top shelf alongside the old device – an act of reverence – and flung in the wire – an act of frustration. There they sat, so similar but not quite the same. In his excitement to get the new Window in his posession he had noticed that it was slightly thinner, there were some slight differences in its design but, most frustratingly, he had failed to spot that it took a totally different charging cable.

More banging, the voice louder and more insistent, 'Bevan Hughes!' He slid the panel shut and the wire he had hurled in so unceremoniously caught under the door and it jammed. 'Shit!' he muttered and bent down to yank it free from the runner as a nervous sweat sprung up acorss his forehead. He shut the panelling, ensuring it was properly closed. Standing up he held a breath and slowly exhaled, trying to calm. Another barrage of banging and he raced to the front door while swiping the back of his hand across his brow to wipe away the little beads of guilt that had sprung up all over it.

He opened the door as casually as he could. There on the doorstep stood two J3 guards. A panic rose in him – the game was up! *I bet Vulture sold me out*, he thought. He was a J1 banquet main course, for sure.

One guard was about a foot and a half taller than the other and wore a pair of thick–framed driving goggles; the shorter of the two a tatty captain's hat. Both were clearly well–built and athletic, their muscular physiques obvious through the tight fitting white and black guard uniform. They sported the '3' tattoo under their right eyes and had close-cropped haircuts. They were each armed with a sub-machine gun casually held by their sides. Behind them was Teddy.

'What's going on, Grizzly?' Bevan asked ignoring the two guards.

It was the shorter guard who replied though, his deep voice a contradiction to his small stature. 'You are to come with us now, Hughes. You are wanted at the Central Bastion.'

'What? Why! I'm just an electrician.'

'Look, sparky, it ain't our place to question our orders, and it sure as shit ain't yours to question me. Now get your jacket and come with us.'

'If it's Central that wants us, why are they sending J3 and not J1 elite to collect us?' Bevan replied, pushing his luck.

'I'll not ask you again. I'll blast off your big toe and drag you there.'

There was a mini–standoff as for ten seconds Bevan just held the guard's stare. The taller guard thumbed the safety off on his gun and Teddy spoke, trying to defuse the situation. 'Come on, Bev. Don't be stupid. Let's just go see what's what, eh?'

Bevan smiled. His arse crack was sodden, he was so afraid, but he would not show it. 'Yeah, sure, of course. Lead the way.' He grabbed his jacket, tugging it on over his shoulders as he stepped out and shut the door.

'We ain't leading you anywhere, volts. Get in.' The shorter guard pointed towards an old black 4×4 parked up at the kerb. Its tyre tracks were clearly visible in the dust, debris and slush of the unused road behind it. It had a J1 stamp in white lettering on the side panelling and on the bonnet there were painted two red eyes – the red eyes of the Shrouded.

'Haha, look, Teddy. They really are trying to be J1s.'

'Just move!' yelled the short guard and poked Bevan hard in the back with the barrel of his gun.

Bevan had never been in a car before and despite the fact he was nervous about their intended destination and, perhaps most worryingly, that it appeared the Shrouded were somehow involved, he allowed himself, just for a moment, to be excited about getting a close–up look at a new machine. His mind boggled with the number of moving parts there must be to make these things work. This very thought occupied and distracted him entirely as they drove in silence the relatively short trip across Axiom to the Central Bastion.

They travelled north through J17. All the way Residents scampered from the vehicle like startled birds, or peered out of their windows at the growling metal beast, all surely wondering what would befall those it was transporting. It was not often that a J1 car came and collected a Resident of any Jurisdiction.

They crossed the Jurisdiction border gate into J5. As they travelled the roads of the Jurisdictions of the Corruptibles, Bevan heard Teddy snicker to himself. He turned to look at his lifelong friend, a look of complete confusion on his face. 'What the hell could possibly be funny?' he quietly hissed.

'Not been here since we graduated. Didn't think I would again till Lil Ted's,' he said, his voice hollow, his stare vacant as he reached up and ran his fingers across his '17' tattoo.

'Shut the fuck up back there,' the little J3 yelled, twisting in his seat to glare back at the two of them.

They spoke not a word more as they passed school after school after boarding house after training compound after school, until finally they were crossing another border gate into J1. The car accelerated as it tore up the main street, heading directly for the Central Bastion, which loomed high above them. Bars, brothels, abattoirs, munitions factories and breweries sped by, a blur of neon and sin.

They pulled up sharply outside the main gates. The taller guard who was driving spoke into the intercom, 'Whiskey, Indigo, November, Delta. J3 to J17 returning with requested package for Madame De Sanctis.'

A voice answered: 'Acknowledged and received. Please proceed.' The gates began a slow slide open on huge steel runners. They were old and rusted and made one hell of a racket, squeaking and grinding their way across to make way for their car.

Teddy took the opportunity to nudge Bevan and whisper, 'Shit. *Requested by De Sanctis?* What's going on? They must know about –'

Bevan cut him off, 'I dunno, but I think we'll be OK. Why all the fuss if she just wanted us dead?' he said rather hopefully, not truly believing it himself.

The shorter guard spun around in his seat again, raising the gun in their faces. 'What the hell did I say before? Were you told you could flirt with one another? Huh? Shut the fuck up gossiping, ladies!' They instantly fell silent again.

Bevan glanced out of the window. He'd only been here the once before, on that day after Evelyn was taken, but he was in no fit state to take much notice of his surroundings then. Now, with tension rising in the back of the car, he took it all in.

There was nowhere else in all of Axiom like the Central Bastion and its surrounding area. A circular expanse a half mile across in diameter, there were guards patrolling everywhere, perched high in watch towers and sat at sentry huts and heavy fortified machine-gun nests. *A bit overkill*, Bevan thought; there hadn't ever been a single incident of a threat against the De Sanctis regime in their entire rule, and he presumed it was more a show of power than it was actually functional and necessary. There was a lot of electrically charged metal fencing topped with barbed wire, and as at the Farms of J13 they were used for sectioning off specific areas and buildings. Unlike the rest of the city, the tarmac all around was perfect, no cracks or crumbling pot holes here. There were no oil lamps either – the whole area was lit by huge electric lights held aloft by thick metal columns, their harsh white light spilling down in perfect circles on the dark ground. The snow wasn't allowed to settle; a team worked incessantly to keep everything clear and clean. It all somehow looked new. There were more cars here too, all parked up in fleet formation and gleaming, all carrying the same J1 lettering and cruel red eyes on the bonnet. There were also some vans and a few massive trucks for transporting troops en masse, an oil tanker and a bulldozer. He could see at least four generators that could be heard humming even from inside the car. They kept everything here with power at all times. Bevan wondered, perhaps wishfully, if it was these they had been asked in to assess, repair or replace.

They journeyed up a purposely designed zigzagging road with four-foot drop-offs at each kerb. It didn't allow for a direct approach to the Central Bastion. On either side they saw guard lodgings and store houses for general supplies, food and arms. All the while, the view out of the front window of the car gave glimpses of the Bastion itself. As they got closer and closer, it rose ever higher above them, filling more and more of the view out the windscreen. It was an imposing structure, three colossal chimneys set into the front of one, even larger, cold, hard, featureless block of a building. It had one huge steel door and just a handful of windows, each with a set of bars. From the centre of the building, rising up ever higher behind the middle chimney, was a tall, sleek rectangular tower. Up and up it rose, its flat sides impossible to scale. Just a couple of feet from the pinnacle there was a vast window, as wide as the tower and, Bevan guessed, as tall as an entire storey. From down here on the ground, it reflected back the twinkling of thousands of oil lamps in the vastness of the city below like a clear winter's night sky full of countless stars. That was where they were heading, to the room that lay behind that glass; he knew it.

The car stopped suddenly again, coming to a halt with a jolt. 'Out!' ordered the driver. Stepping from the car, they were instantly greeted by another set of chaperones. These guys, however, were more hands–on. They wore a similar uniform to all the J3 guards, but they also wore a hooded top that partly shadowed their faces. They had '1' tattoos under their right eyes and on each of their eyelids were tattooed the same evil red eyes they'd seen on the car that brought them here. These men had been handpicked by General Stricken, Bevan knew, and all were raised, trained and housed in J1 to be the military police, the secret service and elite guard of Axiom. All had to be at least six-foot-two tall. All were expert marksmen and super–proficient in hand-to-hand combat. They each carried a mod-ified assault rifle that could be set to either deadly accurate single fire or a barrage of automatic gunfire at the flick of a switch. Each of them also car-ried a belt of throwing knives. These were the Shrouded.

Each Shrouded clamped one hand on the captives' shoulders and took one of their wrists in the other. Bevan's guard said in his ear, in a very controlled voice, 'Walk slowly and precisely in the direction that I lead you. If I feel a hint of resistance from you, I will take this arm out of its socket, leave it dangling uselessly at your side, and I will lead you the rest of the way with your other one.'

With this threat, he gave a slight nudge in the direction of the door and they began walking towards it with the same careful manner in which the guard had just spoken. It slid open, revealing a room seemingly empty and devoid of any character or furnishings. They stepped in and the door slammed behind them. A moment later there was a small 'ping' and a hid-den elevator door in the far right corner opened. 'Get in!' instructed the Shrouded guard. Bevan and Teddy moved inside and turned to face their guards who remained outside. As the door started closing, Bevan's guard very slowly blinked and gave a grin. His red eyelids coupled with the sinister smirk had the desired effect: Bevan was scared.

As soon as the door was firmly shut and they felt themselves ascending, Teddy spoke, 'Can they know we've been trading with Vulture?'

'No I don't think so; they'd have raided my house.'

'Then why the big show, the guards, the Shrouded, the car. Why does *she* want to see *us*?'

Bevan hesitated a moment then said, 'Shit, they might know something else.'

'Know what, man? Bev? They might know what, dammit?'

'I stole produce from the Farm. Well, I mean I just took some unwanted cuts, that's all.'

'What? Why?'

'I didnt think anyone would care. I just wanted some more meat to trade down at the Merchants' Quarter!'

Teddy slumped against the wall and banged his head backwards against it in frustration; a dull banging sound filled the small elevator. He let out a big sigh. 'If we don't die today, you best have got some life-changing, earth-shattering gadget or something in exchange for your ill-gotten burgers, you damn idiot.'

'If we don't die today, I swear I'll make it up to you. I'll never put you, Monika or the kids in this position ever again, but I did get something. And I just know that it's important.'

'Well, something I know for damn sure is you're the stupidest clever person I know!' said Teddy, lightening the tension as only he could. Though he was still scared about what this meeting would bring, Bevan knew his old friend still trusted him and he suspected was also now curious as to what that Window would do.

The elevator slowed to a halt, they heard the same inappropriately happy-sounding ping and the doors opened. They were greeted in the same manner as they were at the front door by two more of the Shrouded and led down doorless, windowless corridors that turned from left to right and back again every thirty yards or so, until they reached the door to the main control room and the office and home of Eleanor De Sanctis.

One guard opened the door and the other spoke. 'Go in and sit down. Place your hands on the table and don't move. Only speak if directly asked a question.'

They stepped into the room and the doors closed behind them. Bevan took a moment to take in their new surroundings. Off to the left was a bank of control panels. There was an array of meters, dials, buttons, knobs and blinking lights – it was a mind–boggling, tantalising collection of electronics he would have loved to have investigated. He did not allow his eyes to linger long though. Directly in front of them was the gigantic glass window they had seen from the ground. Bevan felt that from here one could see forever: he felt sure he could make out the edges of the city and the unknown land that lay beyond, the horizon and even further. It was all he had never allowed himself to consider and all that, in truth, terrified him. Nothing good could be found outside of Axiom, he was certain of that. His gaze continued past the window, off around to the right, and his eyes beheld a huge table. Sat on the other side of it were General Curtis Stricken and Eleanor De Sanctis.

He had seen her just once before and never again since, but she had left an impression. It was on the day of his graduation ceremony. She graced just one or two of the many that took place each year, as a guest of the highest honour. She would appear, often unbeknownst to the students and their watching parents, and would give no indication as to why she chose these select few to attend.

The ceremony was not so much a graduation as it was a cattle branding. The students would be taken out by their Teacher to the central square of the Jurisdiction of the Corruptible. The parents would gather in front of the main stage ready to take their child home for the first time in many years. Each student would have to climb the stage and stand before the other Teachers and the Tutor while they recited to them for the final time the words they had heard countless times before. They would read through the roles and responsibilities given to Residents of their particular Jurisdiction. The words reserved for the guards of J3, the carpenters, smiths, oil–riggers, bakers, butchers and other trades of Jurisdictions 7, 9 and 11 and the words which Bevan and his class mates spoke, the words of the electricians of J17. At the end of the reading the student would give a single nod to acknowledge and thank those who had taught them their life skills. In response, the Tutor would reel off a variation of the same basic premise outlining how well they had done in their training and how they would go on to be model Residents of Axiom. They would then leave the stage and gather in a holding area. Once all had recited their words they were then called by name back to the stage one by one, and here they were placed in a stock with their hands and head restrained while a tattoo of their Jurisdiction's number was quickly yet accurately drawn under their right eye. The student was now a Resident.

Bevan recalled climbing the stairs to the stage as a completely focused twelve–year–old student. He had come face to face with the senior members of the Jurisdiction of the Corruptible before and they had not fazed him. He knew what was in store after the reading and he was already bracing himself for the pain of his tattooing. Teddy had gone before him and not even flinched. He could be as tough as the bear, he thought.

He had read through his own words with the assured confidence that came from practice and repetition. He stood with a stupid grin on his face in the holding pen, his fear of the needle and the ink masked by a feeling of pride. However, when his name was called and he approached the stock, she appeared, walking up behind and standing next to Tutor. Bevan's composure gone, he stood there listening but not hearing the words being recited to him. He allowed himself a quick glance at her and knew then in that fleeting second that Eleanor De Sanctis was, if nothing else, two things: a formidable and powerful woman who scared him; and unerringly beautiful, which scared him even more. After that, the tattoo was agony.

Now, seventeen years later, he found himself looking at that face again and he felt precisely the same feelings. His cheeks flushed red very slightly – the woman was stunning and terrifying. Teddy took the lead and walked over to the table, sitting down and placing his palms flat on surface, Bevan followed his friend's lead.

Now that they were seated, she spoke. 'So I understand you two are rather industrious, would you agree?'

Bevan sat staring at his hands on the table, feeling his palms getting sweaty.

Teddy answered, 'We are both very good at our jobs, yes.'

'That is not what I asked. I said "industrious". You seem to partake in some interesting projects as well as carrying out your roles, as you yourself suggest, to a very high level.' She left the accusation hanging in the air. Bevan knew the game was up; she knew about his theft of the meat, must think that Teddy had been in on it with him. He felt immense guilt. Any moment now, Stricken would surely stand and fire his pistol into them both, and the Shrouded would return and haul away their bodies for processing. He had to say something. Monika and the kids could not be deprived of their father because of his foolish act.

'Wait! You need to know that I –'

Stricken spoke quickly, cutting Bevan short, 'Shut your mouth! This isn't a time for you to speak.'

Eleanor held up a hand to quieten her right–hand man and lowered it to come to rest on his forearm, a calming touch. She continued, 'I need to know what? That you are the one who is constructing additional rooms onto your home, using valuable resources that could be used for the greater good of Axiom? Or that it is you who has rigged his home to steal electricity from the city?' Neither man wanted to answer her. Bevan was relieved that they didn't appear to know about his theft, but it was scant consolation, as he knew there was now nothing he could say to save his friend. They were both guilty of crimes he had completely forgotten they'd been committing for months. He was certain they were both dead, regardless of the admission to their individual crimes. Eleanor changed her tone though, 'Of course, Residents have been executed or Farmed for lesser infringements of the law, but I've a particular interest in you two and your skills. I even instructed the General to come unarmed, in case he got carried away and killed you both!' She let out a faint laugh and gently tapped Stricken on his arm. Bevan allowed himself a brief glance at Stricken's holster, which was indeed empty.

They sat opposite her, utterly confused, a touch relieved yet still more than a little wary that they were not out of this just yet.

She carried on, 'You may not know this, but the city's most precious resource is that which we cannot possibly hope to replace: oil. It is not for nought that we ration it so strictly. The reservoir is emptying, and only the right conditions, pressure and hundreds of millions of years will bring more. It *will* run out and when it does the the lights will go out, electricity will stop, which means the Farm fences will fail, the UV houses will go dark – food will be a problem. The water treatment plant will no longer function – clean water will be a problem. The main gate will no longer lock and the whole of Axiom will be vunerable. A solution must be sought. In seventeen days' time, General Stricken will oversee a project beyond the walls of this city.' Bevan and Teddy were dumbfounded – why was she telling them all this? Expeditions beyond the walls were unheard of. 'Several weeks' journey westward from here, there is a wall of ice of unimaginable depth and size. The winds which race towards it and funnel down its vast edge are almost constant and they are strong. You shall both be part of this project. You shall head up two teams. You,' she addressed Teddy, 'are to lead on the construction and you,' her attention shifted to Bevan who shifted in his seat – he hoped he hadn't shown a thing other than surprise, but the thought of getting outside the walls was beyond exciting; out there was everything he'd read about on the broken Window – 'will oversee the means for generating constant electrical supply via a wind farm – a collection of huge wind-driven turbines. You'll no doubt fully grasp the marvels of engineering to make sure this project is a success.' She let the magnitude of this order sink in; they could not quite believe what she was saying. She swivelled in her chair to face away from them; the well-maintained furniture made not a sound. She stood and glided across the room, collecting a glass of red wine from the edge of a control panel on her way, and stood before the massive window. She gazed out over all she ruled.

Curtis Stricken stood up and spoke: 'Get up.' They did as they were told, both holding expressions of dumbfounded amazement. 'Cars will collect you tomorrow morning and you will return here for a thorough briefing. Now get out!'

Chapter 6

Eleanor waited until the door closed on well-oiled hinges and the frame silently accepted it. She turned away from the window and moved across the room and stood before two frames on the wall. One contained a dog-eared, sun-bleached photograph of a stern-looking man. He had a good strong chin, a thick crop of black hair and well-kempt moustache. His eyes were cold, emotionless. The plaque below indicated that this was the 'Founding Father of Axiom: Roberto Julius De Sanctis'. The other frame housed a piece of paper that looked even older than the photograph alongside it. It was torn from a cheap spiral-bound pad and across it was written a list. An untrained scrawl listed the 'Principles of Power'; they were the defining rules underpinning all of his beloved city's society. They were alone, so she spoke freely to her right-hand man. 'Tutor wasn't wrong though, was he, General?'

'The fool was disrespectful to you and lacking in his abilities. All creatures can be broken.'

'Watch yourself; that creature is my son!'

'My apologies, ma'am. What I meant is the new Tutor will be able to get Ben to a level that he can succeed you and fulfil his birthright.'

Eleanor let out a sigh. ' I would have thought you of all men would know when a creature should be put down!' She licked a thumb and rubbed away a smudge from the image of her ancestor. 'The child is broken, he is not a De Sanctis and he is not capable of this great position.'

She casually sipped her wine and returned to the window to look out over Axiom, her city and the city her great family had created. Below her, the Residents were going about their daily tasks, working hard to ensure this speck of civilisation continued to function. The endless dim twilight covered everything and the countless oil lamps flickered in the dusk, their yellow light the only colour in a sea of grey hues and slushy black snow. The window was a thick glass, but the industrial din of Axiom filtered through – the clanging of metal, the hiss of valves and the hum of generators. Eleanor smiled slightly to herself; it was a beautiful thing, this city, and a wonder of life in the dead expanse beyond its walls. Whenever she had such a difficult decision to make, she would stare out over all she ruled and it always prompted her to make the right choice.

Her great-great-great-great-grandfather had had the control room changed to incorporate the window. A whole panel of systems and monitors had been removed, rewired and set up in a room a floor below to free up the entire exterior wall for a single sheet of glass. It was an eye out onto the city and in turn it let the populace know they were always under the gaze of the ruling De Sanctis. Eleanor, like all of her predecessors, knew precisely how to operate the power plant, and the panels that remained were only those essential to a safe shutdown. The room had been split in two. One side housing the controls doubled as a chamber for council. There was a large pentagonal table with ten chairs around it, one for each of the heads of Jurisdictions and one for Eleanor herself. No-one had sat at this table for some twenty years: Eleanor didn't hold council; she was supremely confident in her own decisions. The walls were lined with images of past rulers of Axiom in amongst the old flaking and retouched safety and instruction posters and signs. The other half of the old control room was her private bedroom and living quarters; the number of people other than Eleanor to have been in this room could be counted on one hand.

She ended most of her days reading the old journals of those who had come before her. She kept them as secret as a girl documenting the trials and tribulations of teenage life. They gave her insight into the world as it had been before. Gave her knowledge of how things worked. She was an intelligent woman, she fully understood technical content, but she was fearful where others might be curious. She saw the errors of those who had led the old world to its demise. She was steadfastly determined to preserve the Axiom way of life. Her father and his father before him and so on and so forth, they had all done their duty. They had put Axiom first and followed the Founding Father's doctrine. She was a De Sanctis and she would do what needed to be done.

The Central Bastion had housed a De Sanctis family since the city was founded. When the tidal locking began and the world changed, when the natural disasters came thick and fast and the bombs began to drop, Roberto Julius De Sanctis had been a team leader on shift at an oil–fuelled electrical power plant. Roberto was a career man. He had no wife, no children; he was an only child of now-deceased parents who themselves were little more than children; he had no family at all. He had sat at the base of a pitiful funnel of inheritance; he mourned them not a little. Roberto also had very few friends. If truth be told he wasn't a particularly nice person; he was antisocial, openly spoke of his dislike for people and in his spare time read the doctrines of communism, Marxism and fascism. Lenin's *'Left-Wing' Communism: An Infantile Disorder* was a particular favourite; he regularly read and re-read Marinetti's article 'The Fascist Manifesto' and had begun his own work that was inspired by, questioned and completely (mis)interpreted *The 48 Laws of Power* by Robert Greene. He loathed the society in which he lived, found people's morals deplorable, despised what he perceived as warped standards and priorities. He watched the final TV broadcasts with interest and a degree of excitement: he didn't see the end of it all as a bad thing; this was a natural cull. As he saw it, humankind had had its time. Roberto was a 'prepper'. For years he had prepared for the end, to be ready to benefit from chaos. He knew that the masses would be scrambling around and over one another to first work out what on earth was going on and only then would a small number survive. He knew that he could be a leader, knew that knowledge was power, and was determined to be knowledgeable in the things that mattered when society stopped providing. He schooled himself in the basics of engineering, physics and chemistry. He learnt the means to grow, rear, prepare and store food and purify water. He understood how to source, refine and utilise materials.

He regularly took double shifts, triple shifts even. In the beginning, it wasn't uncommon for him to stay overnight at the plant in the staff accommodation. Soon it became a rare occurrence that he'd leave the compound and travel back to his apartment in the city. The only time he took any annual leave was to go on hunting and fishing trips alone; he found great pleasure in living off the land and connecting with nature.

He'd worked his way up from an office junior position until he headed up a team that kept the plant ticking over and functioning as it should do – maintenance, asset management and technical repairs were all areas that Roberto majored in. He knew the job inside out, knew the plant intimately, and it made him very good at his job. He was a good leader of men; despite his social deficiencies he was able to effectively formulate and delegate workloads and tasks. Getting the job done was the most important thing to Roberto Julius De Sanctis, and he didn't mind if he annoyed people on the route to success. Eventually, rumour was that he was due a promotion to make him the most important man on site; the current foreman was due to retire and the firm had been hugely impressed with his dedication and levels of performance.

It perhaps wasn't a surprise, then, that as the world ended and everyone else decided they'd spend it with loved ones in their homes, or jack in the job and flee the various and terrible natural disasters and wars, Roberto chose to stay at the plant.

When everyone had gone, he had single-handedly kept it running. The plant was an isolated building in the middle of a desert sat atop an underground lake of oil. The nearest city was eighty–odd miles away. It had drilling platforms for extracting the oil, onsite refineries and storage silos. It was encircled by a wall, with a single security gate the only access and exit point. There were a handful of onsite amenities, a gym, a single–screen cinema, a petrol station, a kitchen and diner, a doctor's office, a power substation and a small collection of housing units and a security hut. It was set up in such a way that it could be capable of being wholly self-sufficient for up to two years. Before the end came, however, when the world was still frivolous, during business as usual, the complex was receiving regular fortnightly deliveries, and stock onsite was such that even a fully manned station would require nothing from the outside for nearer ten years. Following the departures of all of his colleagues, though, the deliveries had stopped. There had not been any word from head office and for two months Roberto was alone, had not seen a soul.

He'd scoured every inch of the compound and secured a small stash of firearms, sealed away all food and water provisions and first aid supplies, and holed himself up in the control room that sat at the summit of a large tower rising up from the centre of the compound. It was the most secure part of the entire site – he named it the Bastion.

As the third month began, a small group of military personnel arrived, accompanied by their families and a ragtag bunch of civilians they had picked up along the way. Their ramshackle convoy of battered Humvees, MPVs and a city bus that still insisted that the next stop was 'SB17 Merryweather Road' pulled up to the entrance and patiently awaited a greeting. The soldiers carried sidearms only, any heavy weaponry they might have once had now abandoned or cannibalised. Roberto had watched them from his control tower through his security cameras for just over a day before he decided that this was a threat he could handle, perhaps more an opportunity than a danger. He knew that while he had a head full of knowledge, skilled hands and stubborn, steadfast resolve, there were gaps in what he had learned and essential tasks he did not enjoy. And perhaps most importantly to Roberto, these strangers could be the first Residents, the first followers. They would be the first subjects of his well-conceived fledgling regime.

This group at his gates had been through a lot, and they weren't looking for any further conflict. They were in poor health, many carried injuries and perhaps more detrimental to their survival (and what played in Roberto's favour) was the fact that they were without a plan or destination; they were travelling aimlessly. They sought sanctuary.

They spoke of the terrible things they had witnessed and heard. Roberto took them in but they were there under his rules, it was his community and if they didn't like it they could leave – no-one ever left. He had found his first subjects, the first Residents of Axiom. As the only one who knew how to work the power station he was in a unique position: this knowledge was invaluable. He also held all the security codes, all the keys and, after he confiscated the newcomers' firearms, all the weaponry. Though some questioned his rules privately, no-one dared to risk being thrown out. The compound was secure and had a sense of order and routine that people needed and craved. It had a good supply of food and clean water. Roberto didn't waste time in asserting his authority and demonstrating a ruthless streak. His rules were frowned upon by most but still the existence inside the compound was so much better than the chaos beyond its walls.

As more people arrived so the compound began to change – people came with various kinds of expertise and their skills were well utilised. More buildings were built; the surrounding area was pillaged of any useful materials – wood, steel, stone, brick and plastics, guns, grenades, rockets and bullets, canned food, bottled drinks and packets and packets of provisions. Teams would venture out and pillage the nearby cities for these supplies. They even brought back large machinery on flatbed trucks to complete various tasks (those for which they were originally intended and new purposes they were modified for). The entire area that had become known as Axiom was secured, the walls and fences reinforced and defended. Guard towers were erected, gun turrets mounted upon them and minefields were planted along the single road which led up to the single gate. He recruited a smaller group of close allies, empowered them to enforce and promote his doctrine. They began to section off the compound into distinct areas of production, housing, farming and education – everything they needed to provide for themselves, to be wholly self-sufficient and self-reliant.

These were the physical infrastructure changes. The societal changes that had taken place at this time began to shape the hierarchy which would develop, take hold and govern the city for ever more. Roberto found that the new world was only survived by the fittest, but also that it was often the meanest and the most ruthless who found their way out of the chaos and to the gate of Axiom. It was these individuals who shared his vision and his theories and ultimately enforced his laws. They were fledgling J1 and the first of the Shrouded. At the other end of the pecking order were those who were not comfortable with the new regime, who were vocal in their opposition or simply came with nothing to contribute to the cause. Roberto (and his new sidekicks) made these poor individuals the first of the Farm's herds.

There were a few violent clashes in the first year or so. Mobs would arrive from the world outside and seek to enter and take what was not theirs to take. Roberto and the Residents had dealt with them all swiftly and brutally. Such was their fortified position and armoury, they were easily capable of repelling attacks. Some of the survivors were brought in to be made examples of. Others were taken out into the wilderness and left nailed to posts; their rotting corpses, contorted in their death throes, acted as warning signs to would-be enemies to turn back. There was literally nothing more precious than the city and the existence they were carving out for themselves in this new world.

As the Residents saw it, this life simply could no longer happen anywhere else. Those that arrived at the gates seeking shelter and civilisation were given it and integrated into life in the compound.

Roberto had a clear plan of how his city would develop and function. He had felt certain he understood the flaws of the old societies and would not allow them to become a cancer in this one. He classified people as animals that had blindly followed the orders and manipulation of past leaders and their corrupt media empires. The greatest illusion was that of freedom of choice. As long as people felt they were in control of their choices, they were obedient and happy in their existence. He knew it would take time, but he banned all forms of literature and confiscated and destroyed all electronic devices with Infinity SatNet connection. All the trivial things these people once held dear, that once dominated their spare time and their thoughts, would be forgotten, and only those things that mattered would be held in their consciousness – new ideas which would only be beneficial to the greater good, to the many and to the city. And which would all be of Roberto's creation.

Roberto chose a wife. It wasn't love but he understood the need for an heir to what he had created, someone who would love him unconditionally and someone who he could completely manipulate to his will and ways of thinking. Someone who could continue his regime. His son and the many generations since had followed in his footsteps and continued his doctrine. They were, all of them, all of the leaders in the history of Axiom, completely revered and feared by their people.

After a while no–one else arrived and after a while it was decided by all that there was no need to leave. Certain things were outlawed, certain things became law, De Sanctis law. Quite quickly some things were forgotten, while new ways were adopted, and slowly – very, very slowly – as some things were forgotten completely and those new ways were accepted without question, it all just became The Way Things Are.

And the compound became Axiom.

Eleanor had read about it all in the records kept by Roberto and those who had followed in his footsteps. It was up to her to ensure their way of life would continue for as long as she was able and when the time came she needed to know there was a successor as driven, ruthless and determined as her. Ben was a problem.

She felt a mother's love towards the child, a natural instinct that she wished she didn't have. She knew that this could not be enough, that he could not and would not be her successor. Nothing and no–one was bigger than Axiom and only one of her blood could rule, but it couldn't be Benedict. He would not be able to adopt this most important of roles. Eleanor drew her gaze back from beyond the pane of glass and stared at her own reflection for a moment. She was a suitable ruler in every way. Her parents had always been quick to compliment her on her appearance as she had grown tall and slim yet curvaceous. Her long black hair was full of body, her lips a deep red and her eyes large, dark hazel and edged with perfectly shaped eyebrows and long lashes – just like her mother. She had her clothes tailored such that they accentuated her body shape. Her blouse was fitted and cinched in at her small waist and buttoned up the front to contain a buxom chest. She wore a pencil skirt and heels. Power dressing. She was an attractive woman. Benedict had, she mused, follwed suit genetically when it came to physical prowess but he was not of strong enough mind and will. His simplistic view of the world would simply not do. It had become clear he was not like other children. Yet as alluring and beautiful as she was, she was merciless, unforgiving and deadly in equal measure. She was a praying mantis, a black widow spider and a queen bee. She turned back to Stricken, who had remained at attention in front of her desk. Her mind was made up and she stood to address him.

'Principle 9: Your blood is your strength and your weakness, do not be afraid to bleed. Not the Farms though, Curtis,' she said. 'He'll face a swift end and I'll not have him consumed.'

'What would you have me do?' Stricken asked.

'This new project beyond the walls of the city, it could last some time, months even.' Stricken's left eye twitched almost imperceptibly, it was the only indication that he was surprised by the revelation; only the water gatherers ventured out and it was a very regimented 'there and back again' task. No—one went out, and certainly not for any length of time. This was bound to be quite some task for him and his forces to oversee. 'Once the workers are familiar with their tasks and routine has settled in,' Eleanor continued, 'you will take the boy out there as if to join the project. When you are halfway there give the boy a dose of Click and put a single bullet in his head.'

'I shall of course see to it personally, ma'am,' said Stricken with a nod.

'Of course,' she replied, returning the nod. She sat back down in her chair and swivelled back around to stare out of the window. The general knew this was him dismissed and turned to leave. Just as he reached the door she called out, 'Curtis... ' Neither of them turned to face the other, and she said to the thick glass window, her lips curled into a seductive smile, 'I will still require a successor. We will have to try again.'

Still facing the door he replied, 'Of course, Eleanor.'

Part Two

Excerpt of Log 717... reported by 'Gatherer and Assessor' Ensign Chung Zhang... Here continues recordings of project 'Unaccompanied'... Herein lie documented ping tests originating from attempt 001.001.0.001 to present denomination – 192.168.2.101. All subsequent tests have been conducted with single number increases to ensure no possible IP addresses are missed... no reachable host target has been found for some considerable time... My search continues for a response... Upon identification I shall report the location of the host for phase 2 – 'Removal process'... search time in an attempt to identify the 71st target is ongoing but one suspects that likelihood of success is highly improbable now. Search time since 70th target to date stands at 6 years, 11 months, 23 days and 17 hours...

Part Two

Chapter 7

She was running. Running hard and as fast as she could. And she'd made good progress. No mean feat when trying to remain as quiet and stealthy as possible. With each step her rifle gently knocked against her back and her side–arm on her hip; her breath was fogging the cold air and her feet were crunching in the snow. Directly ahead there was a wreck of an old car – she hit it at full pelt and slid across the bonnet on her backside, leaving a smooth trough in the snow. She landed and didn't skip a stride. The warehouse directly ahead: that was her destination – it should offer a perfect vantage point.

As she approached the old service entrance door she could clearly see that it was barely clinging to its hinges, the wood all rotten to hell. She slung her rifle round in one smooth motion and held it before her. She clattered one strong boot-clad foot into the latch side and it burst asunder. She stepped into the vast old warehouse and scanned the interior, ready to fire at any hostiles within. Nothing. No–one. It appeared that it had once been used to store and manufacture clothing. Several huge looms occupied the centre of the floor space and around them giant spools, around which the materials would have been wound and fed into the machines. The entire place was thick with dust. Everything else that was not bolted to the floor had been pilfered. Satisfied that she was alone, she raced across the room and began to scale a metal staircase which zig-zagged its way up a corner of the warehouse. At each floor a walkway led off to service the various basic office spaces and storage spaces. Her feet clanged on the steps and she was fearful she would alert attention, but frankly this could be make or break. If the conversation she had not long since overheard was to be trusted, she could be about to complete the first part of her mission.

She had been listening in on a group of Click addicts who were squabbling about all manner of things which all seemed inconsequential and of very little interest. That was until one of them began to voice his concern about a Resident that was rumoured to be aiding Ferals. An old wives' tale, the others had snapped back – everyone had heard that one, but it was impossible. There was no way in or out other than the main gate. That story had been doing the rounds in the underground world of J15 for years. Even she had heard about this, but it had never been proven. It was, as one of them so eloquently put it, horseshit, bullshit and dogshit all shit on by gossipers until you couldn't tell which shit was which and what the hell the story was in the first place. The lead gossiper, though, was insistent: apparently he had seen them himself. Seen them coming in through a large sink-hole, a sinkhole which, if accurately described, she felt sure she knew the location of. If he had been keeping count of the days right, he rekoned they would be coming through again today. They began to bicker as to whether this was all a load of rubbish, who even cared, whether they should get in on it, whether they should try and stop it. As a fight broke out amongst them, she was already spinning on her heels and taking off across the Jurisdiction to get in position – it was the best, or rather the only, solid lead she'd had. She'd stopped at the point at which she felt she was high enough to observe without being seen, but low enough to listen in if words were spoken. She'd moved along the walkway and holed up in a fourth–storey office, began the arduous stakeout.

Three hours later she was still looking from a shattered window, scanning up and down the street below her. It was a bottleneck, a perfect spot. Opposite her and running the full length of the street were more high–rise units, warehouses and office blocks. To her right, one end of the road ended with a huge pile of rubble, the remains of what was once a refinery. It was a colossal mass of concrete, steel girders, glass, and timber all entwined. The road had once split off into a T-junction, but the pile of destruction completely blocked the end of the street. She peered through her rifle scope and, starting at this end like she had done countless times over the last few hours, scanned left, her shoulder joints creaking from lack of activity.

A rusty red truck lying on its roof, the tyres long plundered. A bent road sign, its message completely removed by time and the weather. Next, on her side of the street, there sat an old guard hut, the windows all smashed and the door left wide open. A burnt–out car, its driver slumped against the steering wheel, a very long time dead and decayed. An old set of tracks in the dust and snow came out of a door in the building furthest down on the left–hand side, but they stopped abruptly in the middle of the road where a dark patch of old dried blood stained the ground – a mysterious death. At the far end of the street, another collapsed building half stood on the precipitous edge of a deep hole in the ground. The other half of the building had crumbled and slid down, swallowed by what looked like a great screaming mouth in the tarmac.

She adjusted the focus of the scope very slightly and clicked her neck off to one side. This was starting to feel like it could be a long stakeout.

Rosalyn Torres was, she knew, hands down, the most deadly sniper in all of J3. It was for this reason that she was in the position she was, why no-one else would be given such a mission. To be staked out in the most dangerous part of Axiom hunting the most dangerous Residents alone. She had never missed a target. 'We bring the cold' were the words she uttered before squeezing the trigger, words she had said 161 times over the twelve freezes and melts since her graduation. 161 rounds had been fired from her weapon, an old school AWC .50 calibre she had named 'The Cold Bringer', and each shot had resulted in a death. Not one miss. She remembered them all. Fifty-eight Ferals, forty-six Click addicts, twenty-six members of the Farms' herds, sixteen beasts that had roamed too close to the walls, nine rioters following the failed harvest of her nineteenth year (those were the kills that brought her the initial recognition and acclaim from her peers), five illegal traders and four heads of escaping cattle.

Each and every one of their faces was seared onto her mind's eye forever. All of them had the same completely unsuspecting look, oblivious to the fact that they were living their final moments. The bullet always carried out its deadly task so efficiently. Their bodies would drop out of her scope's field of sight, replaced by a slight mist of blood before she was able to see whether for a fleeting moment they were shocked by their undoing. They never told you in training, but Rosalyn thought in hindsight she should have known – a sniper will always see, with complete clarity, those they kill and they will, every one of them, forever haunt their dispatcher. Her victims were ghosts in her dreams. Their dead faces sought her out when she was helpless in her sleep and chewed away little pieces of her conscious and her self-worth.

Torres was widely revered, held an almost legendary status amongst her fellow J3 guards as a hugely reliable and effective harbinger of death, one that the Bastion made very good use of. She was pretty sure she was earmarked for induction into the Shrouded by her superiors – it was a grisly procedure involving Click, a scalpel and a tattoo gun but one which was deemed a great honour to endure. She'd even seen the half-completed paperwork, confirming that her suspicion was just a few sheets of paper and ink from being a reality: it had been spread all over the desk of her commanding officer when he'd summoned her to the meeting just shy of six weeks ago.

Normally when such a command came through she would be full of a combination of excitement and trepidation. Who would they task her to kill? Where would she be sent to and for how long? This particular time it had been something of a blessing. Her current post was testing her. It was basically just endless patrols of J9, and for a few reasons it had been a hard slog for a couple of months.

It did not utilise her skills. She was a proficient hand-to-hand fighter and a crack shot with a small firearm, but then so were most J3s; the skill that set her apart was how deadly accurate she was with her rifle over distance. Her talents for sniping were wasted here and she felt frustrated and restricted. Furthermore this assignment involved constant companionship. No beat-cop patrols alone. Every day was shared in the company of another guard. She much preferred to be on her own; these fools would always attempt to engage in inane conversation – the weather (which never changed!), their boring lives and families, unfunny jokes and tales of how damn heroic they were when breaking up a bar fight or arresting a Citizen for a crime as heinous as stealing a cup of water from the shower barns. The effort of appearing to be entertained and civil was terribly draining.

Perhaps the worst thing of all, though, was that their very presence here intimidated and worried the regular Citizens and Rosalyn saw no sense in it – though that, she was told, was precisely the point.

'Nothing keeps a flock of sheep compliant like fear, so get out there and look mean and unapproachable... Or just act natural, Torres,' her Captain had commented.

Rosalyn Torres openly admitted she was not the most sociable of creatures but she saw no sense in making others feel uncomfortable and threatened for no reason. In truth, crimes were very rare. The prospect of the Farms was so terrifyingly real that it was deterrent enough.

So when the call came, she virtually skipped to the headquarters for a briefing. She stood before the broad wooden desk of Captain Benitez, or, as some of the less wise corporals had nicknamed him, 'Captain Cube'. The last man caught calling him that he'd had thrown in a trash compactor, and laughed his head off when the machine was done and spat out a perfect square mass of waste material, rusted metal, bones, flesh and blood.

He sat behind his cluttered desk, arbitrarily reading the command from a piece of paper in front of him; he could not have looked more uninterested if he tried. Benitez was a squat individual who had all the dimensions of a box, as wide as he was tall and his head sunk into his shoulders on a short neck. He really was a man of right angles. His stubby legs finished with feet that were too long for his height, such that he always held them at ten to two. On his round head he wore his uniform cap, which covered a thinning receded hairline, the elastic of it digging in deep to the soft flesh above his ears. He wore it low on his forehead, almost resting on the protruding eyebrows which overhung his small deep-set beady eyes. As he licked a chipolata of a thumb to aid him in turning the pages of the brief, Rosie stood before him, marvelling at how perfectly centrally his squished nose sat on his face – pock-marked and red from too much alcohol.

Never taking his eyes from the document, he sniffed hard, hocked, held the globule of filth in his mouth and revoltingly swallowed. Completely oblivious to this disgusting act, he continued to slowly read to himself. Torres stood before him waiting for his command and allowed her eyes to wander across his desk and there it was: a J3–J1 transfer form, and her name was scribbled in the top box. It was followed by her vital statistics, age and date of birth. A half-completed checklist, so far full of ticks. Benitez spoke and her eyes whipped back up to meet his. He proceeded to explain her assignment.

'You're on your own again, Torres. J15.'

'J15, sir? There is nothing there, I don't... '

'Err shhh, I am not finished and anyway... ', another sniff, 'it is not for you to question why. You are a puppet and I'm pulling the strings.' He mimicked the action of playing with the child's toy but managed none of a child's enthusiasm for play. 'You are to case out the dead Jurisdiction. Says here stealth is paramount, so you are not to be seen but you are to see all.' Another deep sniff. 'We have received unconfirmed reports of Ferals using J15 as a catflap into Axiom. They are coming in at their leisure and making off with all kinds of resources – grain, oil, meat... people! Just last winter we checked all the perimeter walls – there are no gaps, no holes, no goddamn backdoors. Find out how the hell they are getting in and out.'

'Then kill them all. Yes, understood, sir.'

'No, no killing! Observation only. Find out where these vermin are wriggling into our city. Wait. Observe. Then follow them out!'

'Out, sir? Beyond the walls?' Rosalyn's heart began to beat faster. Was the prospect nerve-wracking or exciting? She was not sure.

'Yes, Torres, was I not clear? I feel like I was being quite concise and slow just so you could keep up.' Benitez yawned.

Rosalyn clenched her fists at her sides. Oh, how easy it would be to smash her gun butt into that bull's-eye of a nose. 'Clear, sir, sorry sir, what should I do when I'm on the outside?'

'Well I was coming to that before you interrupted me with foolish questions.' Another sniff and his running nose gurgled its way back up, defying gravity. 'You are to follow, find out where these rats are nesting, then report back.' Another sniff. This time he swilled from cheek to cheek and Rosalyn held back the desire to yack. 'Then we may instruct you to take a small unit back to the nest... then you are to cull them all, particularly the Feral bitches. We don't want any more Feral kits being born now, do we?'

'When do I start, sir?'

'Torres, are you still here?' With that final demeaning line, Benitez returned his eyes to the document on his desk and did not look back up.

She had done just as she was instructed to do for near on a month. She had sat still as a stone, the snow settling on and all around her for days at a time, just watching. She had kept moving from position to position throughout J15, being careful to cover her tracks and leave no evidence of her presence. She had seen the odd group of Click addicts fighting, scavenging and salvaging what little valuable or usable materials were left, and she'd witnessed two Citizens conduct what was undoubtedly an illegal trade exchange. She would normally have killed them all, but a shot fired would change the whole dynamic of the disused Jurisdiction. She would be revealed. She wanted them going about their business as they would at any other time. They needed to be completely at ease in their surroundings with their guard down.

So she watched… and she saw nothing.

Until now. It was timely, as luck would have it: the sighting came perhaps a day, two days max before she would have had to abandon post and return for provisions.

She very nearly missed him. Rosie was preparing to start the scan back up the street when a hooded figure emerged most unexpectedly from the hole. It was nothing more than the top of a head at first, the face obscured by the hood – someone was peering out and over the edge of the hole at the street in front of them. They were sitting so very still themselves and Rosalyn hoped she had not given herself away with the swaying movement of her rifle. The figure's arm came up and waved to someone behind him down in the ground, a beckoning motion to follow him up to the surface. The wind dropped and the road was silent as a crypt. You could hear a pin drop.

Rosie held her breath and heard the figure speak; a man's voice, it was no more than a whisper. 'Coast is clear. Let's move.' 'Alpha target' she named him in her head.

He hoisted himself up and out on to the road side, stood for a moment, surveyed his surroundings, and then, leaning back down, he helped first one then another companion out. 'Bravo target' and 'Charlie target'.

'Where the hell are we? How far is it to the door?' Charlie asked.

'Not far, not far, boy. You just follow me now, quickly and quietly,' Alpha replied.

Charlie and Bravo hesitated a moment. Charlie spoke again. 'What guarantees do we have that you can provide what we need?'

'You don't have any guarantees, boy. I don't give out guarantees! You know I've supplied the goods before – that's good enough! I know just the target – it'll be the perfect snatch and grab – so quit the questions, boy, and let's move! It's not safe stood out here in the open, gossiping like old women at the market! If Clickers find us, you are on your own, boy, and believe me, I'm the only one that knows this place better than those junkies do. I'll get away, you two will be a tasty mid-afternoon snack.' Alpha half coughed, half cackled the last sentence out.

'Don't get ahead of yourself, today is just pure reconnaissance. We're scoping out the route in and out. You show us the way in from the Land Reclaimed, to your door and into the active Jurisdictions... we want a glimpse of the target too... OK? Then we report back and when the time is right, we'll come and get her.' Charlie said, reasserting his dominance. It was clear he was the one in charge. Alpha was the service provider, Charlie the client and brains, Bravo the brawn.

'Fine, fine, but move your Feral asses. It doesn't change the fact we're bickering out in the open when we should –' Bravo suddenly stepped forward and with frightening speed drew a dagger from an unseen scabbard hidden up his opposite sleeve, grabbed Alpha by the throat and pressed the blade inside the hood, presumably, Rosalyn thought, just below his eye.

'Watch your tongue or it'll be us dining on a mid-afternoon snack of liver of human trafficker! Liver's our favourite, isn't it?' he asked Charlie.

'Mmm yeah, delicious,' Charlie responded while withdrawing his knife and prodding into the lower abdomen of Alpha. 'The Clickers can finish up the flayed remains we leave of you too.'

'OK, boy, OK, I didn't mean no offence. Just trying to move this little excursion along,' Alpha said, looking for a way to defuse the situation while squirming a bit in the grasp of Bravo.

'Then move along, little tour guide,' said Bravo as he released his grip and slipped his knife back into its concealed sheath.

Charlie did likewise. 'Yes, come on – quickly and quietly now, isn't that what you said?'

Alpha stood before the other two men and at his waist Rosie watched him very slightly flex his fingers, a surge of tension. He was not happy about how they had just treated him and she felt certain he was about to attack them, but instead he threw his arms up into the air in mock defeat and said, 'Well, that's all I wanted, boy. Let's go, this way, follow me!'

Rosalyn maintained position. She would wait for them to return; they had said they were coming back this way.

Sure enough, just a few hours later they did, though it was only Bravo and Charlie. They came clambering over the rubble at the far end and stalked their way down on her side of the street keeping close to the buildings. When they reached the hole they slid down into it and disappeared from view. As soon as they had done so Rosie stood, slung the Cold Bringer over her shoulder and drew her silenced firearm from her thigh holster. She turned and slid down the ladder behind her to the ground floor and moved to the door to peer out. Nothing. Not a sound and no sign that her movement had been detected. She slipped from the doorway and approached the opening in the ground in a crouched position, with weapon raised and heartbeat racing but still the epitome of stealth. At the edge of the precipice she could hear below the muffled conversation of the two Feral men. She began her own slow, steady, silent descent. She paused from time to time to ensure she hadn't been heard, but based on the conversation faintly echoing below her in the gloom, Bravo and Charlie remained oblivious to her pursuit.

At the bottom the hole opened out into a large cave full of debris. She tiptoed her way after the sound of her targets. The underground cave was full of the remains of the collapsed half of the building above. As she ventured deeper in, though, it became clear that it was also being used as a makeshift storage area since there were neat piles of all manner of other seemingly useless bits of kit, mechanical parts and machine components from the surface that would have all once kept J15 a throng of industrial activity.

The two intruders unknowingly led the way and Rosalyn followed. Through an old wooden door in the cave wall and down deeper along a sloping maze of tunnel systems, until quite unexpectedly they turned a corner and emerged out into the world beyond. The Land Reclaimed as the Ferals called it, as for all of the manipulation and abuse humans had imposed on the earth in laying claim to it, nature had begun to take it back.

Only a handful of Axiom Residents had stood this side of the wall and Rosie suddenly felt very exposed, very small and insignificant in the vastness of the space before her. Fortunately, though, it was not completely open space: she could follow Bravo and Charlie with plenty of cover. For the first half mile out from the wall there were strewn the countless shells of old rusting vehicles of all shapes and sizes, large pockets of thick, tall grasses and the odd bush or pine sapling winding its way up and out of the chassis of this or that old car, reaching upwards for the dim light. Rosie pulled up her scarf to hide the steam of her breath in the cold air and ducked and weaved, moving between and behind all the obstacles, always out of sight. Until she reached the tree line.

So often she had sat guard in a tower looking out at the wilderness beyond the wall, just scanning up and down the tree line; she had never thought she would one day be walking out and beyond it. She leant her back against the nearest tree trunk and stared back at the immense scale of the city and the wall looming menacingly over everything inside and out. Rosie knew, though, that her next steps took her beyond anything she had ever known or seen. That mixed feeling of excitement and fear bubbled up in her stomach and her heart hammered away in her chest. She took a deep breath and rolled herself round the trunk and into the Barrier Woods. As a child of Axiom you were never taught much of the Barrier but, as a student reached graduation age, tales would begin to circulate amongst the Jurisdiction of the Corruptible of the monsters, human and animal alike, that would creep out from the darkness of the pines and scale the walls to snatch you from your bed. As she took her first steps into the old woodland, Rosalyn thought that it felt like all those tales could well hold an element of truth. Yet what she also thought was that everything she had ever seen emerge from the wood, everything she'd spotted through the scope of a sniper rifle from atop the wall, she had shot at, and all of them had died. Though as she followed the two Ferals deeper and deeper into the Barrier, and as the trees became taller and broader and their foliage denser, so the light grew dimmer and those childish fears of monsters began to tease at her sense of logic.

For four hours she pursued them. Four hours of stealthy pursuit, flitting from tree to tree, from fallen trunk to thorny bush, from patches of ferns to clusters of boulders and only once did they break conversation, pause and look about them. It was the precise moment at which she was crossing a more open part of the wood, a break in the trees and it was all she could do to throw herself on the ground and remain as still and quiet as possible. She hoped that from a distance in the low light she would appear to be nothing more than a rut in the ground. She held her breath as Bravo took two steps forward, very definitely looking in her direction. Another step, Rosalyn decided, and she would rise to her knees, draw her pistol and kill them both. A snap of a twig off to her right took hers and the Feral's attention.

A monster in the gloom?

They spun to face it, while Rosie took the chance to roll sideways and stand up against the trunk of a tree and draw her sidearm. She peered around to see if she had been seen just as a huge stag burst from the underbrush into the clearing. He was majestic. A huge head of antlers a full six foot across, his coat a deep shiny red, he stood tall and defiant with chest puffed out, eyeing up the two Feral men. This King of the Barrier let out a snort and a cloud of his warm breath burst from his nostrils. Rosalyn was in complete awe. She had only ever seen such beasts from a distance through the sight of her rifle. A great white bear sharpening his claws on a tree, huge cats with strange markings skulking through the wreckage outside the wall, small packs of bickering, snarling wolves, wild cows with shaggy fur and large horns lumbering along the tree line. Up close, though, she could not help but marvel at the healthy buck and despite the two dangerous

foes just twenty feet from her, a smile spread across the face of Rosalyn Torres. Charlie ruined the moment though. As he slid his blade
from its scabbard the scrape of steel on leather broke the silence and
the deer swiftly turned and with a crash of branches leapt back in to
the bushes and bounded away and out of sight.

The two Ferals had continued onwards, with Rosie as the shadow
that followed. Eventually though they had emerged out the other side
of the dim–lit oppressive air of the Barrier. She lingered in the shadows as the two men stood on the edge of a field of crops discussing
their next move.

'I'm spent. Let's just rest at the farm for the night then move on in
the morning,' said Charlie.

'But we're expected back inside a week. That puts us off schedule,'
Bravo replied.

'To hell with the schedule, if I don't get some rest I'll not be in a fit
state to protect you from all the big bad monsters between here and
home.'

'The only reason I'll need your old arse looking out for me is if we
report back late and the boss sets the rest against us for a lack of punc-
tuality!'

'Calm down, one night won't make any difference, especially when
we get back and let the boss know precisely how we can get in and
take what we need,' Charlie ended with a confident tone as he strode
off into the crops and towards the old house on the hill with Bravo
trailing after him.

Torres assessed the situation. She could continue to pursue them
but her provisions were low – no, she would return to Axiom and
report to Benitez. The Ferals would return and she would be ready.

Chapter 8

Bevan was laying on his back staring up at the ceiling. The last ten days had been something of a blur and he was just as mentally exhausted as he was physically. His body ached; the muscles in his arms and legs were burning from the exertion. J3 Guards, overseen by J1s, had them keeping good pace through long–distance runs and short–sprint bleep tests. They had been lifting weights, climbing ropes and walls, and crawling through ditches. When they weren't working on fitness, being pushed through various cardio drills or building muscle mass and bodies capable of surviving the tough task ahead of them, they were being briefed in detail on stage sections of the overall project plan. Or the teams had been busying themselves devising complex electrical circuits and wiring topologies. Tutors arrived from J5 to conduct refresher courses in construction and engineering principles. Routes through the wilderness were formulated; logistical requirements for the journey out to the ice mass were assessed and put in place. During all of this Bevan continued to formulate his own logistical requirements for fleeing from the project and seeking out Efran and his Solacity. He'd review the maps and try to work out the best points at which escape might just be possible.

The training had begun the morning after the meeting with Eleanor De Sanctis. Just as Stricken had said, it was early. Long before the alarms began to sound to signal the start of the working day, the same metal, snarling machines with their menacing red eyes had arrived and taken them back to Central. The powers that be had obviously decided they didn't require the show of intimidation of the previous day and once inside the gates they were not guarded. Stricken had met them at the entrance to Central personally and after instructing them to follow him he had led them in silence across the compound and into one of the smaller storage units.

It had been completely stripped out and refitted for a new purpose. The walls, floor and ceiling were still cold, hard, dark metal and there were no windows. Inside, four free–standing lamps provided ample light for the relatively small space. There were gym weights and two combat dummies, one of which had an arrow protruding from its abdomen, the other an axe casually left embedded in its head. There were racks of more primitive weapons as well as advanced firearms, a bookshelf stuffed with rolled–up and bound documents and a large trolley full of circuitry, solder, wires and electrical devices. In the middle of the room was a large table, an incredibly detailed map of Axiom drawn directly onto its hard black surface, in the centre. Every documented building, road and walkway was drawn out to scale. Overlaid on this was a secondary map of the electrical power infrastructure of the city. All the space on the outside edges of the table, Bevan guessed, would be drawn out as they reported back on their journey beyond the walls.

The plan for Project Wind was, in theory, quite simple. Teddy's construction team would leave first under the cover of night and get a week's head start. They'd be accompanied and supervised by a small unit of J1 and J3 guards. It was estimated that it would take around nine days to get out to the site. Here they would very quickly build some temporary houses and a mess hall for the workforce that would follow. They'd also erect two guard towers to be manned in shifts throughout the project, to offer protection from Ferals and wild beasts. It would also ensure they could keep tabs on the workers. They should be complete for the arrival of Bevan's team, who would then hook up the batteries and generators. Once the power was switched on, they'd all work together to assemble the wind turbines. They would take some eight months to complete, and a further ten to route the electrical cabling back to Axiom.

The wind turbines would need to be transported in the fleet of large trucks they had seen parked outside the Bastion. They had been built in secret and came in several parts and each component would need to be joined together at the site. With this new resource, Madame De Sanctis also hoped that eventually they would be able to sustain larger yields of crops under bigger UV houses. The existing sheds were greedy with the electricity and they were dining on a dwindling resource – the oil *would* run out, but the wind would blow forever. The most obedient and easily influenced Residents were surely those that were well–fed and happy. They might even be able to redevelop and expand the city as a result.

In the storage unit, they had been introduced to their teams. Teddy would lead on the physical construction of the infrastructure itself, support platforms and the site's housing. These simple structures would be occupied by engineers, and eventually a permanent set of Residents, to form a security force to protect the vital installation from Feral raids. His construction team consisted of some forty–five large burly men and around ten equally physically imposing women from J7, 9 and 11. After a whirlwind introduction of names, credentials and greetings, the constructors left the storage unit to continue planning and training for the project. Bevan had not seen any of them since, including his best friend.

Bevan had been given a smaller team of just six other individuals, five of whom were from J17, one woman and four men of varying ages. He recognised all of them from his home Jurisdiction but this was the first time he'd ever spoken to any of them. Initial impressions were positive though – they seemed in good humour and it was obvious from conversations that they were very skilled electrical engineers – so he had faith that they would get the job done and get it done well. The sixth member was just a boy, probably no older than eleven or twelve years old, Bevan guessed. He must have been very near to undertaking his graduation.

Stricken had arrived with him shortly after the others had finished their introductions. 'Another one for your team, Hughes,' he had said and shoved the boy a step forward. 'Smaller hands will be useful for some of the more intricate circuits.' With that he gave an almost reassuring pat on the lad's shoulder and left them.

This unexpected and unusual addition to the team was quiet, shy and nervous and suffered from tremendous social anxieties. These traits were not particularly conducive to building team rapport, but it was clear that he might indeed prove useful.

As soon as Stricken had left, the boy had given a very slight nod and rather awkward glance at Bevan and walked past the group to the trolley box of electrical equipment. He immediately sat down on the floor cross-legged and set about deconstructing and reassembling a broken circuit breaker. Bevan left the group talking amongst themselves as they stood around the table map pointing out where they lived, other places they knew and other such inane chatter. He walked over to the sixth member of the team, stood over him and watched the boy work, impressed with his speed and accuracy but also puzzled by the faint zapping and crackling noises he was making with his mouth as he brought the complex piece of kit back to life.

'Hi, kid. I'm Bevan,' he said extending his hand in greeting. The boy fell silent and shifted nervously. 'You know I'm supposed to be in charge, but I don't see it that way. I mean, you can fix stuff just as quick as me, if not faster! Perhaps they've chosen the wrong guy to be the boss!' He laughed, trying to encourage the young lad to engage with him. Bevan reached into the box and brought out a piece he knew was needed and sat down next to the boy. 'Here, try this part,' he said and handed it to him. The youngster took it from him, quickly snatching it from his hand, being especially careful not to make physical contact, and began soldering it in place on the circuit board. Bevan continued, 'You know, I think you and me are going to get along. I love making this stuff work too. I get just like you, full concentration, head down, mind on the task at hand, excited about what lights it might have, what job it might be able to do for me, what noise it will make.' Bevan made an electric shock noise and the boy laughed a little but immediately grimaced at the sound, his eyes shifting rapidly from side to side. He looked both embarrassed and worried by this tiny show of emotion. Bevan made the noise again, 'Zzzaap!' and gave a playful nudge with his finger in the boy's side. Quick as a flash, the lad seized his finger and twisted it painfully.

His grip was strong. Bevan let out a slight yelp that fortunately the others didn't hear and gritted his teeth to stifle a louder whimper. He let out a relieved sigh when the boy released him from his grasp.

'No, I don't like touching, no,' the boy said.

'Ouch, oh, OK, I'm sorry, I was just playing,' Bevan stood up rubbing his sore finger, 'but I bet it makes that noise when it's finished.' He bent down and made the noise again by the boys ear – he laughed awkwardly again and turned to look up at Bevan. A fleeting glance, no more.

His long dark hair hung down across his forehead, partially obscuring his equally dark brown eyes. He swept his tousled hair back up into a neat fringe, 'Hi, Bevan. Yes, my name's a "B" name too. My name is Benedict.'

'Now we appreciate your help in this little task, we really do, but we aint gonna be setting you free with no automatic weapons,' said the stern-looking yet uncharacteristically friendly guard named Albert Goode-Dooher – or 'Buddy' as he was known to most – as he tossed Bevan and Benedict a bow and an arrow each for the archery drill. 'That's not so say these won't do some serious damage if you know how to use them, and with a host of beasties and Ferals out there you may need it,' he finished with a wink to little Benedict.

'Guns are betterer, yes,' said Benedict in a sulky voice crossing his arms across his chest.

'Exactly why I'll have one out there, and you and Bevan will have bows. If you boys decide to play silly buggers, I'll have some six hundred rounds a minute. You my little friend will have one shot to stop ol' Albert, so pay attention,' he said while chuckling and ruffling the top of Benedict's head which in turn pushed the boy's hair down over his eyes.

'No, you, no!' Benedict yelled rearranging his hair and scowling at the guard.

'You won't be shooting no–one and nothing with your eyes hidden in that silly hat!' Albert laughed back at him.

'Hey, show us how then, Buddy,' said Bevan, stepping between the two before the boy got angry. In his short time spent with Benedict, he'd learnt that the boy's fuse could be short and his temper fiery. On more than one occasion his frustration had got the better of him. He had completely trashed a circuit board they had been working on because he singed the end of his finger on a soldering iron. Another time one of the other team members had laughed when he had tripped over some loose cabling. The same guy – twice the boy's age, twice the boy's size – had found it difficult to laugh at anything through his broken nose and chipped teeth the following day.

'OK, it's simple really, it's all about the breath and absolute focused concentration on the target,' said Albert as he fitted an arrow to the bow string and pulled it back taut. 'Now to begin with we shall be aiming for the stomach on the dummy, it's the biggest target and you two are just novices,' he said with a sideways smirk at Benedict. 'Now focus on the point you want to hit, I don't mean the general area, I mean the exact point, just a space that the tip of your arrow-head would cover, block everything else out... and hold... your... breath... ' They watched as he steadied himself, took a long, slow inhale and held it. Without warning he released the string and there came a satisfying whistle of the air being cut by cord and arrow, followed by a thud as it found its mark on the dummy directly where you would find the belly button on a man. 'And out pour his guts,' said Albert looking a little too smug. 'Now your turn fellas, Bevan you go first, show this whippersnapper how it's done,' he said with a playful nudge.

Bevan fitted an arrow and stepped up to fire. The bow felt heavy in his hands. It was a fine polished carbon that his sweaty palms were struggling to keep a hold of. The arm holding back the string began to shake a little at the strain. He did as Albert had done, slowed his breathing until he found himself holding it. He stared across the room at the stomach of the dummy, squinted. Waited. Fired. The arrow flew straight and faster than his eye could register. He re-focused to see it shuddering away with the force of impact. Right in the crotch.

Albert roared with laughter, 'Well that'd slow me down and my wife would be fuming, but it'd not likely kill me', he raised a hand, about to clap it on the shoulder of his younger pupil but stopped short, presumably recalling the way Benedict had reacted previously, 'Come on. Your turn, lad.'

Benedict raised his bow, looking decidedly uninterested.

Bevan knelt down beside him, 'Take your time, little man. Show Buddy he'd need more than a machine gun.' He saw a smile in the boy's eyes, pleased for the encouragement.

'Yeah, yeah, I will Bevan, I'm a good shot I am, yes.' But he rushed it. No sooner had he taken in a breath than he'd fired. Bevan sighed, even Albert's patience could be tested. Benedict needed to take the training seriously. The world beyond the wall was not a playground, so he feared that these new skills might well come in useful. His sigh though was premature and his frustration quickly turned to suspicion. The arrow was lodged very deep directly between the eyes. Albert stood alongside them, his mouth open wide in astonishment at the unerring accuracy of the shot. Bevan hid his suspicion and surprise with a smile. Was this tattoo-less young boy more than a spy? Was he a skilled assassin?

Loud, slow, purposeful clapping was suddenly heard from the door-way. It filled the metal container and drowned out the din of conversation. Stricken stood there, flanked by two of the Shrouded. He was applauding Benedict's marksmanship.

'It would seem your training is paying off,' he said to the boy, but making sure everyone in the room heard. He continued, this time addressing them all though, 'As a reward for your commitment to the project and the future of Axiom, Eleanor De Sanctis has arranged a party for you all in Jurisdiction 1. A week from now you will all join us in celebrating this great undertaking, you will be making history and securing the future of our great city.' He spoke slowly and kept lingering, unnerving eye contact with each of them one by one as he spoke. 'You will eat, drink and be merry, you'll have one day to recover in the familiar surroundings of your homes and this great city, before we set out beyond the walls. I'm sure you realise this is not an invitation, your attendance is not optional.'

With that he walked out, leaving the whole group feeling anxious and in no way in the party mood. Enforced fun was almost certainly anything but fun and the sort of fun enforced by Stricken and the Shrouded could lead to severe punishments if you were perceived to be ungrateful or not in the party spirit.

Chapter 9

It was a week out from Violet's fifth birthday and Rosalyn Torres and her daughter stood in their modest kitchen preparing the mixture for Violet's birthday cake. All the previous week they had scoured the J7 Merchants' Quarter for eggs, flour, sugar and butter to make a simple sponge all covered in icing. All four ingredients were extremely hard to come by but J3 was one Jurisdiction where guards (themselves Residents of J3) tended to turn a blind eye to the illegal black market goods that found their way out of other Jurisdictions through the secret trade routes of J15 and into the general supply lines. There was a fractious agreement of convenience between the law enforcers and the crime bosses of the trade. The Merchants' Quarter was bustling, the bosses got rich and from time to time the J3 were able to demonstrate they were making a difference by apprehending and making an example of some low-ranking scumbags.

The shopping trip had been the fun kind of treasure hunt that Violet had so loved, her tiny hand clasped in Rosie's as they wove their way through the crowds of buyers and sellers. An assault on the senses, the market place was full of smells – raw and cooking foods like bread, meat and stews, chemicals such as paint, antifreeze and oil and, mixed in with it all, the pong of people and the livestock for sale, their body odour, shit and harsh perfumes to cover up the other two. All the sounds made little Violet's head spin – there were the whispers of dodgy dealings, the yelling of tradesmen, the laughs and shouts of negotiation combined with the clatter of hammer on metal, saw on wood, cutlery scraping and chinking on crockery, chickens clucking and pigs squealing. It was all taken in at waist height by the young girl. Spray of snowmelt as big boots stomped by, a swish of fabric in her face as a woman sped past. She loved it all. Together they were the perfect team for disarming the tradesmen with their good and adorable looks and the tale of a birthday cake.

'That's it, sweety, keep that stirring and I'll crack in the egg. It's going to be the prettiest cake for my prettiest princess, eh?'

Rosie had never thought it possible that she could be so naturally maternal. Being a mother to Violet had come so easily to her – it was fuelled by a love so complete and all-consuming that it was impossible to be anything other than besotted and devoted to the girl. Right there in that moment as she baked a cake with her daughter, she reflected that not so long ago it would have been a scenario she could not have even imagined.

A sniper was a lonely job, she operated alone and the solitary years had made her cold and unapproachable. She could not recall the last time she had laughed. Rosalyn accepted her role. She had perfected an expression that warned others from even trying to engage in conversation with her, and completely de-sexualising herself was a conscious decision. She wore her uniform loose, trousers cinched in at the ankle and stuffed into her boots. A T-shirt instead of a vest top, covered with a baggy sweatshirt. Her only tight article of clothing was a bra that flattened rather than accentuated her bust. Rosie had been named because of her deep red hair that, if left to grow, was thick, shiny and curly, but instead it was shorn, cropped close to her scalp and almost always covered by a tatty old regulation J3 uniform cap. Her Jurisdiction tattoo was just another smudge on her ruddy, bruised and often grimy complexion. Her small button nose, defined chin and high cheek bones were strikingly, classically beautiful but it would take a lot of scrubbing up for these features to shine through. If she'd ever wanted them to.

Even her daughter's birth hadn't improved her social skills. Many marvelled at the fact that she had managed to ever get pregnant. 'It'd be like fucking a snowman, she's so cold,' was often the joke in the mess hall; 'Yeah, or a Click addict, she'd not feel a thing' others would comment.

The act itself had been completely nondescript. Rosie didn't even know his name. A rare posting out on the city wall, watching the wilderness for approaching threats with 'some guy', and it just kind of happened. Some fumbling to undo zips and belts and half pull down trousers and underwear, a few thrusts in the dark, in the cold, not even a kiss exchanged, and it was over.

'Well that ought to sort out that sexual tension we were building up, eh?' he had said afterwards while stuffing himself away and zip-ping up his fly. Rosie had not felt any tension but it was, she reflected, the longest watch period she had gone in her career without firing the Cold Bringer. Had she come to rely on the buzz of the kill? Perhaps that was why she had let him, why she didn't snap his fingers the instant he dared to 'accidentally' stroke her hand. It wasn't her first time, but it was the first time she'd seemed to instantly forget every detail of the act the moment he had grunted his climax and slid away from her. She had only even seen him twice since in passing, and never again spoke another word to the father of her child. Not even to tell him his seed had taken root.

The child grew inside her slowly to begin with, it seemed. She had gone about her day–to–day duties never even realising she was just months away from a miracle. Roll calls, target practice, patrols, even excursions beyond the wall and never once did she feel like she was with child. She was blossoming but no sign of a bump. When the vomiting started, she had visited the infirmary. She had told herself it would be no good to be doubled over retching up your guts when you should be scanning the perimeter for threats. The nurse, a haggard crone with a face that resembled an old creased leather bag, had cackled and poured scorn on Rosalyn for her mistaken self-diagnosis. While she had set about tattooing Rosie's wrist with the mark all women received when pregnant (a permanent sign to signify they had birthed their one permitted offspring) she had harped on incessantly, asking anyone who might care to listen, how could a real woman not recognise her body's signs? What sort of mother would she be if she was oblivious to the precious package she carried? What man would sow his seed in a woman so clearly not cut out for motherhood?'

But the nurse was wrong, so wrong. The very second she was told she was pregnant, Rosie changed. She had felt it so keenly, like an epiphany. She was, in that very moment, suddenly full of purpose like never before. As she stood there with the nurse wittering on around her, her hands had involuntarily moved to protectively cradle her stomach, the tiny suggestion of a bump now so obvious, an indicator right there, literally under her nose. For the first time what her touch registered was now clearly an engorged stomach, a slightly raised tummy, the skin taut and her bellybutton not quite as deep as it once was. Her fingertips brushing against the coarse shirt of her uniform, she felt like she could even feel the tiny heartbeat inside. She already loved the child more than anything else in her life. This life inside her was more precious than her own and she fully intended to make sure that her baby knew love and knew the good things in life. She was removed from active duty with immediate effect, something that, had it happened the very day before, would have torn her world apart, devastated her. Now though, as she watched the nurse sign the paperwork, she felt elated: she could dedicate all her thoughts and efforts to nurturing her baby inside her, bringing it into the world and raising her.

Her.

Rosie knew it was a baby girl, could sense it. Standing there watching her life change, Rosalyn Torres did something she had not done for longer than she could remember: she smiled. Smiled and cried. A single tear of joy escaped and trickled its merry way down her cheek; a clean line of happiness left in its wake on her mucky face.

Seven months later almost to the day the smile was gone. It was replaced by the face of labouring agony. A pleasure-pain phenomenon, it was so unexplainably glorious in its ability to provide feelings of utter happiness while simultaneously those of sheer physical anguish. Mercifully it didn't last long; fifty–nine minutes and seventeen seconds after contractions began Violet Torres was born. Rosie lay back, unclenched her teeth, drew a forearm across her sweat–dappled brow and accepted her daughter into her arms. Violet wasn't crying, (she was always such a good girl) and when her searching mouth found the teat, mother and child were one again. Rosie's smile returned as she looked down into her daughter's tiny face. While she knew the baby's eyes were far from fully functional yet, it was as if they saw one another completely, not just in the simple physical way but in a way that Rosie was certain was an unbreakable bond. She was Violet and Violet was her. The baby's tiny hand wrapped around Rosie's index finger and the single happy tear made its escape again and ran down her face. The tear teetered on the tip of her nose before detaching and dropping the short distance to plop almost audibly onto Violet's forehead in some sort of private and personal baptism.

The following four years and fifty weeks were the happiest of Rosalyn Torres's life. Relieved of her duties Rosalyn completely dedicated her every waking (and dreaming) thoughts to Violet. They were never apart, inseparable. She would speak to Violet as if she were years older than her approaching five. Always telling her how special she was, how much she loved her and all the things she would one day teach her and all the things that they could do together. The usual trials and tribulations of parenthood were just challenges that Rosie relished, embraced and conquered with a happy heart.

A sniper always prepared. Preparation was key. Rosalyn's ability to think ahead of the game, to know what her prey was thinking, to know their intentions before they themselves did, was one of the reasons she was so good at what she did. So often she would be there lying in wait as her victim came wandering obliviously into her crosshairs.

Violet's voice suddenly chimed in and cut through her reflection of who she once was. She looked down at her and smiled, 'Pardon, sweetheart?'

'I want to make little birds on the top, mummy.'

'Yes excellent idea, and what noise do the birdies make, little sparrow?'

'I'm not a sparrow.' The little girl screwed up her face, a host of little wrinkles creasing across the bridge of her button nose. 'I'm a princess. Birdies go tweet, tweet, tweet.'

'Tweet, tweet, tweet, yes! Well done, Violet and yes, you are the most precious thing of all, Mummy loves you so very much. Now who can that be? Keep stirring, poppet. Mummy needs to get the door.'

Rosie opened the door while wiping off her grubby hands on a towel. Stood before her was a J3 guard. She knew the face but not the name. The man who stood beside the J3 spoke first. He was dressed in the garb of a J5 Teacher with a medical specialism, a deep purple cloak with a white sash adorned with a red cross, and '5-t' under his right eye.

'Rosalyn Torres, I am Martin Catlow. This is your formal notice to report to the Jurisdiction of the Corruptible for the induction of Violet Torres a week from today. She must arrive with two full sets of clothes, a pair of sturdy shoes; all should be plain and unadorned. Not one accessory or sentimental object will be permitted. Do you understand?' he said with unwavering authority. Rosie's shoulders sagged; she stumbled and caught herself on the doorframe.

It must have been the love that clouded her knowledge of what she knew was going to happen all along. The love had blocked out the formality that all parents of Axiom knew would come. An inescapable law of the city.

'But, but she's my baby. You can't take away my little princess,' she said, surprising even herself with her shrill tone.

'She is not yours any longer; she is a youngster of Axiom and she will join us to learn her place.'

'You're both for the Farm if you don't show, Torres,' piped up the guard.

'You can't, please you can't, please I can, erm – I can keep her secret, yes she can stay inside with me forever, no–one need know she is here.'

'For goodness sake, woman, compose yourself!' Catlow sneered. 'You have one week to finalise her departure. Say goodbye. She will be returned to you a Resident in nine years.' With that they left. They walked away and did not look back as Rosalyn collapsed to her knees and sobbed.

'Why are you sad, Mummy?' A tiny comforting hand on her shoulder. She had not heard Violet approach.

'It's OK, sweetheart, I'm OK. Mummy is just a bit sad because, erm... Mummy is sad because we are leaving – *yes, we are leaving!* We'll have to travel a long way, but we will be together forever, just you and me. Far away from here in our own house, a house that we will make our own. And Mummy will always, always keep you safe.' She hugged Violet close to her and in her head started putting together a plan. Step one – get out of Axiom.

They didn't hang around. No sooner had their unwanted guests left and the idea to flee came into her head, Rosie composed herself and wasted no time in putting it into action. She rose from her embrace with her daughter, ruffled her hair and moved to the bedroom. Here she shook open a duffel bag and into it she put several sets of clothes for Violet; just a spare pair of trousers, long sleeve top and a jacket for herself. In amongst the garments she threw in bullet clips for her pistol and the Cold Bringer and a knife and flint. Violet stood in the doorway observing. Rosie looked up and smiled. 'Anything you want to pack for our adventure, my love?'

'Can I take Philly with me Mummy?' Violet asked as she dashed across the room and plucked the soft cuddly toy who had been perched upon her pillow.

Rosie's heart soared – such innocence. 'Of course you can. Here, pop her in the bag. Right, I'm ready, are you ready?'

'Yep, ready. Leeeeet's go!' she said with a little hop and a clumsy attempt at a fist pump.

Before leaving the house, Rosalyn opened up the oven and in with the half-baked cake she tossed the oil lamp retrieved from her bedside table. The house would burst into flames and when the blaze had died down she hoped there would be some sifting of the ashes in an attempt to determine if they had perished in the fire. It could offer a small delay to the inevitable pursuit.

Hand in hand, they left the house, with Rosie walking as casually as she could appear through J3. Rosalyn kept a good pace and Violet skipped alongside her, oblivious. They reached the Jurisdiction border gate and joined a small queue waiting to cross over into J7. Rosalyn feigned to scratch her lower back with her free hand and checked her pistol was just so that it could be swiftly drawn if required. Her other hand, which held her daughter's, grew clammy with a nervous sweat. Behind her she heard the scuff of a boot on tarmac and she instinctively moved Violet between her and the individual approaching. As she spun round, she reached for her weapon, only to quickly change her stance to collect a dropped bag of flour and hand it back to the clumsy young baker boy who had joined the back of the queue. She exchanged a smile with the boy, who thanked her, as she turned back to face forward so she found herself just one place back from the front.

A J3 sat behind a barred window of the dimly lit guard booth and behind her, stooping forward to get a good look at the man seeking passage across the Jurisdiction border, stood another, more senior, supervising J3 who Rosalyn did know – known simply, yet oddly, as Small Eye. They were quizzing the man who was carry two large bulging sacks of hair ready for processing into clothing.

'Take hold of a sack in each hand and pick them up at the same time,' Rosalyn heard Small Eye say. The man glanced over his shoulder and flashed a nervous apologetic smile at the rest of the queue, which was growing due to this delay. His tattoo told her he was a J9. He did as he was told, lifting each bag barely four inches from the floor. 'Higher. Shoulder height and hold them there until I tell you to drop them,' Small Eye demanded. J9 did as he was told and the J3s waited. It did not take long until his left arm began to visibly shake while the right was completely straight. Small Eye took a step backwards out of sight only to re-emerge from behind the booth and approached the J9. 'Put the bags down and do not move. Jenny-Li, get out here and bring a knife,' he instructed his colleague without breaking eye contact with the man. Rosalyn took a moment to glance over her shoulder: several other people in the queue were keeping close tabs on the interaction at the booth and more than a few were drifting away, merging back into the Jurisdiction. Some she guessed were simply avoiding seeing anything they may not have wanted to see, while others she noticed were discarding their own packages in places to be retrieved at a later date. Her training was so engrained, there was a voice inside her that was screaming at her to apprehend these criminals of the city. She ignored it, felt Violet's hand held in her own – she gave it a little squeeze and received a squeeze back in return. It did the trick, it silenced the voice, and she focused back on the task at hand – cross into J7.

Ahead of her, the junior J3, Jenny-Li, was passing over her knife to Small Eye. He took it and knelt down. He plunged the knife into the right-hand sack and it passed through the contents and the tip appeared the other side with barely a sound. He withdrew it and with the same motion stabbed at the left-hand sack. There was the unmistakable pang of steel on steel. The would-be smuggler turned to flee but they were on him in a flash. Jenny-Li tackled him about the waist and he fell to the ground. Small Eye joined in to subdue the J9, but they were struggling. He was fighting like his life depended on it – it did.

'Wait right there, poppet,' Rosie said to Violet as she saw an opportunity. She joined the fray and between the three of them they managed to restrain the man. As they stood him up the border chief, Small Eye instructed Jenny-Li to escort him to the holding cell and call in a J13 farm hand to come and collect him. He turned to look at Rosalyn properly and now he clearly realised just who she was.

'Rosalyn Torres!' He was, she supposed, a bit star struck. Amongst her own, she was a known person, more than just a number.

'Good work, er... ' She extended a hand and waited for him to introduce himself.

'Spender, ma'am, err Onesiphorus Spender,' he blushed a little, 'unusual right? It's a really old name – my great, great grandfather's...I'm rambling though, most just call me Small Eye.' He ran a finger around his right eye. 'Got a good idea for detail me,' he said before extending his hand to meet Rosalyn's and firmly shake her hand, 'Where are you heading to?'

She tapped the muzzle of the Cold Bringer, which was protruding up over her shoulder. 'Need to get some oil to clean her up.'

'I see, sure sure, of course, yeah. Head on through.' He extended an arm and showed her the way through.

'Thanks Charlie, I owe you one' she said. 'Violet, come on poppet.'

One border crossed, one to go. From J7 into J15 and from here she knew the way out of Axiom. Back to the spot where she had followed the Ferals, the tunnel underground and the door to the outside world. She knew that this one would perhaps be easier in some respects, harder in others. There was another guard booth to the only entrance left to the old Jurisdiction. All others had been permanently sealed off. She'd passed through this gate just twice previously, once on her way into her Feral monitoring mission and once on her way out. Both times it had been manned by a single guard, so sour faced and rude she felt comfortable knowing he would be collateral damage in her exit strategy. She made straight for the gate. Violet was, mercifully, still in good spirits and kept up with Rosalyn as she whisked them through the Merchants' Quarter. As they neared their destination, Rosie knelt down before her daughter, 'Wait right here, OK. I won't be more than a minute or two. I need to pop across the road there and speak to the man in charge. He is going to let us through and on with our little adventure, OK?' Violet nodded enthusiastically.

Rosalyn was true to her word. No more than ninety seconds later, she was back by Violet's side, picking her up and marching through the guard booth and into J15. Violet didn't appear to register a thing but Rosalyn caught the metallic smell of blood in her nostrils as they passed through the booth.

Time was not on their side, so Rosalyn moved Violet around onto her back and the little girl clung on as she upped the pace to cover the ground quicker. She drew her pistol and moved with purpose. She kept as quiet and as out of sight as possible so as not to draw any unwanted attention, and arrived at the edge of the sinkhole without incident. 'Right, hold on real tight now. We are heading down there.'

'Wow!' whispered Violet.

'I'm tired, Mummy. Can we stop? Please, can we stop, Mummy?' Violet's enthusiasm for the 'adventure' had well and truly waned.

They could not stop. Not yet. Not for perhaps another four hours. Four hours should open up enough distance between them and the city perimeter; they would have travelled far enough to find some cover, and then they could stop. Violet could sleep and Rosalyn could watch through the Cold Bringer's lens for pursuers.

'Soon, sweetheart, real soon, I promise,' she lied.

'I'm scared though, I want to go home.'

'Nothing to be scared of, poppet, nothing out here but you and me on a nice walk, a walk all the way to our new house where we will be safe and sound, a house that is just for you and me,' she lied again. 'In fact, we'll find the perfect place and we'll build a house. Doesn't that sound like fun?' she asked the small child, without the faintest hint of excitement and through a feigned smile she hoped would help to mask her own fear and urgency to press on. 'Together we will make our own little world.' She squeezed Violet's hand a little tighter and again smiled reassuringly down at her daughter. Rosie hated being untruthful to the girl; they were not safe and she too was scared, if she was honest. Violet's tiny fingers clasped inside her own felt so delicate, so fragile. Still, Rosalyn had confidence that her own strong, dangerous hands could protect them both. These hands, which had been calloused by conflict, which held the grip of a pistol or a knife just as comfortably as they currently did a five–year–old girl's hand. They would be OK – and *definitely* OK in four hours. They had that time window, that head-start… if their absence had gone unnoticed.

The light snowfall of the previous evening had mercifully begun to melt away in regular patches – summer was certainly on the way. They kept out of the white stuff that remained for the fear of leaving tracks. They moved from one dry patch of ground to the next but it made it slow going. She hoped they had enough time.

Four hours' march from the wall, she knew that there was a crumbling, ancient farmstead from the time before. It stood atop a small hill with a steady, yet fairly shallow, incline to its summit, surrounded by fields of a yellow flowering crop that grew waist high and somehow managed to grow abundantly in the dim light and cold clime. No–one could approach unseen; it would be the perfect resting place for a short while. Though as Rosie and Violet hurried through the Barrier wood hand in hand Rosie felt anything but confident of her next move. What they would find at the farmstead she really could not say.

Chapter 10

It wasn't the nightmare that had woken him prematurely. Bevan had lain awake for nearly half the night; he'd barely slept. He was lying on his back staring up at the ceiling, while on his chest he was turning over and over in his hands the item he'd secured from Vulture. This had been his routine for a few weeks now. He'd made progress with the Window. Returning home from shift each night he had settled into a very strict routine which consisted of a quick flannel down to wash away the grime from the day's toil, a simple meal hastily assembled and consumed – and then he would open up the secret storage space and set to work. Having taken it apart he was fairly certain everything was as it should be inside. It had required some tweaking of the circuitry; there were a few broken elements which he had replaced from his collections of spares and a bit of soldering of some loose connections. The cracks in the bottom left corner of the glass front didn't go all the way through. It should do what it was supposed to do... if he could find a way to get some power into the thing!

Initially it had all seemed like it would be easy. The first night he arrived home with the Window, he'd rifled through his box of various cables and neatly balled up in the bottom was just what he needed. It was a white plastic coated cable, yellowed by time and at one end badly frayed, but he had hoped it would still work. He plugged it in and after a little delay it shone into life. The screen on the device had instantly lit up very faintly and the same round shape depicted on the back appeared in white in the centre of it. It hadn't made a sound, and neither had Bevan. He had held his breath and heard the thud of his pulse in his ears. After a moment or two the round logo disappeared, only to be replaced with a circulating group of lines, like a fast-moving clock. It was a timer, a countdown to the big reveal of the unknown treasures of the Window – Bevan's excitement grew. The screen turned a hue brighter and a sentence spread across the grey background in white lettering:

'IPad Infinitum, always connected to the global Infinity SatNet –
Be The Inspiration!'

The lettering faded and there on the screen was a picture of a man and a woman. He was wearing a smart shirt but with the top button undone and a bow tie loosely draped around his neck, and in the button hole of his blazer jacket he wore over the shirt there was a purple flower, its colour intense against the dark fabric. He smiled out at Bevan, mid-laugh, his teeth white and gleaming, his happiness captured in this moment. The woman too was clearly smiling but she was not facing out towards Bevan. Her eyes were closed and she was planting a loving kiss on the man's cheek, and her hand reached across and was placed gently against the opposite cheek. She was wearing a bright white, spotless dress with an ornate pattern in the satin across the bodice. Her hair was a wonderful mix of light browns and dark blondes and it was all gathered up and secured in the most ornate of knots. She was beautiful, they were beautiful, the occasion was a glorious one and they reminded him of all the incredible feelings he had felt on his own wedding day. Tears had welled up in his eyes. The woman was not too dissimilar to Evelyn, and the couple's love for one another was so evident. Bevan slowly scrunched his eyes tight shut and squeezed the tears out. He'd sniffed once and when he opened his eyes he shifted his focus from the background image to the foreground of the Window's display.

Overlaying the picture were ten different icons each with their own label. There were 'Camera', 'Photos', 'Clock', 'Contacts', 'iTunes', 'App store', 'Settings', 'Safari' and 'Mail' but the one that drew his eye and his finger was 'Maps'.

Though his finger had barely made contact with the smooth glass surface, the image instantly changed. The happy couple disappeared and Bevan was amongst the stars. He was looking at an image of the whole world and then the Window was dragging him down. The image was pulling him down, thundering through the clouds and there was blue and green everywhere. He hurtled towards the green, and the nearer to the ground the Window took him the more the green gave way to greys of concrete, roads, buildings. It was a city, a vast city, and the image just kept going. Pushing through the concrete jungle, the sights – colours, people, cars – everything was just a dazzling assault on the senses to Bevan. He had not been able to blink; he was taking it all in. Finally the image slowed until it zeroed in on a well-kept balcony of a simple apartment in the middle of a tower block. Two boxes appeared in the centre of the screen. In the top one it read: '*You are home*'. The bottom had a flashing ticker alongside '*Where to?*' Bevan had tapped the bottom box and a panel of letters appeared.

There was only one place he wanted to go. He wanted to go wherever Evelyn was. He had begun to type her name. E. V. E. The Window tried to second-guess him; it began self-populating the box and offered other options below:

Eversham...

Everdene Street, Shillingworth, PO7...

Eversholt Road, Upper Hants, LK7 4BZ...

He tapped the first option and the image once again began to move. This time it rose rapidly back up above the high-rise buildings and from this birds'-eye view it drew a neat blue line across the streets. It showed the way from the Window's 'home' across the city to 'Eversham'. It was at this point that two things had happened. Firstly, a realisation had dawned on Bevan. The icon's name, 'Maps', the street names it proposed... the ancient city had been real, the whole world mapped out. The Window could show him a map of the entire world and it could show him how to get from point A to point B and everything he might encounter in between. Second was the action which Bevan had chastised himself for since. As he swung around on his bed, the Window in his hands was still plugged into the wall – and the old frayed wire snapped and its complicated connector had dropped to the floor. In his haste to retrieve it he had brought one clumsy, heavy-soled shoe down upon it and it was crushed. He had felt the wire go taut and give up, and he had heard the ping of the delicate metal fibres shearing apart and the intricate connector making contact with the wooden floor of his home. He had felt the soft metal driven flat under his weight. He'd turned back to look at what he had just done, left the Window on the bed and got onto his knees to see if the cable could be repaired. It could not. By the time he admitted defeat and returned to the Window it had died, its brief charge expelled. He grabbed up a pillow and yelled obscenities into it, furious at himself.

He had got past that moment of anger, frustration and depression. Now he had seen a glimpse of what it could do his desire to find another way to get the Window working was stronger than ever.

Typically he could manipulate another cable and plug and hook anything into the grid, but such was the connection on the cable for the Window nothing he'd tried would work. He knew what he needed was the precise adapter for this precise piece of kit. The thought of getting hold of the adapter had been consuming him and utterly depressing him; since surely such a find was nigh on impossible.

Bevan had kept staying up late working on the Window and there was no such thing as a day off for any Resident of Axiom, so he was exhausted. The little sleep he had been getting was inevitably interrupted with nightmares of Evelyn. He knew he would not be able to get any proper sleep (even the nightmare-filled kind he had become accustomed to) until he had managed to get this device working. The dilemma which was keeping him from dozing off now was that he knew if the power cable existed anywhere it would be in J15, but he couldn't give a clear enough description of the socket and its corresponding cable, or indeed trust that Vulture would be able to find the plug on his own. So he needed to go with him, and therein lay the problem. Or rather problems. He faced two huge challenges. Firstly he needed to escape for just a day from working on the Farm fences and secondly he needed to convince Vulture to let him go along on a foraging trip. To top it all off, accomplishing either challenge would land him in serious trouble if caught by the guards, or even worse the Shrouded. That said, he felt certain it would be worth it; this gadget, this piece of kit, the Window, was the most complex item he'd ever worked on. He had daydreamed about the other tasks it could perform – and she was alive, he just knew it, and if anything could help him find her out there in the vastness beyond the walls it was this. He felt certain the Window was the thing that would lead him to Evelyn.

As he lay there in the dark bedroom, his breath puffing lightly in the cold air, he heard a guard patrol crunch by in the snow outside in the street. He decided then that he would try, and to hell with the consequences – what life was it without Evelyn anyway? He had to get this remarkable device working and had to get it working soon. The day of the party was looming and with it the start of Project Wind. After that he would be beyond the confines of Axiom and he would need the device to guide him if he was to make a dash for freedom. Without any power, the Window in his bag would be as useful to him as his fellow workers would be welcomed as companions. They were pleasant enough, but they weren't friends. They would also be chaperoned by guards, who would ensure no friendships could be forged. It was not going to be a fun outing.

Then there was the boy, Benedict. Bevan had grown quite attached to him. He had strange ways and he was more than socially awkward, but as Bevan had come to understand him, he had really come to enjoy his company. They shared their love for electronics. They bounced ideas off one another and taught one another new things, and not just about electronic devices. Bevan was sure Benedict felt more comfortable in his company and spoke to him in a manner far surer than he was capable of with others. For Bevan it was the feeling that he was in some way fulfilling the role he was destined for – a father (figure). It made him both terribly sad and yet terribly fulfilled as he recalled what felt like a conversation from forever ago. A conversation he and Evelyn had had.

A young child had slipped in the snow. Bevan had been holding hands with Evelyn as they were making the commute to shift, and he broke away just in the nick of time to catch the toddler. The little boy was shocked, scared at what had nearly happened and he began to cry. His mother had been talking with someone nearby and turned to return to comfort her child, but by the time she had made it the boy was giggling and had quite forgotten about the peril that had nearly befallen him. Bevan was making the youngster laugh with a simple little trick where he made it appear as if his thumb was splitting in two. His mother stepped in and thanked Bevan who ruffled the boy's hair before they went on their way. He rose up from being on one knee, and Evelyn pulled him into an embrace, held him there and whispered in his ear, 'You are going to make an incredible father, Bevan Hughes.'

'Oh, that's nothing – you wait till you see me when it's my own little un,' he'd replied with a smile.

They'd pulled apart a little and kissed. She smiled at him and asked, 'Is that you saying you are ready for one?'

He'd brought a hand up to her cheek and said, 'With you I'm ready for anything and I want everything that can be had.'

'I want a son. He will be just like you. The very best thing he can be.'

Bevan let out a short laugh, 'Nope, I'm afraid not. He will be a bit of me and a bit of you and that is the *very* best thing, us together.'

'Well then', she'd said with a wink, 'we'll have to get started on this plan tonight.'

Bevan recalled with a feeling of deep regret that they had not started to try for a baby that night. He'd been late back from shift and she was already fast asleep. Life had got in the way for another week and then she was taken. He was conflicted. It would be a wrench to leave Benedict; he seemingly had no-one else in the whole world. He never spoke of a mother or father, he had been plucked from J5 for his talent for restoring gadgets and manipulating circuitry, to be used as a tool to carry out a task. Bevan was sure that once that task was complete he would be thrown back into the box with all the other tools the regime leading Axiom was forging to help build its own future.

Still, the boy would be OK, he told himself. Evelyn, though – she was out there, Bevan felt sure of it, and he was determined to get away, determined to search for her. He had to get a new cable and get the Window powered back up.

The next morning he put his plan into action and discreetly set up part one. He had taken his first risk, and only time would tell if it would pay off. For six bangers he had convinced the guard at the clocking-in booth to overlook the fact that the man who would appear the following day and check in as Bevan Hughes was not Bevan Hughes. He was the only one who could put a face to a name. The others patrolling the Farms would just be given a number, a headcount. Providing the expected number of Residents were working on the faulty fencing they'd not check any further... he hoped.

Incredibly, for just two patties of the old cattle's flesh, Louie Summerville had agreed to take his place at work. Louie too had had a daughter taken by Ferals some twelve years ago, and when Bevan said he needed the time to see if he could get Evelyn back, Louie could not decline. He felt a little bad for not divulging all the details to his colleague, particularly when he was also taking a risk in covering for him. It was a white lie; he was not technically playing on the trauma of another, as who knew what the Window could really do?

Now the morning for action had arrived. The shift alarm would sound in little under an hour's time; he would leave when it sounded so that he was out and about when others were. A lone figure walking in any Jurisdiction outside of working hours would be greeted with suspicion. He set about getting ready. He could convince Vulture to take him – he was a greedy creature and Bevan always had a knack for playing the fear or greed factor in most people. Who knew, he thought to himself with a wry smile as he pulled on an extra pair of socks, he might even welcome the company.

The only thing was, Bevan wasn't sure entirely where they would be going and what one might need for such a trip. Vulture had never disclosed where he found the goods he traded or the lengths he had to go to in order to get them. He felt sure he must know a way into J15 and into and between the alleys, connecting corridors, alcoves, passageways and secret pathways that made up the blurred boundaries of the Jurisdictions. The secret places where goods were traded out of sight, on a larger scale, or because of a more sensitive nature. Bevan also knew that, aside from your basic rations – food, water, oil for your lamp, clothing and electricity, which were all provided by the central bastion – nothing in Axiom came easily... or legally.

Once he'd washed and dressed he began filling his backpack and checking off the list he'd prepared:

- Bottle of water
- Dry-cured meat strips X 8 – personal emergency food
- Patties X 4 sausages X 4 – for trade
- Mini pickaxe
- 1 extra pair of socks
- 1 additional jumper
- Coil of 12' high tension cable

• The Window

He sat on the edge of his bed staring at the front door. He was fully dressed, including his coat and hat and boots. He had his backpack slung across one shoulder and his legs were jigging up and down with anticipation. In his hands he held his father's pistol which was loaded with five bullets in the magazine. He ran his fingers over the gun and thought back to the day he had found it. His father had not long passed away and before the home was reallocted he had secretly visited in the dead of night to collect any items of value. The gun and seventeen bullets had been stowed away beneath a loose floorboard. He'd stood looking at them for some time – the ultimate contraband. Were they more trouble that they were worth? Should he just leave them where they were? In the end he had decided to take them, fearing they would end up in the hands of someone who didn't truly grasp their deadly potential. This was the first time he had handled them since the day he took them. His father had of course just been an electrician like himself and quite how he could possibly have come by such an item Bevan would now never know. He was known to be something of a gambling man though, and it was entirely possible he had won them in a game of cards, drunk on poli after a long shift. Either way the gun was now Bevan's and it terrified him. He had seen them fired plenty of times before, heard the deafening thunder, seen the horrible mess they made of a man's flesh. He would take it with him but feared he might not have the courage to unleash that terrible power by pulling the trigger.

He drew in a slow long intake of breath to steady his nerves and attempt to stifle the adrenaline that was beginning to course through his veins.

The alarm sounded.

Bevan rose, slipped the pistol into the back of the waistband of his trousers and concealed it with his shirt. He stood on the spot for the briefest moment and exhaled. No turning back now.

Out in the street, others were starting to leave for work. He pulled his hood in tight and kept his head down as he crossed the street and ducked straight into the nearest alleyway. He'd not said a word to Teddy, so he couldn't be implicated in anything if Bevan was caught – it was better that no-one but those who'd taken a bribe knew anything. Getting off J17's Main Street fast meant any awkward encounters would be avoided. Weaving his way through the backstreets and electrical infrastructure, he was barely noticed – just another Resident ducked down against the wind, hurrying to his shift. The sky above was grey. The sky was always grey. The clouds looked heavy though, and there was a quiet in the air, a stillness in the atmosphere which so often signalled that a big dumping-down of snow would shortly commence. Underfoot the remnants of the last of such snowfall had frozen over, thawed, turned to slush and refrozen. They crunched and squeaked loudly underfoot. This and the sound of his own pulse pounding in his head were the only sounds which Bevan could hear.

It didn't take long to reach Vulture's street. He stood in the shadows for a moment surveying the surroundings. Surely no–one could know his plan, no–one would be watching, but the paranoia was setting in. The Shrouded were aptly named: they were not easily spotted. They lurked and they killed with terrible efficiency and he was just an electrician; he would not stand a chance.

Not a sound, just the soft whistle of the wind cutting through the silence which had fallen just as heavily as the imminent snow was certain to. He tried to hold his breath, but the puff of it was too easy to see, the sound of it too easy to hear.

Then movement off to his right just a few houses up – did someone duck back into a doorway? No, there it was again, a loose panel caught in the wind. He let out a deep exhalation, nervously chuckled and told himself he was being too jittery. Relief set in – it was just a panel swinging in the wind. His muscles relaxed.

A scrape. Right behind him. He froze, entire body rigid as instinct readied him for a fight. He spun round on the spot and in the same motion unhitched the pickaxe hanging from his belt, raising it high above his head ready to strike.

'Woah there, boy, *pick* a fight with someone else, ahaha,' cackled Vulture, pleased with his simple play on words.

Bevan breathed another heavy sign of relief and lowered the axe, 'Shit, Vulture I nearly pierced your beak with this then,' he said re-hooking the axe to his belt. 'Listen, I need to speak to you about our trade a few weeks back, I really need –'

'No exchanges or refunds, you know the rules boy. Damn, it's not like I can return those steaks. Well, not in the same condition I can't!'

'Gross! Look it's not that – it's great, it's just that I need another part to make it work.'

'OK, well, step into my office,' Vulture said motioning for Bevan to lead the way to his home.

Bevan took another swift look up and down the street then stepped out and made his way across with Vulture following close behind.

Inside they again walked down the corridor and into the middle room. Vulture had had something of a tidy up, it seemed. The table was clear of any debris, the chair tucked neatly under it, and the bed was clear except for the neatly rolled up sleeping bag. The huge rug in the middle of the floor was still filthy, but it was smoothed out flat. Vulture strode into the room and as he did so he threw a handful of nuts, bolts and screws from his pocket on to the table which went scattering everywhere.

'What do you need then?' he asked as he began to wriggle into the sleeping bag.

'I need to come with you to get it.' Bevan got straight to the point; the room looked better but it smelt worse, so he wanted to be back out in the fresh air. In the corner sat a bucket which likely contained the aforementioned steaks and everything else Vulture had eaten since.

'Are you out of your damn mind, boy?' Vulture spluttered with surprise at the request.

'I can't explain the part I need. It's weird, like nothing I've seen before. You'll not even know I'm there. I'll do exactly as you say, exactly.'

'No. No chance.'

'OK, look.' Bevan reached into his back pocket and brought a cable and the squashed connector. He held them out before him. 'A cable like this. Specifically like this, not similar but one exactly like this. The connection got squashed so it looks different when, you know, it's not squashed!'

'I dunno, boy. You are a good client, but I work alone. What you got in the bag? Just some meat ain't gonna do it.'

Bevan reeled off the list of items, leaving out the pistol and bullets. 'I'll give you the meat now and you can have the rest when we get back? Fair trade?'

Vulture eyed Bevan up through squinted eyes and he began clicking his tongue on his lip again. Bevan stood before him waiting patiently for a decision. He could tell that Vulture wanted the stuff, but he was, in fairness, probably good at what he did precisely because he worked alone, because he could be a ghost and a shadow and just the feeling of a presence. He'd slip in and out of rooms, hurdle fences, run through already broken window frames and barely leave the glass which was clinging to the edges tinkling. He would rummage through rubble and not make a sound. 'No.' He spoke, interrupted Bevan's imagining of his J15 forays and stopped clicking. 'No, you tell me what you want, I'll see what I can do... alone.'

'Electricity – twenty-four seven! I can get you it.' Bevan was playing his last card and making a promise he wasn't sure he could keep. It would be difficult to find the time outside of shift and even more so to re-electrify a building that sat on a street cut off from the grid for so long. It was also risky: A, because if caught doing the work by guards he'd definitely be Farmed; and B, because if he couldn't do it the very skills Vulture employed to scavenge valuable goods for trade made him an excellent killer. It wasn't just his ability to source illegal goods that made him notorious.

Vulture's eyes widened and he fidgeted in his sleeping bag. 'You could do that, eh, boy?'

'Sure, it's easy when you know how,' Bevan bluffed.

'And all that other stuff too?'

'Yeah, course. Hey, with electricity you'll be able to do product demos to prospective buyers eh?' He knew he was winning him over; Vulture couldn't sit still from the excitement. He stood up and let the sleeping bag drop to the floor around his feet, he stepped out of it and forward, just a foot away from Bevan. Vulture reached into his pockets. His long-fingered, skeletal hands came back out clutching something in each – a bunch of three rusty keys in one hand and in the other an ugly-looking homemade stabbing weapon. He held them up and waggled them in front of Bevan's face.

'Then let's go, but you watch your step out there, boy. You give me away or draw attention and you'll only be coming back here in parts. The parts I'd wanna eat!' He slurped in a mouthful of saliva that had threatened to overrun his lips.

Bevan nodded once, slowly and croaked out a single word, sound-

ing a lot more shaken up by the threat than he wanted to admit,
'OK... '

Vulture led Bevan out of the room and down the corridor to the third
locked door. He slid each key into the three padlocks, turned and unlocked
them and slid back the bolts. As the door opened, an old filthy kitchen was
revealed. It was only a small room. On the far wall was a basin and a rickety–looking butcher's cart with something dead and rotting on it. Skew-
ering the decaying flesh was a large knife stood upright, its sharp point
buried deep in the wooden surface, and Bevan was again reminded of Vulture's threat. The wall to the right of the door was full of shelves on which
there were just a few empty tins. The left wall was the exterior wall that
made up the rear of the house and it was bare. Propped against it was a
heavy–looking wardrobe. Vulture walked over and heaved open the cupboard door. There was no back to the wardrobe, and a section of the wall
had been carved out just big enough to crawl through. Vulture smiled
slyly, a look that displayed both pride and cunning. Bevan walked over to
the open cupboard, bent down with his hands resting on his thighs, and
peered through the gap. He could see all the wrack and ruin of abandoned
buildings and streets. Inside the wardrobe was nothing... and everything.
Inside was Jurisdiction 15.

Chapter 11

Her head lolled, rolled and her eyes shot open. In that absolute silence the scraping sound the Cold Bringer made on the rotten wooden window's edge as she leapt back awake felt as loud as if it had actually discharged a round. Rosalyn fumbled with the weapon, readjusting its barrel's balance on the sill, and glanced back down the scope – still nothing and no movement.

Violet – where was Violet?

She wheeled around, spinning on the balls of her feet and remaining in her crouched position. She could see the pile of material on the old armchair, a coat, a blanket, and a sleeping bag slowly rising and falling with the rhythmic breathing of her precious Violet beneath them. Her daughter was still safe, still asleep, still blissfully unaware of the very real danger they were in. Rosie felt an anger begin to build in her chest, a knot of adrenaline mixed with raw emotion, anger at herself – how could she doze off like that? It had never happened before, not once in all her long vigils. Many had been longer. Just her, the Cold Bringer and the never ending dusk. Watching and waiting. And never before had she lost concentration. Yet now during her most important mission of her life, to protect and watch out for her daughter, the one thing that meant anything to her in the whole world, she had drifted off. How long for she couldn't say, but looking back through the lens of the sniper rifle she scanned the field below, the distant tree line and the patches of snow, none of which appeared to have been disturbed. Everything was still, the wind was nonexistent, an ominous hush had descended on the ancient farmhouse on the hill.

She had known tiredness before but this was something else. They would have to move on soon. They had been here too long. A few days had passed and Rosalyn's original intention had been to stay put for no more than a few hours. The initial race from Axiom had taken its toll on young Violet, though. They had made it to the house just fine, but no sooner had Violet drifted off into her first ever sleep outside the city walls than she began to bark a horrible cough. A nasty cold had taken hold of her and she was in no fit state to travel. Once the child was better and refreshed they would push on and maybe then find somewhere she could, just perhaps, grab more than the single hour of shut-eye in every twenty-four she had been allowing herself. Rosie stood slowly, her knees audibly popping back into life having been still in a crouched position for so long. Placing her hands on her lower back, she arched backwards, stretching, and then rubbed her aching red eyes. Picking up the rifle, she walked purposefully but quietly across the room to the adjacent kitchen, careful not to wake the child. She needed to check the back of the house again.

They had made the rest of the journey through the Barrier without incident and Rosie was relieved to have made it this far unscathed. As they had worked their way through the forest, part of her had hoped the stag would return. She didn't know why it seemed even a remote possibility, but she liked the idea. Violet would have loved to see him.

They had reached the farmstead on schedule. They could afford the three hours they had planned to be there, but then they should have left to maintain an hour's lead at least on any pursuers. The fire at her home must have done the trick in buying them some more time, though: she had seen no sign of any pursuit. Emerging from the trees and crossing the open field was the worst part of that initial journey outside of Axiom. Not only was she exposed, in plain sight of anyone who might be loitering on the edge of the wood or holed up in the house on the hill, but she'd also had to momentarily leave Violet's side. She had insisted that the small child curl up into the bowels of an old fallen tree before heading out across the field to check the house was unoccupied. If anything happened to her, Violet was to stay as still as possible. 'You must not call out, sweetheart. Whatever happens you must remain silent as a little mouse, OK?'

'Yes Mummy, I'll be still as a stone,' the little one had replied with a cheeky smile.

'When I call for you, you come to me, OK – not running, but like a little fieldmouse, sneaking through the grass?'

'Sneaky little mouse.' Her grin widened. 'Yes, Mummy.' Outwardly Rosalyn showed no sign of emotion but inside she allowed herself a small smile of her own; such innocence was a rare thing in this world and it was all just a fun game to Violet. Bless her heart; in this game the losers died. She wondered perhaps if she should have told her daughter this sobering truth, but Violet was both her strength and her weakness; there was no–one else for whom she would ever sugar–coat the stark realities of life in Axiom.

Fortunately the house was empty and quiet as a crypt. Once she was satisfied no–one was lurking within, she called for Violet to follow. From the elevated position of the house she could cover the child with sniper fire if need be. She had watched her mousey brown hair snaking through the grass, sweeping the scope over the surrounding area. Nothing else moved. Violet crossed the field without incident. No sooner had Rosie drawn her in through the front window and into an embrace than Violet had asked to sleep. That's when the coughing started, her nose running... and her mood was difficult to say the least.

Countless years of neglect had taken their toll on what must have once been a beautiful home. From the front it was the typical design of a child's drawing, one large central front door, two large square windows downstairs and a matching pair above on the upper floor. It was the perfect abode for a family, a set of parents and their two children. The solid external brick structure still stood relatively intact but for some crumbling mortar. The footings had subsided a touch and the house stood wonky, the right side dipping some four feet deep in the dirt. A section of the tiled roof had given up clinging on, and had slid off and down into the rear garden, leaving the loft space exposed to the elements. So one half of the house was rotten inside. The large hole had allowed countless years' worth of rain, sleet and snow to tear through the ceiling, rotting the flooring and finished its destructive work in the stone basement. A thick smell of mould filled those rooms. All wood and fabrics had long decayed and the lower ground floor was now filled by a stagnant pool of water which Rosalyn guessed was probably six or seven feet deep.

The side of the house with the roof still above it had been quite well preserved; the heavy solid oak doors had all been shut when Rosie first entered, and together with the stone walls they had done a good job of keeping the elements at bay. The front room where they had entered through the window had the remnants of what was once an expensive carpet underfoot but the dull brown, dusty, threadbare remains now cracked underfoot and disintegrated. The wallpaper all hung from the walls, curling down on its own weight at different heights. Ferals had torched the sofa, the bookcase and every precious volume that once stood on its shelves; they had been piled within the huge fireplace which was the focal point of the living room and set ablaze. There was still a leather armchair, which Violet now slumbered on. The chair was all torn and peeling and the cushion was completely flattened. In the corner, a large square black device from the time before was lying on its smashed front, the wires on the back torn out and cut away. In the kitchen there were more signs of Ferals. They had removed every single cupboard door to burn and had pilfered every utensil and piece of crockery. As with the device in the living room, those in the kitchen had all been discarded on the floor, their wires and any other useful elements, like blades or heating elements, removed. Also strewn amongst the debris on the floor were several used Clickers. The pantry, Rosie imagined, would have once been full of all the most delicious foods: herbs, spices, meats, fruits and vegetables – all manner of items that no longer even existed – but now all that it stored were thick layers of dust, the skeleton of a large rat and piles of mouse shit. She had tried the door directly off the corridor and the kitchen to find a small water closet tucked in under the stair with a throne remarkably untouched by the passing of time. There was 'evidence' that Ferals had been in there too however. She had shut the door immediately.

She leant on the old chipped, scum-caked butler sink and gazed out of the back window. Across the field it was much the same view as the front, a gradual slope downhill into a field of crops which spread out below until it touched the imposing wall of trees that was the Barrier. Midway down the hill there were the remains of the charred frame of a burnt–out barn. Weeds and grasses had moved in on the fertile scorched earth and, where there would have once been just the dusty floor, the former interior of the barn was now the greenest, lushest part of the old farm. As she stared she could feel fatigue taking its grip again. Her shoulders sagged, arms and neck ached and her legs burned. Her eyes got heavy and their lids threatened to close when suddenly something caught her attention. Something red, something dancing in amongst all the green of the former barn's floor. A slight shake of her head wakened her senses, and she focused on it, and as she did so, some more red flecks appeared... or had they always been there? Tiredness *could* play tricks on the mind. Rosalyn swung her rifle across from her back and braced it into her shoulder to peer down the magnified scope. All she could see was green. Grass. Bushes. Weeds. Leaves. Green. And then there it was again. A fleck of red caught in the slightest hush of a breeze. A small red papery flower with a black centre sat proud atop a thin hairy looking stem... and another, and another. She had seen them before, grown in batches in J1, she understood their seeds could be used to develop a favourite narcotic of the guards. She was not aware they could grow wild. The way they merrily danced in the wind mesmerised her and while she stood watching them she decided she would pick them before moving on. Nothing was given attention in the Jurisdiction of Stricken and his minions without holding some value; perhaps she would work out how to manipulate this little plant and trade the produce.

The creak of a floorboard in the other room tore Rosalyn from her daydream. She spun on her heels dropping the Cold Bringer, which swung to her back on its strap. In the same motion she drew the pistol from the holster on her hip and brought it up before her, aiming at the door to the adjoining room. The room in which her daughter was. The door was ajar by just an inch or so. The dull gloom of the outside world, dimly coming through the front window, filled the room beyond with a grey light which seeped through the crack in the door and left a shaft across the floor which touched the toes of her boots. No further sound came from within. Rosalyn knew that had Violet woken she would immediately call out for her. They were no longer alone in the house.

She wanted so desperately to burst through the door and check on her baby, to make sure she was safe. Her training and tactical know-how kept her natural instincts from taking over, though. She would not call out. Another creak from the front room nearer to the door, and in a split second Rosie made the decision to change tactic. As silently as possible, she withdrew, tucking herself into the pantry, pulling its door almost closed and peeking out through the thin slit with a full view on the living room door.

The barrel of a gun appeared and four dirty fingers with gnawed nails grasped the edge of the door, slowly opening it inwards. Next to come into view was a heavy looking, mud–covered boot and a leg dressed in black. The exact same boot and trousers that Rosalyn wore herself. Regulation J3 guard uniform.

They had found her. Found them both. As the door swung open with a barely audible groan, the guard entered cautiously, eyes firmly fixed down the iron sights of his weapon. He was young, with a shock of orange hair, freckled skin, defined jaw bone and green eyes. Eyes that betrayed him. Rosalyn saw the fear in them, his lack of experience. Backing him up was his partner, following closely behind, wearing a combat helmet with the visor down. Long golden locks tumbled out from the helmet and down the shoulders. This woman too was a rookie – her position was off, and the gun trembled slightly in her grip. Rosie didn't know whether to feel insulted or relieved. These two would not leave this kitchen.

They ventured farther in, swivelling to move back-to-back and sweep their weapons around the room. As they circled their way across to her position, she holstered her pistol and withdrew her hunting knife from its sheath on her thigh, braced her back against the shelves and her arms to either side of the small cupboard space, and waited. Another half a yard and she would attack.

Two more steps from the ginger rookie brought him within striking distance, and with all her strength she thrust one leg up, kicking the door to the pantry wide open, slamming into his back and sending him sprawling forward, knocking his companion to the ground. Both were shocked. Both, she knew, were dead. As he staggered forward, she grabbed the back of his head by his hair, pulling him upright and towards her while drawing the edge of the knife clean across his throat. As his blood sprayed up, splattering the ceiling, his lifeless body fell, and Rosalyn went down with him. As the female guard whirled around, all she saw was her partner on the ground, too slow to recognise that not one but two bodies lay before her. Rosalyn grasped the gun in the dead man's hand and fired four bullets into her chest. A muffled cough of pain and surprise came from inside the helmet as the J3 girl left this world.

Before the second guard's body had even hit the ground Rosalyn was on her feet and rushing through into the living room with the small sub-machine gun held out before her. She stopped in her tracks. Sat in the chair where Violet should have been was Benitez. More worrying still were the two Shrouded who stood behind him.

'Even the most inept guards can be useful, if only in their dying.' He smirked. 'You're rusty, Torres! I didn't think you'd give us that much time dispatching those two green fools.'

'Where is my daughter?' she demanded.

'Well now, you see, that would have been a simple answer, had you not so foolishly taken matters into your own hands. I would just say, "Where all children are in Axiom, the Jurisdiction of the Corruptible, of course, learning her place in our great society."' He raised his arms in tandem with his mocking tone.

'I will not ask you again,' Rosalyn threatened, aiming directly for his smug face.

'Now, now. Calm down. Do you think I would be so cruel as to deny a mother a final sighting of her beloved child? See, there she is.' He pointed one fat finger in the direction of the front window. Rosie dared the briefest glance out of the window. Her eyes left Benitez's for less than a second. It was long enough though – she took it all in.

Looking through the broken pane and beyond, at the bottom of the hill and the edge of the field, she had seen a patrol of five J3 guards. Two of them stood either side of Violet who sat on the ground. She was still huddled in one of the blankets, floods of tears running down her face, wide-eyed with terror and confusion. Their weapons were drawn and aimed at her. Rosie's stomach knotted and her throat tightened, she felt like she needed to vomit.

'When a pet bites the hand that feeds it, it can never again be trusted.' Rosie barely heard Benitez as anger and fear gripped her. 'And one thing is for damn sure, I would never trust their whelps either – treacherous genes breed treacherous offspring. You did this, not me.'

She knew what this meant, his final verdict, and she could not let them harm her child. Springing into life she shifted her aim to the Shrouded on Benitez's left, but this simple readjustment was time enough for them both to anticipate, and as the bullet skimmed past his arm they were on her. As they clattered into her, one Shrouded locked her arm and dragged the machine gun away as bullets peppered the fireplace, smacking into brickwork. The other wrapped around behind her, tearing the sniper rifle from her back and slinging it to the ground as she struggled with the first assailant. The second then moved back in and grabbed her in a chokehold. She thrashed furiously in their grasps like a mad old cat in a bag, but their strength was uncanny. At the point she thought her arm was going to break, she released her grip on the weapon, and in the same moment the Shrouded at her back tightened his own around her throat. She made a small gasping sound and her vision went blurry. Her legs went to jelly and her heart rate slowed. Her body was shutting down, trying to conserve the oxygen still in its system. She knew that in a moment she would black out, and she hoped she would never wake again because she knew Violet would be gone.

'Alright that's enough.' A distant voice, murky and blurred as if heard underwater. 'Let her be.' A merciful release and the air rushed back into her lungs; she gulped down huge inhalations of the wonderful life-giving oxygen and things began to switch back on. Her vision returned and the voice could be heard more clearly. Benitez's revolting sneer. 'This bitch has been muzzled; let's put down the puppy!' He raised a walkie-talkie to his mouth. 'Do not waste ammunition or alert any bloody Ferals to our location. Get it done.'

Rosalyn assessed her situation. She was somehow still on her feet but in the hold of one of the Shrouded, with her arm held up behind her back. The other stood to the left and slightly behind them, inspecting the Cold Bringer with keen interest, Benitez was still seated awkwardly trying to clip the walkie-talkie back onto his belt – partially hidden beneath his bulging waistline. All three of them were making the grave mistake in thinking she was beaten and finished.

Her loose hand went to her hip and slid the knife free from its casing. Swiftly she thrust the blade back and upwards, feeling it part ribs as she stabbed through her captor's chest. She left the knife where she had plunged it and was free. The second Shrouded was so preoccupied with the sniper rifle that as he looked up at the commotion, it was too late. Rosalyn's gloved fist was already too close and quickly making a complete mess of his nose and teeth. As he reeled back, clutching at his face, she snatched up her sniper rifle and spun to see an empty chair – Captain Cube had wisely fled. Racing to the window, she brought the gun up and looked down the sight to the bottom of the hill.

Her life fell apart as she was faced with the most devastating choice imaginable. Her daughter was going to die, this was certain, but Rosalyn could choose how.

Three guards stood over the wailing little girl with large rocks held over their heads, ready to rain them down upon her. Rosie knew she could not shoot them all before at least one of those rocks did its evil work. She aimed at Violet's head. The perfect kill shot.

'We bring the cold and take the warmth' she said with icy, measured professionalism, tears streaming down her cheeks. And fired.

Part Three

This document contains herein and proceeding the four overriding governing laws of Solacity Biome.

Agreed, signed and ratified 17 June, 2035 by the Leadership Committee.

1. There is no money. The city will provide for you. You in turn will provide for the city.

2. There are no material possessions. You have what you are provided. You must care for, reintroduce and circulate items into the wider populace as and when they are required and requested by your neighbour or the Leadership Committee.

3. Work is voluntary but the city cannot and will not carry passengers. Your quality of life is dependent on the work put in.

4. All crimes are punishable. There are no distinguishing levels of severity of crime. There is law abiding or there is wrongdoing. There is only one punishment, and there is only one chance – exile and absolutely no re-admittance.

Chapter 12

'Now, before we start on through that hole, boy, I need for you to understand how this works. You move precisely when I do and you step precisely where I step – shit, Bevan, you should be inhaling and exhaling at the same time as me, OK, boy?'

'Yeah look, no worries. I'm fine, I know this ain't a game.' No worries? In truth Bevan's back was sodden from nervous perspiration and his mouth was bone dry from anticipation. He knew crawling through that hole was signing his own death warrant if caught… *if* caught, though, and they'd be in and out in no time, it'd be fine… or so he kept telling himself.

'Then let's do this, boy, follow me… and follow me precisely, remember.'

They shimmied through the gap on their stomachs and stood upright on the other side of the wall. Stood in Jurisdiction 15.

No–one had lived here (legally) for seventy years, no–one had cared for the buildings or their surroundings and it had been left in a hurry. Under direct orders from the then ruler of Axiom, Eleanor's father, Theodore De Sanctis, all Residents were to leave to be relocated and were given just one hour to do so. They might not have been so compliant in their relocation, and might not have left so willingly, had they known that all but a few who were deemed useful were relocated to the Farms. Axiom did and always would have a finite amount of space for Residents to occupy and so relied on its laws for procreation and population control. With the Jurisdiction becoming unsafe for habitation there was nowhere else for these individuals to move out to. Some tried to stay, but were soon flushed out and removed by the Shrouded. People were moved out and a new wall had been built around the Jurisdiction to keep it off limits. Since that time everything had remained just as it was left and the elements had ravaged it all. The cold and the frost and the ice had wrenched buildings apart, cracking walls and joists, which had fallen to pieces. The unstable ground had also crumbled in on itself in other areas and entire neighbourhoods had tumbled into the ground, leaving gaping holes full of debris. As buildings toppled, a thick dust was flung into the air and had settled on all exposed surfaces. It was once a Jurisdiction of production and manufacturing, a highly valued and wealthy Jurisdiction. There was no currency in Axiom, but all bosses made sure that their workers would produce more than enough goods for them to take advantage of, and so they were rich in terms of their possessions, their wealth lay in their power to trade. The work that once took place here was now spread out across the rest of Axiom and production bosses were far more closely governed. Theodore had always feared that should a rebellion come it would manifest itself in J15, where the fat cats would begin to get ideas of grandeur, confident from the power they wielded in their isolated slice of the city. He taught his daughter well and she promptly ensured that the manufacturing and productions bosses were aggressively policed by J3s and watched closely and covertly by the Shrouded.

In amongst the old houses there stood, in various states of disrepair, factories, workshops and processing plants and their giant crumbling industrial chimneys. It was not like the mass automated production of the forgotten days; there were no vast production lines of robotic arms and the huge machinery for making huge machinery. This was a derelict world of simple mass-produced items. The manufacture was made more efficient by the division of labour on a construction line. There was an occasional machine, a press or a blast furnace, for example, for performing the most simple tasks. Most things of value – tools, good metal, solid wood and the like – had been plundered by Vulture and those like him. Anything left now was rusted, splintered or broken beyond repair. It was a Jurisdiction that offered a reminder and a warning of the Axiom of old to its current Residents.

They set off quietly straight down the street ahead of them, Bevan making sure to step directly into Vulture's footprints in the dusty earth. After about a hundred yards Vulture veered off to cut through a large house on the left side of the street. It must have once belonged to someone of importance, since Bevan had only seen anything else like it near to the Central Bastion or in J1. For a start it was more than just a single storey tall and it was evident from the outside that it had several rooms on each floor. The huge double front doors opened with an initial groan, but then swung open without resistance, and they slipped inside, closing the door silently behind them. The grand hallway was bigger than Bevan's entire house. A creeping vine had found its way in through some unseen crevice in the ceiling and trailed down the wall of the landing above, across the floor, to hang in a great curtain of green which partially obscured the view down the hallway and into the house. Crude drawings and graffiti covered the walls, some of it ('Ignorance = Knowledge', 'The winning days are gone') more intriguing and interesting than others ('Connor, Zach, Josh – Clicking hard!', 'XXX'). The place had been ransacked and all that remained was some broken furniture. They tiptoed through the room, taking care not to disturb anything. Vulture led the way up a now–rickety stairway to a second floor. The boards protested audibly under their weight and as Bevan neared the top a step cracked and fell away clattering below. His hand snatched out and grabbed a hold of the bannister, steadying himself, and left a print in the dust. At the exact same moment that he brought himself up and onto the landing, Vulture grabbed him and, with that surprising strength he'd witnessed before, slammed him into the wall, a hand on his throat and his cruel looking shank just an inch away from Bevan's eye.

'Shhhhhh,' he whispered. They stood there like that for a full minute. Both held their breaths. Vulture never broke his stare, never lowered the weapon, and Bevan's heart pounded against his rib cage and pulsed loudly in his ears. They listened intently. Nothing.

Not a sound.

'You do think this is a game of hide-and-seek, don't ya, but you are running with scissors, boy! Strike one.' Vulture loosened his grip and released Bevan. He turned and walked off down the landing, stopping at the first door and pressing his ear to it. After a moment he turned the handle and opened it. 'Well, come on, boy,' he beckoned.

This room would have been the master bedroom, or so Bevan guessed from the rotting mattress sat atop an old ramshackle bedstead in the middle of the floor. Beside the tatty decaying bed was a dressing table. The mirror was shattered and the two legs on the right of the table gone, and there it stood lopsided. A leak had dripped from the ceiling and a green sludge had accumulated, slid down the top of the dresser and pooled across the floor. These once-cherished pieces of furniture in this grand home were just sad remnants of a lost time of affluence in J15. The room had a sloped roof that came right down to the floor, a large section of which was now gone. It had slid off its frame into the barren garden below and smashed through a child's playhouse. The hole in the ceiling revealed, just some sixty–odd feet behind the house, a factory. This must have once been the factory owner's home. He'd have grown fat and wealthy off its produce.

Vulture walked over to the hole and slipped outside and out onto the roof. Bevan followed. Joining the two buildings was a cable, from the cornerstone of the house over to a fire escape balcony and ladder on the factory wall. They climbed their way slowly across, hand over hand, inch by inch. Falling probably wouldn't be fatal but a broken leg was very possible. The cable felt like ice in Bevan's hands, as he had removed his gloves for the crossing. A swirl of wind set him swinging like washing on a line about halfway across and he tightened his grip and the cold bit harder. Quite why they could not have continued on foot at ground level he wanted to know... but dared not ask. They reached the other side unscathed. Bevan's arms ached. He said nothing but he hoped there was a more simple return route. They climbed another two floors higher on the escape ladder and entered through a window, stepping in onto a walkway that spanned the full length of the factory floor below and across to an isolated foreman's office.

Stepping onto the walkway made it sway, and Bevan was reminded of working on the Farm gangways in the wind, his stomach turning as he looked down the four floors to the ground. He felt dizzy, stumbled and dropped to one knee, a loud clang echoing out through the vast empty shell of the factory. He looked up to see Vulture marching back towards him – he looked furious, his boots thumping on the walkway. He'd obviously given up on stealth, and this worried Bevan more than anything. Vulture continued to bear down on him as he tried to rise to his feet, steady himself and his vision and ready himself to, he assumed, fight.

Thud, thud, thud...

Vulture's footsteps sounded his approach.

Thud – click – thud, thud, – click, click, click…

The footsteps stopped.

Vulture had stopped, and Bevan noticed he no longer looked so angry. No, Vulture looked scared. *Click, click, click.* There it was again, what he'd heard before, mixed in with the stomping sound of boots on steel. Still on one knee, Bevan stared down now through the grating of the walkway, and there he saw them. He saw them looking back up. He saw them seeing him. Click addicts, seven of them. Scattered around their feet were empty Clickers. *Click, click.* The last one of them administered his drugs into each of his thumbs, squeezing them against his forefingers, the other fingers out straight like someone giving the 'OK' sign. He let out a moan of pleasure as he dropped the Clickers into the dust.

'Who's that trip–trapping over my bridge?' he sniggered and grinned, displaying a horrible mouth of bleeding gums and blackened teeth. He pulled a gas mask which sat on his forehead down over his face, and with those words the group broke off at a sprint towards the ladder which would bring them up to the walkway.

Panic set in; Bevan realised he wouldn't make it back out along the cable to the house and so he set off running after Vulture who was himself racing across the walkway to the office. Vulture made it there first; in he dashed and slammed the door shut behind him. Bevan reached the room and grabbed at the handle but the door wouldn't open. Behind him he heard the sound of footsteps on the walkway. They were coming.

'Please, Vulture, please!' he yelled. 'They'll kill me, they're gonna kill me, let me in, gimme a fucking chance, dammit!' the door gave way, it opened inwards and Bevan fell inside landing on all fours. He spun over onto his backside and saw through the doorway the addicts, now halfway up the walkway, running hard towards him. He kicked the door shut, leapt to his feet and toppled over a heavy cabinet to block the door from opening. He turned and grabbed at a table behind him. 'Help me move this thing in front of the door,' he said… and with a degree of horror realised he had said it to an empty room. Vulture was gone. He didn't have time to work out how Vulture had escaped, to even consider how the hell he had vanished, because right then the sound of several bodies slamming into the blocked door was the priority concern.

Click addicts were dangerous. Only well-armed members of the Shrouded would attempt to take them on. They could be found in other Jurisdictions, amongst the other Residents, but only at the early stages of the substance abuse; ultimately they all ended up Farmed, dead or completely dependent on the drug and struggling to survive in J15. They grouped together for safety and to share their poison of choice. A gang of seven like this one was fairly typical. They were always aggressive, desperate for food and goods to trade for more Click.

Click had first been developed as a way of surviving the harsh winters that the first Residents were not accustomed to. It was a prototype that should never have left the laboratory. The device that made the clicking sound that gave the drug its name was basically a modified fingerstick of the kind often used for drawing droplets for a blood test. When pinched between thumb and forefinger the seal broke and made a clicking sound. A tiny needle punctured the skin and sent just a few tiny drops of the drug directly into the bloodstream. Click was, in the most basic sense, a small dose of intravenous anaesthetic; while it numbed the body from skin right through to the deepest tissues, though, the user remained completely awake, completely lucid. They felt a sense of invulnerability and invincibility, a godlike quality. It was this feeling that became addictive, consuming the mind until the addict felt useless without Click, weak and vulnerable. They were of course still human: they could be wounded and they often got injured. Their flesh would still burn, frostbite would eat away at their fingers and toes, illness still afflicted them, but they did not feel it, could not feel anything. As a result many addicts would have mangled limbs from unregistered breaks, gangrenous wounds from untreated cuts and gashes (which also affected their mental state) and pus–filled sores and infections. Their delicate minds and desperate existence meant many would fight and brawl with one another for food and for Click and for dominance within the gang. They were like animals with a pack mentality. They were formidable opponents:

if you didn't strike a lethal blow straight away, they would keep coming; you may as well be striking a block of wood.

The door shuddered again as the Click addict gang piled into it. The cabinet moved an inch with a loud screech on the tiled floor and a set of arms thrust through the gap. Bevan leapt against the door with all his weight and might, crushing them. They must have broken – he heard a sickening loud crack – but the addict did not flinch. This door was not closing again. Bevan slammed the door again and again – at least those arms would be broken and floppy, unable to do damage or wield a weapon. He stepped back and rolled over the table, flipped it onto its side and, crouching behind it, he drew the pistol out from his backpack and checked the bullets, one in the chamber, four in the magazine. He held the gun out in front of him, aimed at the door and in the other hand he held his mini–pickaxe. Head or chest, he thought, head or chest. His heart was racing and the pistol was shaking in his unsteady hand. It went suddenly quiet. Bevan held his breath.

The stillness and silence raised the tension. Then came the muffled voice of the leader from inside his gas mask, 'Ready or not, here we come!'

With an almighty crash, the door burst inwards and the cabinet swung back against the wall. All seven of them rushed in but stopped in their tracks as they spotted the gun. They were of varying heights and ages, the youngest perhaps just eighteen or nineteen, the oldest a woman in her mid-fifties. The gang leader, the one who'd spoken earlier, stood tallest at the back, menacing in his gas mask.

'How good a shot is our dinner, I wonder,' he asked and shoved the old woman forward. She stumbled slightly away from the group regained her footing and came running at Bevan. Just a couple of feet away, he pulled the trigger – nothing. The safety was still on! The others all laughed at his lack of combat nous. He reacted fast, though, stepping forward to meet her and bringing the pickaxe down and through the top of her head. Blood gushed from the puncture wound and from her nose and mouth. The laughter of her companions stopped immediately. She was a dead weight impaled on the pick, though, and she dragged him forward as she fell. As he was falling, he released his grip on the pickaxe and left it embedded in her skull. He landed on her and rolled onto his back, thumbing the safety off on the pistol as two more of the gang descended on him. He took aim and squeezed the trigger twice in quick succession. They too dropped dead. At such close range it wasn't difficult to hit the target. Their shocked, dead faces barely marked. The backs of their heads' terrible messy exit wounds. They both fell right on top of Bevan, though, and the gun fell from his grasp and slid across the floor: he was pinned, helpless and surely, he feared, food for these creatures.

Bevan looked up from the pile of death that lay across him, through a tangle of limbs to see the remaining four Click addicts standing over him, looking down with wicked smiles on their faces. The arms that had come through the door, the ones that Bevan had broken, belonged to a middle-aged man; they hung uselessly at his sides and would take some time to heal. They would never be straight again. Two others appeared to be siblings, a brother and sister, in their late twenties. Even as he laid there, certain he was about to die, Bevan felt sorry for the siblings. He wondered what terrible trauma became them that they ended up here in this state. Both had lost clumps of hair, the boy was missing an eye, and the girl had no top teeth at all. Then there was the group's leader. He appeared even taller and more imposing now. He slid the mask back off his face and Bevan saw that his Jurisdiction tattoo had been crudely removed from his cheek. The entire side of his face where it once had been was heavily infected, swollen and oozing with a yellow pus. This close up he could also see that all their thumbs were just rotting stumps, obliterated by constant injections. They looked as though rats had been gnawing at them.

'Look at this, guys,' the big guy said. 'We scratch around for scraps of food for weeks and nothing but the crummiest morsels and now a whole feast laid right out in front of us.'

'Cut me off a piece – I can't, me arms are all busted!' said the other man, flailing his snapped limbs around in front of himself. The leader stepped forward and drew a blade from his waist. Bevan tried struggling from underneath the weight of bodies to defend himself but couldn't get loose.

'No, don't,' snapped the younger boy, and put his arm out across the leader, stopping him from proceeding. 'He can get his own, or he can't, that's his problem! More for us this way.'

'Hey, I took one for the team to get us in here,' broken arms whined.

'There ain't no team, you cretin! You'll just have to eat without your hands like an animal, won't you?' the girl snickered.

'No team? Eat like an animal?' He mused. 'Yeah, I'll eat like an animal!' and with those words he lunged at the boy next to him and sank his teeth deep into his throat. They fell to the ground, the boy writhing to free himself from the jaws of the man. The girl pulled him away but it was too late. The Click would have masked any feelings of physical pain – the only thing the boy would have felt was shock at the attack – shock and the last few breaths he ever made as he lay in a pool of his own blood trying desperately to suck in air.

'Noooo!' the boy's sister screamed and knelt down beside him, distraught. 'You bastard! He's dead, you didn't have to kill him!'

'Hey if he ain't in my team he's fair game, eh?' said the man, trying to wipe the blood away from his mouth with his mangled left arm.

'That's enough, you clowns we've a fresh one here,' the leader interrupted. 'You can have first choice of cut from this guy, since he went and killed your brother, OK?'

'Scant consolation... but thanks,' she replied standing up away from her brother's dead body, but not before removing four Clickers from his pocket.

The leader stooped down and dragged Bevan out by the scruff of his neck. Bevan struggled and protested but the leader was far bigger and stronger, and simply flung him onto the table.

'Hold him down,' the man instructed. The girl clamped her hands on Bevan's shoulders and put all her weight into keeping him there, as the addict with the damaged arms slumped himself across Bevan's legs.

'I want some belly,' the girl requested.

'Right you are, belly, coming right up,' the leader answered, raising his knife high above his head, ready to plunge down and gut Bevan alive.

Bevan closed his eyes and chastised himself for being so stupid.

Who did he think he was, adventuring into J15 on a mission to save Evelyn? He was just a simple electrician. Not a warrior, not a hero. Evelyn was gone and now so was he, just food for Click addicts.

He heard a horrible cutting sound of a knife passing through flesh and bone, but he felt nothing. Had they given him Click? Was this what death felt like? He opened his eyes. The leader still stood over him, knife held aloft, but protruding from the middle of his face was the point of a blade. It withdrew and he fell to the floor to reveal Vulture.

The girl who had fixated on holding Bevan down looked up at the commotion and loosened her grip. Bevan shot up, headbutting her and sending her tumbling backwards. Before she could even steady herself, Vulture was on her to finish her off. Bevan grabbed the last addict, who was still lying over his legs, by the head and threw him off to the side; he flew and, without his arms to help balance himself, clattered into and over the filing cabinet, hitting his head hard and being knocked unconscious.

'Let's get the hell outta here, boy,' said Vulture appearing at his side wiping off blood from his blade.

'Where the hell were you?' Bevan asked, shoving Vulture in the chest. 'You left me here to die!'

'Calm down boy! I left you to save you, you fool.'

'Where did you go?'

'You are never stuck, boy, you always have options, always somewhere to go. Remember that. And remember this: shove me again and I will have no option but to be quite nasty right back.' He spat the last sentence right in Bevan's face. It was an intimidating threat.

'OK, look, I'm sorry Vulture. Thank you.'

He relaxed his posture, stepped away and began to walk back out of the office to the gangway, 'Well I want that electricity, don't I? Come on let's get that part and get home, not much farther now boy.'

Bevan grabbed the pistol from the floor and followed Vulture out of the room.

Chapter 13

They had travelled in complete silence. Neither Bevan nor Vulture had uttered a word for just over half an hour now. They hadn't put a foot wrong and had moved stealthily and undetected. Their faint footprints in the light snow and heavy dust were just rumours of their presence here. They were ghosts slinking through the gloom of the dead Jurisdiction 15.

Bevan was trailing behind Vulture by some twenty yards. They had come up a weathered wind tunnel of a street, a howling gale throwing the snow into their faces and pulling the breath out of Bevan's mouth, flinging it down the path behind him. The wind must have been almost constantly gusting through this part of the Jurisdiction, since all features had been swept away from the surrounding buildings and there was no litter or dust – it was all blown away. They crept along the cracked, crumbling tarmac in crouched positions for around a quarter mile. Bevan's thighs burned and his back ached, but he dared not change his stance and step out of line; Vulture was not in a forgiving mood. They were flanked on either side by two huge, long-dilapidated warehouses. The windows three stories above them were like great dark eyes on otherwise featureless faces staring down at them. Bevan glanced up at them nervously, half expecting to see figures stood in them, looking back at them, and more than a few times he thought he'd heard clicking. He felt very exposed down in the middle of the old road.

Up ahead Vulture had come to a stop, staring down at the ground at his feet. As Bevan got closer though, he could see clearly that Vulture wasn't staring at the ground but rather into it. He was standing at the edge of a vast hole in the ground. All around the edges the tarmac was warped out of shape and there was evidence of a structure that once stood here. There were a few piles of smashed glass windows and frames, a pile of old roofing tiles and a wall off to the right, still partially standing but snapped in two and leaning in against itself.

'If it's here, boy, it's down there,' said Vulture, not taking his eyes off the hole.

Bevan came gingerly up alongside Vulture, more than a little apprehensive of the ground giving way. He stared down into the utter darkness of the void at their feet. Just over two feet below his feet, visibility was down to zero, the blackness complete. Thick and impenetrable.

'Down there?' Bevan asked his voice wavering slightly, his nerves building. 'But how deep is it? How do you know what's down there?'

'Where do you think that little toy you traded for came from? It was the last thing down there of any use – that and tons and tons of loose wires. I'll bet ya it's down there, boy!'

Bevan sniffed an opportunity, his nerves lifting slightly. 'A bet, eh, Vulture?'

'Yeah, hundred per cent it's down there. You wait till you get down there, you'll see, there's literally countless cables – millions, billions of them, boy. Every length, colour and attachment you can think of.'

Bevan shook his head, 'I don't buy it. There's nothing down there but half an old building and dirt and rocks and the dark. Let's go back… and I'll have half that meat back, since this has been a waste of time.' Bevan turned on his heels and took just one step away from the hole before he heard precisely what he wanted and expected.

'I bet ya, boy. I bet ya it's down there!' said Vulture, with absolute certainty.

Bevan turned to face Vulture, trying his very hardest to hide his smugness. 'Bet me what? You have nothing I want!'

'Look boy, you come outta that hole with the cable you need and… er… and… ' he struggled to think of something, '… and you can forget about that electricity deal! It's cool, boy. I'll just take the meat. Hey, it's been fun. To have the electricity too, see that's just greedy of me.'

Bevan paused for dramatic effect as he feigned thinking it over. 'OK, deal. But it's a moot point, 'cos there ain't no way there's anything down there,' he said as he stepped back towards the edge. He was amazed how simple the double bluff had been. Just by appealing to Vulture's ego, to the man's certainty that he knew all there was to know about J15, he'd got out of completing the task he was sure he couldn't have completed. If he came back with nothing, he owed Vulture nothing, and if by some miracle he found the cable, well then, he had what he came for and he still owed Vulture nothing but a handful of old lady arse steaks.

'So how do I get down there?' he asked.

'It's not so deep as you think, and the sides are staggered like an oversized staircase,' replied Vulture. 'It's quite easy to climb down there, but you'll need light.'

'I've an idea,' said Bevan. Vulture stood and watched as he rummaged in a nearby pile of what was once a section of the factory roof. He selected a shaft of good solid wood beam, around a foot and a half in length, took the spare pair of socks from his backpack and wrapped them around the end. Marching over the street to an old rust encrusted car, he lifted the hood. It made a crunching moan of a creak as the old hinge allowed movement for the first time in forever, and huge chunks of rusty orange metal fell away onto the engine and the ground, crumbling into dust. Unscrewing the plastic cap to the oil tank took some effort, as time and the cold had caused the old thread and cap to more or less fuse together. With it off though, he thrust the sock-covered end of the pole into the reservoir and withdrew it; it had soaked up some of the liquid.

'You'll be wanting this boy,' said Vulture coming up alongside him and sparking a lighter. The flame licked at the oily socks, instantly took hold and burst into a large flame. A perfect torch.

Bevan walked back over to the hole, sat down and shimmied over to the edge. With his legs dangling over, he couldn't even see his feet in the darkness. He leant forward with the torch and the light of the flame cut through the black. Just a couple of feet or so below where he sat was an outcrop, and off this there looked to be a section of metal panelling that he figured he could quite easily slide down onto the next level below. Beyond this, the light could not penetrate and the darkness took over again.

'Here, hold this,' Bevan said to Vulture, handing over the torch while swivelling around onto his stomach and easing himself out over the edge. He shifted back and dropped down to arm's length. Hanging for a brief moment, he wondered to himself for the second time today what on earth he was doing. It was as if when they took her, when his beloved wife was snatched away from him, they'd also taken all his common sense. Just six years ago, he'd led a simple happy life of a married Resident of J17. A man who was good at his job, who came home to a beautiful wife, who was the envy of his neighbours. Today he was a man pitied by those same neighbours for all he'd lost and the obvious way in which he struggled to deal with it. Today he'd taken the lives of three sick addicts and was now hanging over a precipice about to drop into the unknown and unseen... yet... yet something told him that he'd begun on a path that he could no longer leave, a path that maybe, just maybe, would lead him to her.

Bevan dropped down and landed on a good solid ledge, both feet firmly planted. He looked back up to collect the torch.

'So what do I get if you do find that cable, hmm, boy?' Just inches from his own face was Vulture. Surprised, Bevan took a step back and a piece of the ledge broke away down into the dark – he glanced over his shoulder, scared, but held his ground. Vulture had lain down on his stomach and leant out over the edge. He was close enough Bevan could smell his unclean breath as his lips broke apart into a sickly grin, 'You didn't really think I'd not want a wager too? Not a bet otherwise now, is it, boy?' he said. Bevan knew he'd been a fool to even think he could outwit Vulture – he was a wily old fox. A fox whose coat was wrecked by mange and who'd narrowly avoided the hounds on countless occasions, but who still had all his wits about him.

'You're already getting the meat and the electric,' he said, rather hopefully.

'They were payment for taking you out here, boy, but you wanted to start a bet.'

'Well, what do you want?' Bevan asked, changing tack.

'Your help with something.'

'What "something", exactly?'

'I suppose you could call it another scavenging mission of sorts.'

'I thought you worked alone – you didn't want me on this one!' He was fishing for some more information.

'Yeah, well, boy, you ain't so useless after all, quite tasty with a pistol, eh?' Vulture replied with a horrible little wink of his left eye. Bevan just stared back, looking unsure and unimpressed with the proposal. 'Look, boy, it ain't normally this rough a ride and you've learnt your lesson – keep quiet, as sneaky as a little rodent and we can waltz in and out this old Jurisdiction and no–one will ever be any the wiser. I sometimes come through with, shall we say, more challenging... cargo.' His mouth spread into a nasty grin, displaying his yellow, jagged teeth.

Bevan's shoulders sagged. 'I haven't really got a choice, have I?' he said, feeling deflated and defeated.

Vulture's smile got wider. 'No, boy, no, you haven't.' He handed down the flaming torch. 'Now you best get a move on. You don't wanna be down there when this runs out.'

With the flaming sputtering torch in his hand, Bevan could see slightly further into the hole. Vulture was right: the way the ground had collapsed the walls were like a staircase for a giant; in fact he wondered if this was a natural collapse or if these were manmade. He tested the metal sheet that sloped down to the next level with an out-stretched foot – it felt secure and solid enough. He took another step and the metal groaned a little but held firm as he slid his way down to the next level. Here he found the same set-up – each ledge going down deeper into the void was connected by a metal slide. There was no doubt this route in and out had been purposely constructed. Nine shelves of earth later he found himself on solid ground at the bottom.

He looked back up the route he'd come down. High above him the opening to the hole was just an almost perfect circle of the dull Axiom sky in a canvas of black, the tiny specks of light snowfall floating down. There was no sign of Vulture at the edge. The darkness encroaching all around him was suffocating. Beyond the faint glow of his torch he could see very little. The flickering of the flame made the shadows dance, and the remains of the building and its contents were all distorted to mimic every horrible thing Bevan's mind conjured up. A light sweat broke out on his back. He closed his eyes and let out a slow breath to calm the rising panic. It did the trick. He opened his eyes and strode off purposefully in the direction of a mound of something that moments ago had looked like writhing snakes or worms in the dark; now it was clear to him that this was the pile of cables Vulture had spoken of.

Now stood in front of the cable mountain, Bevan was utterly daunted – there were masses of them! Tons in weight, hundreds of thousands in numbers. It was going to be like hunting for a single specific needle in a gigantic pile of needles. The torch in his hand sputtered, choked, and the light momentarily dipped to just a small circle around him, before flaring back to life and pushing the dark away. This kicked him into action, as to be down here in complete darkness would be unthinkable. Swinging the backpack off, he removed the Window and began grabbing cables and trying their ends in the socket. He worked fast – trying them, rejecting and tossing them over his shoulder. Trying them, rejecting them, tossing over his shoulder, over and over again. The torch sputtered again; the dark was oppressive. This was no good, it was going to take too long, the light was going to go out. Damn Vulture! he thought. Two people would have halved this job. He was getting angry. Frustrated and helpless, he started muttering to himself.

'I've got to check them all, can't leave until I've –' A clattering sound in the dark cut him off short. It was close, had come from the other side of the pile of cables. He held his breath and didn't move a muscle. On his knees, surrounded by useless cables, he now suddenly wished he didn't have the torch. Down here, at this moment, it was a huge 'I'm over here' sign.

Nothing, not a sound. Though Bevan's heartbeat was pounding so loudly in his ears, he doubted he'd have been able to hear anything else anyway. A whole minute passed. He was full of adrenaline and his muscles were taut, tight and burning for action, but he didn't move. His ears strained, listening for any sign of movement… then, there it was again, but not so much a clatter, more a creak followed by a thud. He felt something digging in his side and remembered the pistol, holstered in his belt after the fight with the Click addicts back in the abandoned warehouse. It gave him renewed confidence. Sliding the weapon from his belt, he inched his way as slowly and quietly as possible to the edge of the mound of wires and peered around. He couldn't see anything out of the ordinary. The walls seemed to come together and veer off away from him into a pitch–black tunnel. Again the creak and thud came echoing up from down the tunnel. By the sounds of things it wasn't that far away, so Bevan inched his way towards the opening, pistol raised and torch held out in front of him to light the path ahead.

As he stood at the entrance to the tunnel now, the light flooded down and filled the area before him. Bevan shook his head and gave a wry smile. It wasn't a tunnel but rather a small alcove maybe three foot deep, and cut into the back of it was a door swinging on its hinges just a couple of inches open and closed again, gently pulled this way and that by a slight draught. *Creak… thud…* He lowered his pistol slightly, propped the torch against the wall and stepped towards the door. *Creak… thud…* He was curious to see what lay beyond the old, wooden, handle-less door. *Creak…* His hand touched the cold, damp wood, stopping it mid-swing and causing another 'thud' sound. All around him fell silent again.

'Just push it shut, boy,' came a voice behind him. He spun around to face the person and took a step back, bumping into and shutting the door in the process.

'Shit, Vulture, you scared the life outta me!'

Vulture responded by just letting out another of his rasping laughs, picked up the torch and begun to walk back over to the cable mountain. 'That way, through there, is for another time.'

'What other time? What's back there?' Bevan asked.

'I told ya, boy, for another scavenge some other time, another job, some smuggling… and you'll find out, don't you worry. Whets your curiosity though, don't it?' he said with a smile.

It had too, it really had. Bevan lingered in the alcove for a moment, wanting to turn and open the door, before he remembered why the hell he was down under the earth in J15. 'Well, I think that the "some other time" you're talking about will just be more searching through this lot,' said Bevan, following after Vulture and gesturing to all the wires.

'Nah, we are done here,' said Vulture. 'We've not much light left…'

Bevan started to interject, to plead for just a little more time, a repeat visit if necessary, but Vulture carried on: 'Plus I think this is what you were looking for,' he finished, still walking away, not turning around, but holding out for Bevan to see a two-foot-long white cable. Even from this distance, Bevan could see it was an odd connection. Even from this distance, Bevan knew it was going to fit. He ran up and snatched it from his hand, while in the same motion removing the Window from his backpack and sliding the cable in. It did fit, they had found it!

'We've got to get outta here and home fast, OK, Vulture? I've got to get this thing fired up, OK?'

'Well that's exactly what I've been suggesting, boy. Come on,' he replied, setting off at a slight jog.

Bevan was elated. Once they had clambered back up out of the sinkhole, every slow stealthy footstep back to Vulture's house was, for him, frustration epitomised. Every fibre of his being wanted to just run the quickest route possible – and loudest, if need be. He knew that in perhaps an hour's time he'd be home and he'd find out precisely what this thing could do.

It was an arduous, painstakingly slow journey home, though. Sneaking their way back through J15 went without incident but it went at a snail's place. At the slightest sound, or if he had a 'feeling' something was not right, Vulture kept on insisting that they hide and wait and listen... and wait. More often than not he would drag Bevan into cramped, tight spaces. They ended up in the back of an old wrecked car, an empty, rusty ancient industrial liquid vat, an understairs broom cupboard in a derelict house and on their stomachs lying in snowmelt and mud under a sheet of corrugated metal. Squeezed together, at times Bevan thought he would sooner take his chances with alerting Click addicts or guard patrols than fight off the nausea brought on by Vulture's rank smell, but he caught and held the instinct to yack in his throat and kept quiet and still. After all, the smell couldn't kill him but the alternatives almost certainly would. All Bevan wanted was to get home as fast as possible.

Mercifully they finally made it back to the wall and the wardrobe at Vulture's house. As they agreed, Bevan left all the meat and promised to return in a week's time to start work on the electrification of the old decaying building Vulture called a home (knowing full well he would either be long gone on the project, long gone searching for his wife or served up as the main course in a meal). As he turned to leave, though, Vulture grabbed at his wrist, his scrawny, claw–like hand a vice on Bevan's arm as he drew him in close and whispered ominously through his yellow teeth with acrid breath, 'It'll be about time for another scavenge then too, boy. I might take you on through that door down in the hole that you're so curious about.' He paused and released his grip. 'You know, boy. First that gadget, now that door – you are a curious little creature, ain't ya, boy. It's not always good to know.' And with that he turned and left, shutting his front door and leaving Bevan stood in the swirling snow on the old dilapidated street. He stood lost in thought for a moment, contemplating these words, until a big gust of wind shook him back to his senses. He set off at a full-on run back to his house, remembering why he was so impatient to get home – he had to get some power into the Window.

He burst through his front door, shut it behind him and bolted it shut. He slid open the hidden storage space and delicately plucked the window from the shelf. He knelt at the side of his bed, the cable in his hand and the device lying before him, wondering whether plugging it in was really such a good idea. Vulture's words echoed in his mind: 'It's not always good to know.' Was ignorance bliss? A sense of foreboding gripped him and he was sure that even the lights dimmed, all sound of toil and industry outside his window in J17 went quiet and the air got heavier.

'Get a damn grip, Bevan,' he muttered to himself. He took a deep breath and held it. Flicked the switch on the wall. The cable was live with power. Holding the Window in one hand, the cable in the other, he brought the two together, pausing with the cable just an inch away from the socket. He closed his eyes. Slowly exhaled. Steadied his slightly trembling hands. This was it…

Chapter 14

The cable slid into the socket at the base of the Window.

Nothing happened.

Bevan felt like he could cry. He slumped forward onto the bed and his head rested against the cold glass of the Window. He shut his eyes and he began a low growl of frustration in the back of his throat. It was building in volume and he was preparing to scream at the top of his lungs and to hell with who heard it. He brought his head up; he knew what he was going to do. He was going to smash his own stupid head through the stupid gadget. He opened his eyes and looked down at the damn thing. There in the middle of the screen was the picture of a battery and it had a tiny sliver of red in the base – it was charging. Bevan's scream became a laugh; one of relief and excitement. He sat staring at the Window, willing it to suck up power quicker and properly boot up. He stared and waited and waited and stared. And waited. Time seemed to draw out, and Bevan waited, and his mind drifted. One conundrum felt like it was on the verge of being solved. Soon the Window would have power, and he could find out so much more about the world, and he could find Evelyn.

He lay on his bed, the Window on his chest plugged into the wall, waiting for it to power up. He should have been completely content but something else was troubling him. His thoughts went to Benedict. The boy he would have to abandon, the boy who had become a second conundrum. There was plenty of training for the project still to go, and he was exhausted, but he knew that there was absolutely no chance of any sleep tonight. He simply could not calm down his racing thoughts, let alone shut his eyes.

Since that first morning of their training he had slowly built up some form of trust with the boy who had otherwise only spoken about ten words to the rest of the team (and in truth not many more to Bevan).

Bevan had let the other five get on with their training and planning, just occasionally stepping in to give some direction, break up a disagreement or play devil's advocate in a problem that was up for discussion. Instead Bevan had focused almost all of his attention and spare time on the youngest member of the team. Not just because he had genuinely come to believe he could be the most naturally gifted of any of them when it came to understanding and manipulating electrical circuits, currents and devices, but because he had felt drawn to the boy. It was a combination of intrigue, pity and, he guessed, some natural instinct to nurture, protect and comfort. He sat with him, often in complete silence, for hours at a time, just working on a challenge. Bevan would talk and the boy would make random noises, more to vocalise his own enjoyment of fixing things than in response to the conversation, but Bevan took this as a good sign that he was at least comfortable enough in his company to be himself.

Benedict never spoke of himself and was not interested in (or as Bevan suspected, was not really capable of) engaging in conversation. He would occasionally comment on a sound or colour that he liked, or a shape that he felt looked like something else. He would sometimes become frustrated or anxious, and Bevan had learnt that he could be quickly distracted by conversation, or even better a demonstration of a new gadget he had not seen before. In this way he had warmed to the boy's simplistic view of the world, and felt that he had in return gone some way to building up a feeling of commonality with him. Bevan felt he would go as far as to say that he was growing quite fond of the boy, like the son that he and Evelyn had spoken of. Despite all the positive feelings, Bevan still felt that something wasn't right. It was this doubt that niggled at him now.

Growing frustrated, he sat up in his bed and ran both his hands down his face and over his eyes in an effort to force them shut. He let them continue down his face, his palms curling open his bottom lip and his fingertips pulling the skin tight under his eyes. He left them in this position, his lip drying out and his eyes exposed, and then a possibility began to form in his mind. The fingertips of his right hand were touching something that every person in Axiom had. The one thing that every Resident was given at their graduation ceremony. Every adult except for Eleanor De Sanctis had one. The sixth member of their team, Benedict, did not have a Jurisdiction tattoo but was certainly of graduation age. So why was he not in J5, learning his trade and preparing to graduate? He was also clearly not of sound mind, so why wasn't he already cattle seeing out his days in J13?

'And why the hell does the General know the kid?' Bevan questioned out loud to himself. The thought worried him – and he questioned again – was this unassuming member of his team some kind of agent, sent to keep an eye on him by Curtis Stricken and Madame De Sanctis? It would be all too obvious to cut off his fledgling friendship with the boy; he would have to play this one smart. 'Keep your enemies close,' he said, with a half-smile that showed his pleasure at putting some logical thought to a possible solution as to what had been bothering him so much about Benedict, but a smile that also masked his worry and concern. He had half-solved one conundrum: now on to the next one.

He glanced down and to his utter relief the Window began its startup routine. The logo, the slogan, the timer and then there they were again – the happy couple smiling back at him. This time however there was something new. Next to 'Mail' there was a little red circle with a white '1' inside it. He was drawn to this little red indicator; he reached out with the index finger of his left hand and lightly tapped it. He quickly withdrew his hand in surprise as the image before him swiftly shifted and he was greeted with a white interface, two thirds of which was blank, while the other third had a header 'Inbox for chrisandjane@newlyweds.org', under which there was a small box of text that read:

From: *czhang@yarlung_zambo.cn*

Subject: *Respond and be recognised…*

The party had been in full swing for over six hours and showed no sign of abating. It was now three o'clock in the morning and Bevan had been there since proceedings began. He had not enjoyed a single minute. He suspected that Eleanor had had absolutely nothing to do with the organisation of it either, since it smacked of the notorious parties of J1.

The venue was one of the larger of the many seedy clubs spread throughout the Jurisdiction, frequented by the guards, central bastion staff and the Shrouded. The dancers were likely once bastard children from all over Axiom, bought or traded by the club owners that raised and groomed them for the profession. Or they were those saved from the Farms if deemed attractive enough.

Its low grubby ceiling was sparsely lit with dim spotlights that gave a murky glow over the round tables positioned all around the main stage and protruding catwalk. These were, in contrast, lit with harsh white up-lighters to ensure all the flesh on display could be seen from any point in the club's main room. The music was loud and aggressive – you couldn't hear yourself think, let alone hold a conversation. The only thing to do was sit at your table and watch the seemingly endless parade of scantily dressed dancer girls totter out onto the stage. Bevan couldn't help but wonder as they writhed about in front of him, removing the few clothes they did have, who was more uncomfortable – them having to perform or the audience of regular Residents like himself who were forced to watch. Only the guard contingent were whooping and gesticulating at the poor creatures on stage. Even Stricken's elite Shrouded looked uninterested, and the General himself had stood up and left some fifteen minutes ago.

Bevan had done well to position himself as far from the 'entertainment' as possible. He sat alone in a corner of the room while the celebrations went on around him, sipping on some poli. It was, if truth be told, a foul-tasting concoction of fermented liquid made from root vegetables, barley, hops and the smallest drop of human bile. A favourite tipple of those here in J1, just a few mugs of the stuff would make shy men bold and bold men obnoxious. You felt that your senses were heightened when in fact they were dulled. Under its influence you might sing, dance or fight, or you were equally likely to sleep, philosophise or laugh. Bevan had never really understood why anyone would want to drink it. Until now. Right now, working his way through his fifth poli, he felt certain of his next steps. Clear on what he must do, and clear that tonight he would have to bring Teddy up to speed. He would need his friend's help and in just two days' time Project Wind would be set in motion and they would be leaving Axiom.

First though he needed to piss. Poli, it seemed, also went through a bladder like water through a sieve. He rose from his feet and felt the room tilt, bend and swirl; the drink certainly wasn't helping with his coordination. He took a moment, gulped down another mouthful, draining his mug, and strode off towards the toilets. He staggered his way zigzag across the club, feet tacky on the floor from spilt poli and who knew what else. The music thudded out of the speakers and he could feel the sound reverberating through his chest. More than anything, though, he could feel his bladder full to bursting point, screaming at him to be relieved. Bursting through the door to the WC he made for the trough. He leaned back and let out a long sigh of relief as the flow began. As he stood there, he closed his eyes and set out a plan in his mind.

He knew what he needed to do. He would finish this glorious piss. He would leave the club. He would travel back to J17. He would go to Teddy's home. He'd wake his friend if he had to. Those messages. He had to tell Teddy. Suddenly a crash. Something thrown had broken against the other side of the wall in front of him. Raised voices, a woman yelling, 'You are paranoid. Hughes is just a J17 sparky.'

His attention was grabbed, his adrenaline rushed through his body, wiping away the effects of the poli almost in an instant. He strained his ears, ignored the ammonia stench and pushed his face against the filthy wall, but the sudden flush of the urinal drowned out the ruckus in the other room.

He turned and burst out of the toilet and up the corridor which curved around back on itself. The first door was locked. He tried the next; it too was sealed shut. The third was ajar, but no–one was inside. He entered. It was just one small room, roughly eight foot square. Once upon a time, many years ago, it was probably quite a luxurious room. The carpet beneath his feet was threadbare but was once deep, thick and red. The single chair and a side table were the only things inside, and they were a heavy dark wood, all scratched and pocked with chips and dents. A balding red velvet covered the seat cushion. The wall before him was a glass window. He looked through it and froze on the spot, terrified. Stood before him not a few feet away in animated, heated conversation were Madame De Sanctis and General Stricken. They would see him. Stood there so clearly, completely exposed, so obviously listening in on a conversation that he should not be privy to. Yet they did not.

Bevan resisted the urge to bolt out of the room. He took a moment to compose himself and looked beyond them both at the surrounding room. It was circular and in the middle was a smooth metal pole bolted from ceiling to floor. In the walls were mirrors, some smashed, others cracked and scratched from the other side. Behind the mirrors were booths just like the one in which he was standing. By a stroke of luck his booth's two way mirror was just about the only one intact. He realised then that men would once have sat here in this small room alone, privately watching only the very best dancers and the most exotic of acts perform on the pole in the central space. He moved closer to the glass to listen.

'I do not think it's going to be as easy as you first thought,' said Stricken.

'Oh Curtis, this is not like you, to shy away from killing an animal.' She laughed and turned her back on him, and studied her face in a shard of the nearest broken mirror. 'This must be an excuse – I didn't have you down as the sentimental type. The boy is incapable of friendship.'

'I thought so too, but I'm telling you, there is a bond between Benedict and the electrical engineer.'

'Some of our best guards go missing beyond the walls. No–one will question a boy disappearing on this expedition,' she replied, tracing a perfectly manicured finger along the 'T' zone of her beautiful face.

'But they are inseparable. Even if I were able to take and execute the boy alone, there would be suspicion. The Residents are well trained dogs but even they would question a leader that has her own son killed.'

Her patience snapped and she whirled around. 'Then bury Hughes out there too! Bury the whole fucking lot of them if you have to,' she fumed. 'Benedict is not a De Sanctis, not a leader, not my son! His retarded mind must be a broken gene... from his father's side.' She strode back towards him and thrust a finger in his chest. 'You made this mess, Curtis, you clean it up. Kill Benedict, put the blame on Hughes or just kill Hughes too. Use your bloody initiative.'

A pause. The tension rising.

'Well, that's all I was looking for permission to do!' he said with a smile. She held his stare before a smile also crossed her lips. She grabbed him by the shirt collar and pulled him towards her, forcefully kissing him. He returned the kiss with the same lusty aggression.

Eleanor let out a moan, closed her eyes and threw her head back. 'Let's try again,' she said as his hands went to her breasts, he kissed her neck and slowly unbuttoned her blouse. She grabbed the back of his head and forced him to face her. An intense stare followed before he kissed her forcefully on the mouth again and lowered her to the floor.

Bevan averted his eyes. His head was spinning as he tried to comprehend what he had just heard.

Eleanor De Sanctis wanted him dead.

Benedict was the son of Madame De Sanctis and General Curtis Stricken.

They both wanted their own son dead.

He staggered and caught hold of the back of the wooden chair. It brought him back out of his racing thoughts and to reality. He glanced back into the performance room, his eyes quickly skimming over the writhing bodies of De Sanctis and Stricken and then he saw him.

Stood across the room in one of the booths with a broken mirror was Benedict. He was without his balaclava but Bevan recognised him nonetheless. The child's face was completely pale, his mouth hung open with disbelief, his eyes glistening with tears. He had also heard every word. Bevan also knew exactly how Benedict reacted to stress. Bevan knew he had to get to him before he began yelling and trying to get at his two would–be–murderer parents. He was not a spy, he was not an assassin. He was just a young unloved boy. His own parents would have him put down like a disobedient pet, like a troublemaker on one of the Farms or a Feral raider. He remembered now that before he suspected him, Bevan had felt a connection with Benedict, had wanted to care for the lad, to take him under his wing and help him to harness his funny ways and undoubted skills for learning.

He had to speak to Teddy, but first he had to get to Benedict before they saw or heard him. Fortunately for the time being they were very much preoccupied.

He bolted from the door and around the corridor to Benedict's booth. Opening the door he saw he was still stood there, his shoulders visibly shaking from crying, his hands clenched into fists at his sides, knuckles white with the strain. He was about to erupt into a rage. Bevan knew he had to get him out of there.

He wrapped his arms around Benedict's waist and felt his body instantly go tense, ready to defend himself, 'It's OK, Ben, it's Bevan' he whispered in his ear. The boy went limp and slumped in his arms sobbing. 'I'll look after you, buddy. Come on, let's get outta here,' Bevan said while physically dragging him under the arms out of the booth and down the corridor.

They were at the rear of the club. There had to be a way out, a service entrance or something nearby. There was. Directly ahead some three hundred feet away, an old fire exit. Bevan made for it as fast as he could while dragging an inconsolable, stumbling Benedict behind him. It was a straight, sparsely lit hallway. They had to move quick or they would be seen. As they lumbered forward Bevan kept his eyes on the door, focused on it, its splintered rat–gnawed bottom, its rusted panic bar lock, its cracked and faded green and white sign. All the while he could hear behind him and closest the sniffs and sobs of Benedict, a little further away Eleanor and the General reaching a climatic crescendo and further still, but sounding far too close for comfort, the thumping of the bass and whooping of the guards leering over the dancers in the main room. He reached the door. His arms occupied with the weight of the boy, he kicked at the bar and the door swung open. They stumbled out into the cold and dark grey, the fire exit door slamming shut behind them.

Released from Bevan's comforting hold, Benedict stood on the spot and began to cry. He let out choking sobs and tears ran down his face. They dripped from his nose and chin and made small melt holes in the snow at his feet. Bevan was still frantic to get as far away from the club as possible. His head turned left to right, looking up and down the alleyway, trying to decide which way to go. Left to the pavement of the main road, which almost certainly would be guarded and watched (no–one just sauntered around in J1). Heading right would take them into a more built–up area, a rat run of shanty and brick buildings, alleys, doorways, ramps and steps.

Which way was it back to their training unit? He jogged left to the edge of the pavement and glanced out. Sat at the front of the party venue was a car carrying the mark of the Shrouded, the silhouette of two men sitting in the front seats. That way was not an option.

'Let's go, Ben. Come on, this way,' Bevan said, running back towards him and pointing up into the maze of the Jurisdiction's belly. He tore past the grief–stricken boy, who remained rooted to the spot. 'Benedict, come on, dammit' he said more forcefully than before, marching back and pulling him by the arm. It was an error. In an instant the lad locked Bevan's wrist, twisted and yanked his arm behind his back. Bevan let out a yelp of pain, the ligaments strained to their limits, the muscles on the verge of tearing. 'OK, OK, I'm sorry, I'm sorry, ease up, ease up,' he pleaded.

'You don't grab me, no,' Benedict wailed while wiping the tears away from his face with his sleeve. His grip on Bevan's arm still strong, no longer distraught but angry.

'I know, I'm sorry, I just want to get us safe, eh, get you away from those lunatics!'

'No you, that's my mother, my father, no you Bevan. *No*.' He twisted his arm even tighter and higher up his back, the tricep creaking as it neared snapping point. Bevan took a step forward and bent further over to try and alleviate the pain. 'Oh wow, yes, cool! What's that, yes?' Ben suddenly asked, his grip on his Bevan's arm loosening slightly.

'What's what?'

'Yes, that thing on your back, yes, that shiny thing.'

A wind kicked up along the alleyway and Bevan felt a draught. He realised that his shirt had ridden up, and the Window strapped to his back had been exposed. He sensed a way out. 'It *is* cool isn't it? A gadget I found, I wanted to show you it tomorrow, but let's go take a look at it now? Let my arm go, yeah, little man, we can go back and I can show you it, it's real special.' A rush of relief coursed through his arm and he let out a long sigh as he was released.

'You promise, yes?'

'Of course, I promise,' he said with a disarming smile.

'Brilliant! I want a play with it, yes! Come on then Bev, yes, come on let's go,' Benedict said with a childlike excitement. He took a hold of Bevan's arm and tugged him along down in to the alleyway, 'I came in this way yes, found you when I heard the boom booming party music. I remember the way back, yes,' and so hand in hand they raced away from the club and all the terrible things inside. The start of a journey with potentially ever more terrible consequences.

Chapter 15

Benedict De Sanctis did know his way back. The way back to his home – in the Bastion! This fact was now dawning on Bevan as the young boy led the way through the back alleys of J1, heading straight in the direction of the great tower that was looming before them. This was an easy beacon to steer by, right enough, due to the circular arrangement of the city and its Jurisdictions. From this point Bevan could find the route back to his place in J17. It would not be good to take the boy with him, though. He was surprised the alarm had not already been sounded to announce his missing status. If they found him in Bevan's Jurisdiction, let alone his house, there would be serious consequences. The kind that he would not survive.

'Ben, wait,' he whispered hoarsely. Up ahead of him the De Sanctis boy stopped in his tracks and swivelled around, grinning, still excited at the prospect of playing with the gadget. 'I can't come to your house.' Ben's smile faded and gradually turned into a sulky frown.

'You *promised!*' he yelled. Bevan hared across the gap between them, his feet slipping a little in the dirt and snowmelt, holding a finger up to his mouth shushing him.

'I still promise, OK, but I can't go in there. Your mother's guards will not be happy to have me as a visitor... you understand, right, buddy?'

'You promised, yes.' Quieter now, more sulky. 'And I don't care what *she* thinks, no!'

Bevan wracked his brains, massaged his temples and let out a slow sigh, maintaining his cool, but also remembering what the boy had just witnessed and feeling a sense of responsibility to not make things worse. 'OK.' He scanned around his surroundings. It was still all quiet save for the distant thud of the party music at the club they had fled and various others in their immediate vicinity. Fortunately, at this early hour the place was deserted. They hadn't yet come across a single person. They stood in another thin alleyway strewn with rubbish bags. Simple constructions on either side, windowless walls of brick,

155

sheet metal and wood panels all crudely fashioned together. A shanty of the Jurisdiction, it was all just homes to the whores, Click cooks, poli brewers, snack vendors, uniform tailors and weapon modifiers and personalisers (it seemed all the guards had a taste for custom guns with stupid flames emblazoned along the barrel and such like). They were simple places of business, the fronts of which faced the street and welcomed passing trade. Bevan and Benedict were in the Jurisdiction's bowels though, in amongst all the shit.

'OK, here, come here.' He beckoned the boy over to where he stood and crouched down in the gloom, taking the Window out from his waistband. 'Now, we have a quick look now and tomorrow I'll let you have a go properly, yeah?' Benedict's sulk lightened a touch but he was making efforts to maintain his disdain for the situation.

'Yes, OK, yes,' he said begrudgingly.

Bevan gently pushed the button on the front and the thing lit up. It seemed impossibly bright in the gloom of the alleyway. It was like he had switched on one of the Bastion's great search lights, 'Hey, we are over here!' it seemed to yell out. He felt like it had illuminated half the Jurisdiction and sent a huge beam of light shooting into the gloomy sky half blocked out by his shocked face.

'Wow!' Benedict said, again too loud for Bevan's liking.

He tapped another button on the top of the device and the glass went black again.

'That is the coolest thing *ever*, *yes*!' Ben was growing more excited, hopping from one foot to the other, his hands flexing, desperate to get a feel for this wondrous machine. 'My turn, yes, my turn, Bev.' He snatched it from Bevan's grasp, pushing in the front button and lighting up the world again. Bevan stepped forward in a panic, desperate to shut off the glow he was sure could be seen from anywhere in the whole city. Benedict tucked the Window into his chest with one arm, mercifully absorbing all the light, but with his other hand he clutched Bevan by the throat. A squawk escaped Bevan's mouth like a startled gull, and he once more felt the uncanny strength of this teenager.

'I want a go properly now! Yes,' Ben said. Even in his current predicament Bevan couldn't help but worry at how loudly he was speaking.

'Quickly then,' Bevan managed. The vice around his throat eased off and released. Stumbling back a few steps he hunched over, hands on his knees, deeply drawing in breath while stars danced across his vision. He gulped in fresh air and felt the dizziness in his head subside.

'What's a "Solacity"?'

Bevan looked up at the boy's question. He stood before him staring down into the Window, face all awash with light and a look of confusion. 'What do you mean, Ben?'

'I liked that little red "2", yes, but when you touch it it's no fun, no, just a boring letter.'

'A what? Here, let me see.' He stepped forward and gently extended his hand to take the device. To Bevan's surprise Benedict gladly handed it back over and moved around alongside Bevan to peer excitedly over his shoulder so they could both see the screen. On it there was the image Bevan had seen before, on the night he had got the thing working for the first time. When he had nervously tapped the little red '1' over the 'mail' icon – but hadn't Ben said a red '2'? It was the image he had seen previously but now slightly different. There were now two boxes on the left–hand side – the one that still read:

From: *czhang@yarlung_zambo.cn*

Subject: *Respond and be recognised*

...And now another:

From: *chungzhangman17@mailspace.com*

Subject: *I found you!*

But it seemed that the boy's more inquisitive, less fearful mind had not stopped there. He had touched the top box, which was now highlighted in a light blue and in the previously empty white space on the right there was a message.

Benedict whispered in his ear, an underlying tinge of excitement and anticipation in his voice, 'I like how it moves, yes. Let's respond Bev, yes. What's a Solacity? What's an Ensign? Have you seen a "Biome", Bev, what does it look like? Do you think it will recognise me, yes?' Ben's questions continued but while Bevan hardly heard them he was thinking them all the same as he absorbed the message, reading and rereading it. Intrigue was outweighing his fear. Momentarily forgetting where he was and the need to get both himself and Benedict home he tapped the second box on the left-hand side.

The message they had been reading was instantly replaced by another. Another that felt more personal and set the first message into a whole different context while raising even more questions. It held a feeling of excitement and Bevan suspected a whole lot of trouble and danger.

Bevan glanced at Benedict and a smile remained on his face. He could clearly read, but he was not putting all the pieces together. Bevan tapped back to the first message and read it once more. A sense of foreboding gripped him on this second pass through.

From: czhang@yarlung_zambo.cn

To: chrisandjane@newlyweds.org

Cc: chungzhangman17@mailspace.com

Subject: Respond and be recognised

This communication is delivered to you from the Leadership Committee of Solacity. Yours is the first live IP address discovered for 17 years, 2 months and 28 days. We are delighted to learn that we are not alone. What is your name? What is your current condition? Are you safe? Where are you? Are you alone?

Please acknowledge this email.

If you require assistance we can offer it.

If you would like to collaborate we are open.

We have food, water, electrical power and security. Together we can rebuild this world, for beneath the safety of our solar–powered biomes the world we knew never ended.

Respond and be recognised.

Ensign Chung Zhang on behalf of the Solacity Leadership Committee.

Bevan took a breath and tapped the second message. Benedict tugged at his sleeve. 'Let's respond Bev, yes, let's respond.'

Bevan gently shook his arm and Benedict's hand from it. 'Shhh. Hold on Ben, let me read this, I need to work out what this is all about.' He wanted to bring Benedict into this thought process. 'What do you think, Ben, who is this guy? A goodie or a baddie?'

'Hmmm… ' Ben scratched his chin, an action he obviously thought demonstrated he was contemplating his answer. 'I'd say goodie, yes, a good guy… erm let's respond, yes.'

Bevan's eyes scanned over the second message. It seemed sincere, seemed genuinely worried for their safety.

From: chungzhangman17@mailspace.com

To: chrisandjane@newlyweds.org

Cc:

Bc:

Subject: I found you!

Completely ignore what you have just read! Do not respond. Recognition would be fatal.

In telling you the truth I take the greatest risk. You may not hear from me again, this email could have signed my death warrant, but you must know what many before you have not. The many before you who I did not have the bravery to warn. The many before you who I helped to destroy or enslave.

To respond is to die… to all die. They will spare no-one.

Leave. As soon as possible. Take those you love and leave.

Tap 'Reply' and, if I am not already dead, you can talk to me through this message system. I can help you.

In hopeful anticipation that you will allow me to do so, sincerely

Chung Zhang

'Here, respond here, yes,' Benedict said, reaching in once more and tapping the screen of the Window. His finger tapped 'Reply' and a separate box opened, partially covering the message, and the keyboard appeared.

Bevan moved to push Ben's hand away but quickly thought better of any sort of physical contact again. In this split second Bevan also decided that to hell with it, he was already in deep now – he was on the run with the son of Eleanor De Sanctis in the bowels of J1, he'd gone to the effort and risk of getting the Window working and now he would find out more about what it could do. Could he really be communicating with someone out in the world beyond the walls of Axiom? As he began to type Benedict watched, utterly transfixed. He kept it short and didn't give anything away.

From: chrisandjane@newlyweds.org

To: chungzhangman17@mailspace.com

Cc:

Bc:

Subject: RE: I found you!

Who is this? How can you see us??

What do you mean destroy? How??

Where would we go?

Bevan hit 'Send' and the little box with his message in folded in on itself and whizzed away into the top right–hand corner of the screen and was gone.

'Now what?' Benedict whispered.

'I don't know. We wait, I guess,' said Bevan. He heard Ben begin to count under his breath. He rolled his eyes at the ridiculousness of it but despite himself he smiled at the boy's wonderful naivety. The smile promptly faded as the reality of their surroundings came back into focus. They were horribly exposed. Bevan looked all around them for somewhere to hole up for a little bit. Benedict continued to count. 'Come on, Ben, in here,' Bevan said as he jogged down the alleyway a little and ducked into what appeared to be an abandoned bar. It had been entirely gutted by fire but was still structurally sound. It offered shelter from the elements and more importantly they were hidden from view.

Bevan hunkered down on his haunches. Over his left shoulder Benedict stood awkwardly, shuffling from side to side, alternating his weight from foot to foot while nervously wringing the hem of his jumper in his hands. Usually quick to be irritated by, and subsequently prompt in attempting to calm, the boy's fidgeting, Bevan barely even registered he was there. His mind was spinning.

Benedict continued to count: 'Eighty-seven… eighty-eight… eighty-nine… ninety… ninety-one… ' The Window let out a delicate pinging chime. Ben let out a little excitable noise and Bevan's heart skipped a beat. He unlocked the Window and there was a little red '1' alongside the 'Mail' symbol again.

From: chungzhangman17@mailspace.com

To: chrisandjane@newlyweds.org

Cc:

Bc:

Subject: I found you!

My name is Chung Zhang. What is your name, friend?

I am tasked with finding you.

When you are found you will be remotely or manually destroyed. Civilisations large and small have been removed as we seek to minimise threats and maintain control of limited resources. The world is unimaginably vast but the world is dead and the world is dangerous.

We exist in the remnants of what is left, of what was the pinnacle of human existence. A peak of six million years of evolution that came crumbling down in a relative blink of an eye. Despite all man's technical advances we could not stop nature and when the planet had done its level best to rid itself of us we turned on one another.

It is not that I can see you in the physical sense but your signal tells me you are there, tells me your location and I in turn must tell them.

They in turn will come for you.

Take everyone and leave. Head south west. When you have travelled several days from your home leave the device, it will act as a beacon to nothing and your civilisation may survive. You may be safe to return. You may not.

Chung.

Bevan swallowed hard, a gulp of fear that stuck in his throat. Where could they possibly be safe? Everyone was out to get them, it seemed. Bevan was feeling desperate – he could not leave Benedict now, didn't want to draw Teddy too deep in to this madness, couldn't let the General and his Shrouded even get a whiff of his plan to flee and had no real idea of where he would go if he was to escape. He let out a long breath to steady his nerves, cracked his fingers and set about typing. 'Oh well, Ben, let's make friends. If you don't ask you don't get, eh?'

From: chrisandjane@newlyweds.org

To: chungzhangman17@mailspace.com

Cc:

Bc:

Subject: RE: I found you!

My name is Bevan and this is Benedict. We have plans to leave already. We are no longer safe in Axiom. Axiom – that is our city.

I've come to see that it is a cruel place. I have never realised it until now, never have I really considered that there may be another option. I'm willing to try though. Stay or die, leave and maybe survive.

We cannot return. Very soon we are to be sent beyond our borders to carry out an expedition but we have learned that it is planned that we shall not return. We would be murdered and buried in the nowhere.

Can you help us? Can we come to you? Will we be welcomed by your people? We are skilled electricians – perhaps we can help you?

Thank you Chung.

Bevan

'Now what Bev? Shall I count again?' Benedict asked.

'No. Of course not. Be quiet, this is serious,' Bevan snapped back. His patience was thinning just as his nerves were fraying.

Benedict physically flinched at the slightly raised voice and impatient tone. He crossed his arms defensively and put on a sulky face. 'Don't be mean, no! You are mean, Bevan Hughes, yes. *Mean!*' He yelled the final word.

Bevan leapt to his feet, dashed to the door and stuck his head out. The street was still deserted. He spun on his heels and marched back towards Benedict – he was, he realised, in something akin to 'angry dad mode' and he meant to scold the boy. 'Calm the hell down, Ben.' He had to hiss, to keep quiet but show he was not happy. 'You are going to get us caught here and then we are both in a whole world of trouble. The kind that gets us dead!' He pointed at Ben with the Window in his hand. It was just a few inches from Benedict's face and it chimed once more. A tiny little sound that melted the building tension. Curiosity replaced the anger. Ben snatched the Window and plonked himself down cross-legged on the floor. Bevan let him take it and knelt down beside him. A response from Chung was on the screen and they read it together.

From: chungzhangman17@mailspace.com

To: chrisandjane@newlyweds.org

Cc:

Bc:

Subject: I found you!

My work has shown me that the world and its remaining cities are always ruled by dangerous cruel people. There could be a different way for us. There are some who want to try again, want to start again.

No, it is not safe here either… but your skills are of interest, could be of use… I cannot help you… but there is another who may help you… who may help us all.

I will tell you of Efran Mourdorant…

… He is a man. Just a man. Though he is a man who is willing to do what others are not – his mind is open, he imagines the wider world, he dares to dream of breaching our borders and venturing into the unknown. Beneath our solar domes we are safe. Beneath our solar domes we should want for nothing more. Our salvation, though, has become our prison. Those who lead us are determined to maintain the status quo, to retain power and rule the world – both within Solacity and beyond.

I'm sure you will think that we should be grateful for all we have but it is simply another form of control. They govern us with strict rules all of which are designed to keep the little man in place and the committee in power. We are not permitted to leave, despite there being clear evidence that life is possible outside our biomes.

Efran Mourdorant is not a man to be held against his will.

He has developed miniature versions of Solacity and they are mobile – they can be driven! Within this city he has created a village, but a village does not exist within a city, a village is meant to be surrounded by wilderness and by open space. The Leadership Committee have quashed his plan and shut down his company – they were not aware that we had in fact developed beyond prototype and are at technology readiness level (TRL) 8! The technology has been proven to work in its final form and under expected conditions. The final phase and TRL 9 would have to be a live test – actual application of the technology in its final form and under mission conditions. All testing has been conducted as best we can for the conditions expect to encounter. We are supremely confident of success.

Our mini–biomes are still significant in scale and can comfortably house up to fifty occupants. The domes themselves will very efficiently harvest solar energy from the ever–present sun and power all beneath them. We can move from location to location and avoid detection by the Leadership Committee of Solacity. Safe beneath the domes we can, if necessary, flee into the hottest parts of the planet where no others can venture. We can seek out good hunting grounds for game, areas ripe for crop cultivation. We can reclaim valuable materials left behind from the old world and recycle or repurpose them.

Efran proposes to leave Solacity, to venture out and start afresh with a skilled team of individuals. This will be a new community that is composed of individuals chosen specifically to each carry out fundamental and crucial tasks. It is Efran's firm belief that, despite what history has shown us and the continued failings of both our homes, society can work – it just has a tipping point. He has worked tirelessly to build the perfect environment within which to flourish in this world. Crucially, though, he has also intricately devised the precise requirements and number of inhabitants to ensure effective, efficient – and there is hope also, for harmonious – cohabitation. If every person serves a purpose then everyone will feel valued, be needed and work for the good of his fellow villager... and Bevan Hughes and Benedict De Sanctis, we are very much in need of electricians.

If you are committed to leave then we will gladly have you and I can help guide you towards us. Time is not on our side. It is clear that it is only a matter of time before fabricated charges are brought against Efran and he will be sentenced. We leave imminently and can meet you half way. Leave your home and strike out east. You will come across a city of ruination, a decaying

place from the old world of such magnitude that it cannot be believed. Travel
around it – not through it, for it is not safe – and continue east until you
reach an outcrop perched high atop a vast plateau. Below it one may feel that
they perceive the entire world at their feet, such is its size. God's Balcony it
has been named – you will be in no doubt when you behold it. Message me
again when you are here and I will provide further instruction…

He read the final message just once before clicking the top button
to darken the screen. He looked around, nervous and paranoid that
somehow someone else might have read those words.

'Hey, I was playing with it!' Benedict complained.

'I know, buddy, sorry', Bevan replied with genuine sincerity. He
wanted to keep the volatile young man in check but he himself also
wanted to keep 'playing' with the Window… just not here, not now.

Somehow, as he sat there stone still with Benedict flapping behind
him, so the cogs in Bevan's mind turned. Things were becoming
clearer and the course of action he felt was their only option became
more apparent. An idea sprung up in Bevan's mind, one that would
require a huge amount of trust in a boy who right now he was not
sure he could trust from one sentence to the next, let alone with
his life. The messages exchanged were too compelling, though, and
without Evelyn in his life anymore what other reason did he have to
carry on? What could possibly hold as much intrigue, excitement and
adventure as that set of words and all they promised?

He would play this last hand and he would go all in.

He stood up, strapped the device across his lower back again and
turned to speak to Ben. 'We will play with it again, OK. Not tomorrow, but the next day OK? Right now I really think you and I should
be getting ourselves home before anyone starts worrying about you –
worrying about us, I mean.' He looked the boy directly in the eyes;
Ben was unable to hold the contact and shied away. 'Benedict, we are
going to leave.'

'Hometime, yes, OK, yes.' He looked scared Bevan thought, scared
yet oddly relieved to return to something that he knew, something
that made sense to his simple mind.

'No Ben, I mean we are going to leave Axiom.'

'Yes, on the project, I know, yes.'

Bevan smiled gently. the boy's naivety and simplicity were for once endearing. 'No I mean just you and me Ben, we are going to leave. They will chase us but we will go out there and we will find Chung and we will find this Efran Mourdorant. We will both be safe... do you understand?'

'Mum said that the General should... yes, should k-k-k-' the boy stammered. Tears sprung from his eyes and left snail trails of despair down his face. The reality of the order he had overhead weighed down on his fragile mind like a ton of bricks on a thin plate of glass. It was at breaking point.

'I know, little man, I know, but I won't let that happen! It's exactly why we have to go. Just us two before, that can happen... and I think I know the way out! We'll need a distraction but that can be arranged. When no–one suspects it we will slip away, away from Axiom and we will do as the message said. We'll travel far away and everything will be better, I promise!'

'You promise, yes?' Benedict sniffed.

Bevan hesitated – was he really committing to this boy? He took a deep breath and decided there in that moment that yes, yes he would. Benedict would be his purpose. It would not matter if he himself did not make it but Ben had to – he had to know a good life, the way Bevan had felt with Evelyn. 'I promise, Ben!' he reached out to hug the boy, to let him know he meant what he said, but Benedict stepped back and raised his hands.

'No, no touching, no!' he said defensively and then added, 'Thank you, Bevan Hughes,' with a shy smile.

Bevan smiled back. 'OK, well, you best get home and I'll start working out the next steps... you know only we can know this, yes?'

'Yes, our secret, yes,' he replied excitably.

'OK, well, stay calm and you go get home. We won't go on our adventure tomorrow, OK, we will go the next day. Can you come here again to my house very early, not tomorrow but the next day, little man?'

'Yes. Not tomorrow, no. The next day yes, yes!'

'Good. Remember you need to be here very early, before the call to work alarm sounds.'

'Yes that is very early, yes. I will be all sleepy, yes!' The boy's ability to shift from panic to excitement, from fear of leaving to delight in their plan, both encouraged and unsettled Bevan. He seemed to have no comprehension as to the severity of their fleeing the city and perhaps, he thought, that was for the best.

'And if we want to play with this gadget again we won't be able to go to work, will we?' he said to Benedict with a wink, hoping he would take his meaning.

'But we have to work, Bevan, yes, we must do as we are told and I am trying to be good, yes. Mother told me I need to be good and do my work like the General asks.'

'Your mother? But she was just talking about… ' He caught himself mid-sentence. Reminding Benedict of that horrible truth would not help. '… erm, I know, yeah work tomorrow, I agree, we must all be good, you're right, but I think the next day. Not tomorrow, the next day, we are both likely to be too poorly to work. A bit ill, eh?' Another wink, ever more overtly sarcastic.

'But I'm not poorly no, I'm big and strong and ready to work like the General said, yes,' Benedict responded while folding his arms across his chest, a defiant and proud smile spreading across his face. Bevan was staggered – surely he was repressing the conversation between his parents just moments before, or could he genuinely have forgotten that they were plotting to have him killed?

'Well of course, but I must admit I'm starting to feel a bit poorly, a bit of a headache… aren't you?'

'No, I feel OK, yes. I like work now that I'm on your team, Bev! I hope you don't have that headache tomorrow and can come to work, yes.' Bevan realised he would need to change tactic. He had always been good with reading people; it seemed Benedict was not open to suggestion or coercion and he simply did not understand sarcasm.

'OK, but if we are both working two days from now, well then how will we be able to play with this?' He held the Window up in front of him and waited while the boy's mind attempted to work out the conundrum.

'Erm, well, we can play at work... yes, play at work with it,' he offered, pleased with himself for having been able to offer a genuine and feasible answer.

'Nope, I'm afraid we can't, Ben – we would get in big trouble, eh? This is our secret. We can't play at work, we can only work when at work. You would not be being good, you would be being bad.' He paused, waiting for this to sink in. 'The only way we can be good is if no–one else knows that we are playing with the gadget. So I'll pretend to be poorly. Can you pretend too?' This was it. Bevan knew this would go one of two ways – Benedict would join his charade, throwing himself into the new game with fervour, or he would back away, see the deception, and worst of all maybe go running to mummy. The boy stood before him, a blank expression on his face showing no indication that he had even heard what Bevan had said, let alone the way in which he might sway. Then a smile began to spread widely across his face.

'Yes! Like two games! Pretending *and* playing with the gadget, yes!' Bevan's shoulders relaxed and his jaw loosened as he realised how tense he had been waiting for a reply.

'Yes just like that, it'll be the most fun!' Bevan hyped it up, building the excitement. 'Let's meet at my house. You remember I told you all about it at training, how I'd have you come by to fix some other gadgets I have? You remember where I live, right?' Benedict nodded. 'You'll have to pretend very well, pretend you are very sick, that you cannot go. And then when you you are left alone you can sneak out. And then we can get going on our adventure. You want to meet Mr Mourdorant and Chung don't you? Sound like a plan?'

'Yes, a good plan, yes.'

'OK, great, then you run on now, the rest of the way home on your own and I'll go to my house and then I'll see you... ?' Bevan left the sentence hanging, ready for Ben to fill the gaps with the right information.

He duly obliged. 'Not tomorrow, no. Not tomorrow but the next day, yes. Yes at Bev's house, yes.'

'Good lad,' Bevan said. 'Right let's get outta here.' He held up his hand for a parting high five. The boy left him hanging, spun on his heels and dashed off with a clomping, slappy–footed run. Bevan stood just a moment until Ben turned the corner and out of sight before turning for home himself. He stuffed his cold hands into his pockets and crossed his fingers.

Part Four

Vote Mourdorant!

A Vote for Efran Mourdorant is the sensible man's vote.

The learned man's vote.

The vote that will help to bring about positive change.

If you are yearning for knowledge of the time that once was, want to know what lies beyond the domes, to explore the desert and discover all the mysteries it holds, then vote for Efran Mourdorant as your representative on the Leadership Committee!

Mourdorant's policies will set you free and open up the vastness of the world once again. Countless more jobs will be created through expedition.

Repopulation will bring new wealth and fame to us all – will you be the one of the brave souls to grasp this opportunity with Efran?

Efran Mourdorant will bring the horizon!

Vote Mourdorant!

Chapter 16

Rage. Fury. Anger. Hate. And above all an all-consuming desire for revenge. That was all that was left of Rosalyn Torres. Her every thought was of how she could exact her revenge upon Benitez for forcing her into making that terrible choice. Hating him even more so for the brutal method with which he had intended to murder her beautiful, sweet little girl. She brooded on the many horrible ways in which she *would* murder him. She knew when the time came – and it would come – that she would revel in it. She did not care that this in turn made her just another kind of a monster. She had decided that now she was indeed a monster, a dangerous monster driven by a terrible hunger for revenge. A monster that Benitez should be scared of, one he should always be worried was coming to get him. A monster he should have nightmares about. Nightmares from which he would wake with a start, sweating and checking the room for the monster. Of course she knew his arrogance would not permit him to do any of these things. Benitez would be feeling very pleased with himself, she was sure. He probably would have treated himself to a whore and a glass of wine. His surprise and disbelief when she killed him would make it all the more sweet. These thoughts kept Rosalyn going.

There was one small mercy though; the instant she pulled the trigger and saved Violet from any pain, the world had all gone black. The Shrouded she had punched in the face had recovered and cracked her across the back of the head with the butt of the machine gun discarded by his stabbed and dying colleague. So while Rosie had seen Violet so terribly frightened and helpless (in her mind's eye she could no longer recall her sweet face any other way) she had not seen the infinitely more terrible sight of what a .50 calibre bullet reduced a five–year–old child's head to.

She had regained consciousness in the middle of a beating. Benitez had come scuttling back down the hill from the farmhouse on the shout of 'all clear' from his guard and proceeded to kick her unconscious body until three of her ribs had snapped and he was covered in perspiration and on the verge of an asthma attack. Wheezing and hunched over, he waved a chubby hand and managed to sputter out orders for Rosalyn to be taken to the Farms.

She was in a terrible physical state. Her ribs were incredibly sore; deep purple and orange bruising ran across her torso. The impact from the gun butt to the back of her head had, she suspected, delivered a hairline fracture to her skull – she was getting headaches of excruciating stabbing pain, blurring her vision and cutting through her brain. She had to crouch down, head in her hands, and close her eyes to mask the blurry vision it caused. Despite her own wounds, what worried her most about being in the Farm was the malnutrition so evident all around her. All her around her there were those who had lost so much weight. Their bones clearly visible, with pallid skin pulled tight across them. Almost all cattle appeared to have swollen bloody gums their teeth had given up on clinging to. She feared they were a picture of her physical future.

She had been housed in a 'Slaughter pen' and not a 'Work pen'. She had been identified as one of those cattle that were considered too difficult to manage or beyond physical capacity to be of use. Benitez could have killed her on the spot of course but she knew the man and this would be fun for him – his final punishment, his way of extending her suffering. It also dawned on her, with dreadful revulsion, that he had also more than likely seen to it that, when her time came, she would be destined for his dinner plate.

Had she been in better shape when she arrived she would have had a relatively easy time fighting her fellow inmates for larger portions of feed from the Farmers. Hierarchy in the Farm was simple. She had only been able to observe for a matter of hours but it was obvious that each herd had a lead animal, self-appointed through physical assertion over their peers – the guards never intervened. All were mean yet all were destined for the same fate as all the other Farm animals – the dining tables of J1. In fact Rosalyn had thought it to be a cursed position, since while it was clear the weakest went first it was also clear that should a better cut of meat be required then it was the strongest that went next. It was best to be somewhere in the middle; there was safety in mediocrity.

Her bed was the middle bunk of a triple tier. Above her slept an elderly woman and below a young man. She hadn't asked their names, did not want to know them, but knowledge was power and these two seemed to know a lot about the Farms.

The sleeping hours had arrived and they whispered in the gloom. The woman had been a worker in a different herd, skilled in the art of sewing. Fiddly relentless work had taken its toll though and her now-arthritic hands could barely do up a button on her blouse let alone thread a needle. She was kindly enough, a miracle given the time she had been here. It seemed a sad shame that having lived and survived the harsh existence of a Resident of Axiom she should now see out the last of her days rotting in the Farm, waiting to die. Her crime Rosie felt she could relate to: the old woman had had a child, a daughter, who had died in an accident, and in her grief she had looked to replace the child with another. Not a madness that would compel her to break the law to birth another child but she had instead snatched another who had resembled her own lost little girl. A momentary lapse of sanity, but it was witnessed by the guards and the next day she was Farmed. She had given Rosie the inside information on the Farm and how it worked. It was all very simple, she had said:

Always back the favourite.

Always do as you are told by the guards, never look to curry favour, it will get you nowhere.

Eat fast and never carry anything that others might want, including food.

Sleep whenever you can because you should never reach the deepest depths of sleep, be on your guard always.

Accept your fate and relinquish hope.

Rosie had studiously followed all the old woman's rules... except the last.

Old Lady Top–Bunk had also told her an intriguing story of a time long ago when guards, forced to enter one of the paddocks, had nearly been overrun by the occupying herd. They had been tantalisingly close to breaking free. Rosalyn knew then that there was a chink in the armour. She had a sense of the 'how' of her escape and her other companion on the three tier bunk could well be the hammer with which the chink could be smashed and the thin possibility of escape might become a gaping hole.

The old woman also filled her in on their male bunkmate. He was, she told Rosalyn, a tragic case. He was one of those poor individuals who had been born for nothing else, with no other purpose. He was the product of the Farm. Farm born, bred and raised. A rare thing, but as all animals fight, eat, sleep and shit so from time to time, even in this most brutal of environments they fuck. Fuck. Love–making, no – that was a private act conducted in a place and time where love existed and this was a loveless place. Procreate, no – that was an animal act driven by instinct, yes, but procreating was an act conducted with the foresight for the continuation of one's existence through one's spawn. The Farm was not a place to exist, it was merely a waiting room to die. So when these Farm animals who could not resist the urge to rut in the dark eventually fucked, tragedies like that of the young man came to be.

He had been raised by his mother until he was five years old, then she had been slaughtered and he had been put to work. He'd toiled in the work pens for many years and inherited his parents' animal instincts. The young man fought like a wasp in a jar, ate like a starving dog, worked like an ox and slept like a cat, always alert. These had served him well so far, but his parents' penchant for fucking had also been passed on and now that he was at an age where those hormones were raging he had attempted to act upon it. He had successfully satisfied his urge with a willing partner but he had also successfully roused the shed guards who had immediately re-assigned him for slaughter. As he had whispered his tale in the dark Rosalyn had recalled Benitez's words, 'Treacherous genes breed treacherous offspring.' That scripture held sway here too.

For now, though, the young man was a clear threat to their current herd leader's authority and subsequently the head animal had set about testing her young bunkmate at every opportunity. They (for the leader always had a couple of henchmen) had come for him once already in the short time that Rosalyn had been a member of their herd.

As he was dozing off, two of the leader's cronies clamped down his hands and legs while he himself had placed a grubby hand firmly over the young man's mouth and leant forward to spout and spit warnings and threats directly into his face. Rosalyn had lain and listened. This was not her fight. Not yet. The youth had taken a tremendous beating, but so had the leader and his cronies. They had not expected anything back, but they had left with almost as many bruises as the young buck. In fact their plan had backfired: many of the herd could now see the youngster had real mettle, having held his own against three men at the top end of the pecking order. His rise to leader, Rosie suspected, would come soon and she was also sure that, unfortunately, power would corrupt. He would be as mean a herd leader as the Farms had ever seen, and Rosalyn was determined to be one of *his* allies until such time as the guards took him away to be slaughtered. So when they came a second time she was ready to back the challenger to the throne.

Weak as she was, her ribs a rack of pain, she rolled from her bunk, landing on one of the assailants who held the young man down. As he pitched forward under her weight, his forehead smacked off the edge of the bunk. His body, though, continued downwards with Rosalyn on his back, gravity pulling them all down to earth, and with his head stuck his neck gave up with a snap. She had not meant to kill him but accepted the collateral damage. The death would not go unpunished by their captors – they would likely go without rations tomorrow, but she doubted they would go much further than that. After all, while unscheduled, a fresh slab of meat for the mincers was always welcomed.

She rolled off the dead man and sprung up. The adrenaline was coursing through her and it numbed the pain in her ribs and gave back strength to her legs. With his hand now free, the young challenger had broken loose from the other who was trying to restrain him, and begun pummelling the man in the face with a clenched fist. In her peripheral vision she saw the leader running across the shed to join the fray. Raised up above his head was a makeshift knife, a human jawbone sharpened into a point. She tore a loose plank of wood from the bunk and just in time positioned it between the knife and the intended target of the young man's neck. The bone shank dug into the wood and splintered. The leader hissed in frustration, foiled.

Her bunkmate glanced appreciatively in her direction, knowing she had saved him. Then the ceiling hatches opened and furious guards began yelling down into the shed for them to return to their beds, telling all those within that if they heard a mouse fart from the shed for the rest of the night every other one of them would be shot dead. The leader and his bloodied accomplice slunk off back to their beds and Rosie climbed up into hers. The young man watched her clamber back up above him, grateful for her help. The dead man lay there till the waking hours.

Benedict De Sanctis returned home and his mother was there waiting for him. She was sitting on the edge of his bed one leg crossed over the other, gently swinging before her (Benedict did not know why she sat like that, and always thought it uncomfortable when he tried it – when no–one was looking of course).

She was leaning back on her arms. Her hair was a little tousled and the top button of her dress was hanging loose and open, exposing the beginnings of a cleavage (from the wrestle with the General, yes) and she was smiling (but not her happy smile). It was the smile she always wore before he got into trouble – he saw this particular smile a lot.

'Good evening,' Eleanor De Sanctis purred. 'Where have you been? Not causing mischief, I should hope.'

Benedict felt his face go warm, and worried that he must have turned red. His hands went clammy with sweat. He did not, would not, say a word. (That always seemed to work; she would just get madder and hit him and that wouldn't matter... but then what if now when she hit him she killed him, like she had said to the General?)

The journey back with Bev had been fun. He thought that perhaps it was because he should not be out, it was forbidden. It had been easy to sneak past his ageing live-in warden, Mrs P, as she slept, snoring incredibly loudly in her rickety old chair outside his bedroom door. (She was a strange one, Mrs P. She was always sleepy and she confused her words. He wondered if it was the horrible poli she always drank from her secret flask. Now he had two secrets! Mrs P's flask and Bevan's exciting gadget!)

He just wanted to find out what all that noise was. Parties happened a lot but this one sounded extra special. It had been naughty going out though. He was not allowed out and especially not on his own. He always had one of the General's scary men with him – the Shrouded. He didn't like to fight, but he knew he was strong, he knew he was good at it. There was something in his head that made him fight without knowing that was what he was doing. It was like his body was a switch that, if it was touched by anyone else, turned the violence on. The Shrouded though, they were scary and the fear broke the switch. His mother and the General they broke the switch too.

He wished he had not gone out. It was very sad to hear his mother and the General talk like that... but he had also now seen that gadget, that was very good indeed. He had led the way back home and Bevan had followed him. (Like 'follow the leader', good fun! The smaller children who lived at the school liked to play that, he was a big boy, though, so he always could win that one.) They had gone under fence lines, clambered over walls, squeezed through alleyways, hid in doorways and raced across open spaces and all the while the snow had come down. (It was like some of the training they had been doing with Luis and Bevan's other friends. Ooh snow, maybe he could make a snowman with Mrs P tomorrow?)

Once Ben had spotted two guards stood at the intersection of a street smoking and talking and Bevan had not seen them; he warned Bev. They had stayed well hidden until the two J3s stubbed out their cigarettes and went back into the gambling hall. (He was good at sneaking. Like a little sneaky mouse. He was sure he would do well on the outside fixing the water pipes and stuff. Fixing things was fun. Fixing things made the world quiet, made it make sense. He could definitely do his job. That would make Mother happy and then maybe the General wouldn't hurt him or Bev.)

Remembering his journey home though had distracted him from his mother's question. 'Erm... yes, no, yes, We... I... have... ' he sputtered now, certain he had to say something.

'Erm? Please Benedict, have some conviction in your lies! We? Who is we?'

'I'm very poorly, yes' he blurted with a hint of stubbornness, throwing up his arms and slamming his clenched fists into his thighs. A familiar wave of anger came over him. (She always made him angry. She always tried to trick him with her questions. Why couldn't she be nice like Bevan? He always explained things. Questions were hard. When was the last time her smile was the happy one?)

'What on earth are you blathering about? I did not ask about your well-being, I asked where you had been!'

'Yes, playing with my friend... '

'Your friend?' she tittered, amused by this new fantasy of his. 'Oh dear, but you have no friends. You are too strange a thing for people to understand, I fear.' The last part she said almost absentmindedly. 'So where have you been?'

'I do have a friend I do, yes!'

She rose from the bed and walked towards him, a flowing, floating gait. Her back straight, her strides were regular and her approach calm. Each heeled footstep came down with a harsh clack on the wood clad flooring. Her hands were now behind her back and as she came within touching distance her arms swung out from around her back. (The slap, he thought, or perhaps she would hold his neck until he couldn't breathe anymore... not the ruffling of the hair, that didn't happen very often. No, yes, it would be a slap. And she would kill him.)

Eleanor hugged her son, pulling him in close. His face was buried in her bosom, hers in his tangled mop of hair. (No. He didn't like this, no. No–one should touch, he didn't like touching... but when she did, he had learnt he should accept. His hands clamped to his sides suppressing the urge to push her away. She was even tricking his violence switch.)

She leaned down and spoke into his ear.

'Yes, you do don't you? The General has told me about your friend.

I am glad Benedict, it is wonderful news.' Eleanor held her son's face, a warm hand on each cheek and looked him cooly in the eye. 'I'm very pleased that you will have someone to look after you when you go on your adventure. It's good to know that you will be together, you and this J17 man. I'm sure he will look after you. Are you looking forward to going?'

Benedict broke off the eye contact and looked down at his shoes. The toes were caked in snow which was beginning to melt and pool around his feet. 'I'm very poorly, yes,' he said.

It seemed to Rosalyn that the daily routine in a slaughter pen would be just as simple to grasp as the pecking order was to work out.

The ceiling hatches on the sheds opened and guards began shouting through, pointing their guns at them. She had barely slept; she could not get comfortable on account of her cracked ribs and the complete absence of any form of bedding. The guards continued to shout; they were making it very clear that they had thirty seconds to get out into the paddocks for the day. She hauled herself from her bunk and joined the rest of the rabble as they shuffled outside. Calling them paddocks was perhaps another form of torture: no green fields to roam here, just packed hard earth. Not even a stone, just the odd bone left from a slaughtering and piles of frozen human shit. Hanging over everything like a miserable fog was the half-light of their world and the orange glow of oil lamps. Rosie kept her head up and took in her surroundings. They were fenced in and on each corner there stood a guard tower. Their section was on the edge of the Farm. Looking through the fencing to the inner sections of J13, Rosie could see many, many other paddocks and their respective Resident herds. Some were workers, toiling each day over construction or repair of various items.

These pens, those within which Rosie and her fellow herd members dwelt were, she knew, for herds assigned for slaughter: they served no further purpose than a centrepiece for a meal. They were all dead men walking. An acceptance of this fact was evident by a complete lack of humanity amongst them. In the paddock the pattern of a typical day in the Farm begun to become clear to Rosalyn. The herd huddled for warmth, they fought for space, food and supremacy and feed twice a day. A spoken word was rarely uttered. It was all grunts, hisses and spitting. They ate like animals too, shovelling food into their mouths, barely chewing and squabbling over the scraps. Rosalyn Torres, though, had never allowed herself to be seen as a piece of meat, and she was not going to let environment dictate her fate. She had to find a way out, but perhaps the most difficult thing was that she did not think it would be possible to achieve alone.

The last of the waking hours were upon them and the herd sat in the paddock huddled in a corner. A biting wind was swirling through the compound and they were crouched in the dirt together for warmth. They occasionally rotated their positions from centre to edge, like a group of penguins in a snow storm. A dull orange light pooled around them from the lamp above. Rosie blew warm breath into her clasped hands and the hot air escaped between her fingers, misting in the cold. An eerie hush had descended on the group. They had not moved for approaching half an hour and not a sound had been uttered. The herd of animals was on edge, sensing the tension. The calm before the storm.

The first sign of the storm was the lightning, a dazzling fork of white light on the horizon. A blade drawn in the gloom; the dim light of the lamp would not have shown it, but the harsh illumination from the lightning bolt glinted off its sharp edge. Four cattle over on her right. It was the leader, and he had slid the knife from his boot while crouched down. No time to wonder where on earth he had found proper steel in the Farm – a storm was brewing. A light snow had been slowly falling but just as adrenaline–fuelled perspiration leapt free upon Rosalyn's brow the snow changed into driving sleet. Some of the herd looked to the heavens and Rosalyn readied herself for a fight.

Then came the clap of thunder. The clap that came though was not made by the clouds above them. Rosalyn knew that it was the sound of a .50 calibre rifle being fired – not the Cold Bringer but another like it. The shimmer of the knife had also caught the attention and turned the head of the young man, her bunkmate, her hammer, her escape plan. The bullet had removed his face. The rest of the herd ran in all directions, hoping it was a single slaughter. Rosalyn remained crouched, staring in disbelief at the cruel blow fate had just dealt her.

Up on the walkway she saw a guard fling the weapon to another guard and bark out an order, the details of which were swept away from her ears by the wind. The wind also swept away her last hopes of avenging her daughter as she realised they were all just fish in a barrel.

Chapter 17

The screen of the device went black, yet Bevan's finger remained holding down the lock button. The Window powered down with a happy little chime that was completely at odds with the mood in the room. He stared ahead, a blank expression on his face. Not moving a muscle he sat completely still on the floor, as lifeless as the gadget held loosely in his grasp. Everything he had read from Chung had blown his entire world apart, each email exchange a greater explosion of information than the last. In fact, what it actually did was to make his world seem very small, very insignificant and – he felt with a sudden hint of excitement and relief – a world that was very escapable. Everything he knew, it turned out, was not a lot at all. What he knew was isolated, contrived and wholly insignificant. His mind spun with all the incredible notions, ideas, histories and facts that Chung had gone on to describe. Of all the places, technologies and people that had shaped the world. Bevan wanted to know more and he certainly wanted to see such places, meet such people and live such a life. The day had started off better than he had expected it to and he found himself now, despite all that he had just learned, wondering whether things had just got even better or worse. Every time he got something back from Chung, more questions were raised. But a plan had been hatched. They would leave, Bevan and Benedict together, but now they had a purpose beyond the initial running away. They had a destination and a goal to reach. They would find Mourdorant. They would help him build his vision of a new world.

He had, he estimated, slept a total of about ninety minutes the whole night. He hadn't long made it home and the waking hours were rapidly approaching. After leaving Benedict the night before, he had made his own way home. Haring back across the city he skipped Jurisdiction borders, scaled fences, ducked through openings in barriers, crawled under loose fence panels and slipped and skidded in the mud and snow. He had skirted the edge of the city on his way back into J17 and for a moment was in touching distance of the wall. Off to his right was the colossal door to the city, a great gate of steel that in all his lifetime and that of anyone he knew had never been fully opened. Below it, standing sentry, was a single J3. A brief moment of despair had tugged at him and he had contemplated climbing a ladder up to the walkway above and either jumping from the top or taking his chances with the bullets that would certainly come should he be spotted. What was the point in continuing, he wondered? It all felt so futile. How could they possibly make this crazy plan work? Stricken would kill him and Benedict – there could surely be no escape from that. An ancient device with a message on it – messages exchanged with someone who spoke of untold histories and possiblities – was not going to be able to stop a madman with a gun.

Curiosity, though, was a powerful motivator for Bevan and he had to know more. Shaking his head – and the thought of suicide from it – he had released his hand from the cold steel lower rung of the ladder. Better to die trying, he thought and jogged the rest of the way to his front door, quietly let himself in and slumped down on his bed. He had barely slept.

In less than sixty minutes' time, less than a single hour, he had found himself rocked to the core by two pieces of incredible, terrifying and intriguing information:

1. Eleanor De Sanctis wanted him and her own son dead, and she wanted General Stricken to make sure it was done when they left for the expedition in the coming days.

2. Someone, somewhere had contacted him through the device. Initially with conflicting messages. One offered vague help and promises of a new way of life: the other delivered a warning. There was though, it seemed, a glimmer of hope. A proposal to be at the start of something new. To be a crucial part of starting a new life. Or of course it might be just as likely to kill him as the General under Madame De Sanctis's orders.

He had to put the plan into motion. The alarm would sound to summon him to shift in just over an hour's time but Bevan was already halfway there. As he made his way across J17, doubt that this was the right thing to do gnawed at him like a rat sharpening its teeth on a lump of wood; he could almost hear it. He made his way to work – he had to speak to Teddy. The training and preparation for the expedition had been delayed for a couple of days, as they were experiencing problems with the fences down at the Farms again so the electricians had been called in to make repairs.

The rat was gnawing at the very first part of his plan. They *had* to leave, of that he was certain. He was also sure of how they *could* escape the city. Teddy though, he realised, would take some real convincing to agree to leave with them. His best friend had never particularly expressed any resentment towards Axiom, its ways, its traditions, its laws, its brutality. After all, it was this way, it always had been. In fact, Grizzly often revelled in his existence. He had a loving wife, a son to be proud of and a daughter who was on her way to the top. Bevan knew that were he in the same position, perhaps it would not all be so bad. After all, when he and Evelyn were together it had not mattered where they were or what they were doing, regardless of all else it was bliss and he was happy; all of Axiom was sugar–coated, rose–tinted and dressed up. Teddy had his wife and children and he was content.

Perhaps he could just leave and never tell Teddy? Sure, he would be sad for a time at the loss of his friend, but his family and their love would get him through. Yes, he supposed that might work. After Bevan left, he knew that life in Axiom would go on, this unknown threat that Chung spoke of need not ever find them and so the days would pass as they always had... *if* Bevan left with the Window, which he fully intended to do.

The problem was that Teddy was the key to getting out. Teddy would help, of that he was also certain, but if ignorance was bliss then a complete lack of knowledge when the Shrouded started investigating the disappearance of Benedict De Sanctis was likely to keep his best friend alive. But what other way was there?

Deep in thought with his deliberating and planning and re-planning, Bevan's feet had continued on autopilot to the Farm.

'Bev? What are you doing here?' It was Teddy leaving his shift. 'I thought you were stuck with more archery practice?'

'I... er, yeah, I am... Its just that I... er... I'm very poorly.' Teddy, though, was not a simple minded child like Ben. He was not fooled.

'What's going on?' Teddy asked with a hint of genuine curiosity and bit more more than a hint of concern. Bevan rubbed his temples, willing some brainwave to come to him.

'Listen mate, I need to tell you something… I can trust you right?'

Teddy looked at his friend quizzically, confused by his obvious anxiousness, 'Yeah of course, you don't even have to ask that!'

'What if there was something better? What if there was a place where you didn't have to work like a dog for fear of being beaten, Farmed and eaten? What if we could leave here and live a life without fear? What if Axiom isn't the whole world and beyond her walls is life and salvation and not all the awful death and terror we are taught to believe?'

Teddy's face shifted from confusion and concern to exasperation, 'Oh blow me, not this ol' chestnut again! You're really still rambling on about "the oppressive world in which we live"? The Bevan Hughes remedy to curing the plague of this world? Look man, I've just seen off a monster shift, my back aches, my hands are blistered to shit and I'm going home to my wife. There aint no way I'm standing out here in the bitter cold freezing my nuts off listening to your far-flung ideas of utopia!' Teddy finished with a dismissive wave of his hand, stuffed it back into his pocket and turned to trudge home through the snow and slush.

'Someone outside of Axiom has contacted me!' Bevan blurted out, before immediately shooting a glance all around him to ensure no–one was within earshot. They were alone. Teddy Smithers stopped in his tracks and Bevan left the statement hanging in the air, like a foul gas that Teddy had inhaled, despite his best efforts to avoid it. Bevan was pretty sure that his suddenly desperate tone had made certain that Teddy would realise he wasn't pulling his chain. It wasn't a joke or a lie; and Teddy would surely want to know more. Teddy turned back around slowly and asked, 'What? How?'

'It'll be easier for you to see it,' Bevan replied. 'Let's go to the Haven.'

The Drifter's Haven was a dive bar just a five–minute walk across from the Farms. They'd visited the place for a post–work drink with the rest of their electrical crew a few times over the last few weeks while working on the fences. It was the largest ramshackle construction of wood, corrugated iron and cinder blocks on the tight street that it dominated. The small trading shops that flanked it were single-storey, not much more than a J17 home with a four-foot-square shopfront built out into the pavement to sell wares. The Haven, though, was a five-storey-high square box (six if you counted the basement level where Farm-reared offcuts were prepared in the kitchen for stews for the punters above, who were always working up a mad hunger from drinking too much poli).

It was five storeys high from the outside, but inside there were no definable floors. Rather it was a mishmash of levels constructed on top of, through and intertwined amongst themselves. They were connected by a series of ladders, walkways and staircases. Each level space held anywhere from a large table to seat twenty men to those which could just about hold a couple (though such a couple would certainly not be enjoying any form of romantic pursuit in the Haven).

As they stepped in from the cold they were hit in the face with the combined heat of over a hundred bodies and the massive wood-burning stove sitting in the middle of the ground floor, which was fully loaded and throwing out a fierce heat. The heat was certainly not helping with the smell either – a pungent cocktail of sweat, spilt, stale poli, congealing stew left in the bottom of bowls that were never cleared until closing time, and blood. By the looks of things they had just missed the nightly occurrence that was a fight of some sort, which would always end with red-stained floorboards and often a higher meat content in the stew for tomorrow's guests.

Off to the left and running the full length of the wall was the bar, which Bevan and Teddy made their way over to, removing their gloves, scarves and hats as they did so. A few J17 boys were sitting at a table as they passed and Bevan nodded a greeting while Teddy clapped the nearest on the shoulder with a friendly hello.

'Yo, Bev, thanks for those patties son, my Mrs always goes buck wild once she's been wined and dined on poli and patties,' Louie Summerville said with a wink and a raised glass from the other side of table. 'Boys, you gotta join us, Thompson's girl just had a little 'un and we are wetting the baby's head! Hey, hey, Liv, pull these fellas over a couple of chairs, let's all head home staggering!'

Bevan had continued his journey to the bar with barely a smile of recognition in Summerville's direction and was now ordering two mugs of poli.

'No can do, Louie,' Teddy said, slapping down on his shoulders with both hands this time, 'We've got some grown–up business to attend to, but you enjoy your night boys. Oh, and hey – congratulations Thompson.'

'Yeah, sure man, no worries, but hey don't you two get too "grown up" on those love seats and come crashing down on all o'us,' Summerville snorted, pointing over at Bevan who was climbing a set of stairs up a level to one of the tables for two.

'Ha. Ha. Careful, Louie, I only fuck my best good friend – my wife, that way, sure, but I fuck those who take the piss outta me very differently,' Teddy replied, his huge hands squeezing and pinching down on Summerville's collarbone as Summerville squirmed uncomfortably under his painful grip. 'You take care now,' he said, letting go and walking over to join Bevan.

Bevan had re-positioned the two chairs so that they sat side by side, which meant that no–one could see what it was that he placed on the table in front of them as soon as Teddy was seated – the Window.

He reached forward and touched the single button at its base and it lit up immediately to reveal the image of the happy couple and the peculiar icons spread across their beaming faces. Teddy spat out his poli and lurched back in his chair, the legs of which made a shrill scraping sound against the wooden floor and drew some surprised but wholly uninterested, momentary glances.

'What is it?'

'I don't know, I've called it "the Window". It's kinda impressive, eh? And that ain't the half of it. It's not just a pretty picture show, this thing can be used to *talk* to others…'

'"Others"? Like those you were talking about outside?' Teddy asked, one hand tentatively reaching out to touch its shiny surface.

'Exactly!' said Bevan, with a grin akin to that of a proud parent as he politely stopped Teddy's inquisitive touch.

'How?'

'I dont know the "how"s. I just know it can, look, read… ' Bevan tapped the little envelope icon and up popped the inbox of email exchanges with Chung. 'Touch the front lightly to move the message up as you read. Do not react – I know how hard that will be, but no–one else can know. When you are done I'll tell you what I intend to do and I'll tell you –'

'What you want me to do, eh?' Teddy finished with the blunt, yet not angry realisation that Bevan was not sharing for sharing's sake. Bevan looked at his friend, slightly hurt but certainly undeterred in pushing through on his plan. 'It's OK. You know I'll always do all I can, but this is some major shit right here. Drink up and act as if we are having some completely uninteresting conversation, alright?'

In reality just four minutes passed while Teddy absorbed the cor-respondence in front of him, but Bevan felt like he had been sitting there for four hours while his friend carefully read and took in each written word. When he had finished, Teddy wordlessly slid the Win-dow back across the table to Bevan, raised his glass and downed the poli to steady his nerves, but mainly to hide his shocked expression

'You get it right, just so we are clear? You understand what this guy, this Efran Mourdorant is proposing, yeah?' Bevan did not pause for an answer, he was getting all excited again about Mourdorant's bold plan, 'He is going to create mini–versions of these solar–powered Biomes. When I say "mini" I think Chung is talking about them being big enough to still house a decent–sized community, you know. The exciting bit though really is the new way of life they want to start beneath them and within them! No more De Sanctis, no more J1, J3 or Stricken and the Shrouded – we would be part of *something*! Something that we contribute to and it and everyone else in turn pro-vides for us. They want me, want us, to be a part of that. He's already got some of these Biome things mobile, and then we can go any-where we please. He just needs the right people on board when they make a run for it to ensure it can be sustainable. They need people with a good mind for electonics and electricity – That's me, Teddy, that's us! We'd be protected by the dome, the dome will bring us power, endless power and we can explore and unlock and make use of what's left of the old world.' Bevan spun the Window around so that he could unlock it. He opened the 'Mail' app with a soft touch and flicked through various emails until he found the one he was searching for. 'Look, read this one.' Teddy took the device but didn't so much as glance down at the screen. Bevan barely noticed. To speak freely about all he had learnt was cathartic, a weight shared and shed. He virtually snatched the Window back and opened another email, his eyes excitedly scanning over the text as he spoke. 'In this one he talks about what he knows is out there in the Land Reclaimed. There were megacities, like cities that would envelop Axiom ten times over, and its all just been left to ruin. But there will be so much stuff that's useable, that can be collected and put to good use. He knows all about how to grow different crops, how to domesticate and rear beasts for food. He talks about this thing he calls "the Internet" – it's like some mind-blowingly big book of knowledge, *everything* is on there. Like words and images and facts and opinions and knowledge; endless knowledge all held on and beamed around us on this thing he calls the Inifinity SatNet. There would be no problem we couldn't learn to overcome. We would be... ' he tailed off as he finally looked up and into the face of his old friend.

Teddy sat before him, a wan smile on his face. One of sadness, of hope he felt was misplaced but so wished would be seen to be true for a lifelong friend. It was a smile that knew they would be saying goodbye soon. 'I know what you are thinking... but... I can't go with you, Bevan.'

Bevan locked the screen of the Window and placed it face down upon the table. His excited demeanour immediately dissipated and he reached across and placed a hand upon Teddy's shoulder. 'It was a choice I would always leave to you, I won't force you to do anything, won't even try to talk you around.'

'So why tell me, why show me that? Are my family in danger if I stay?'

'No Ted, not if I leave, if I leave and take the Window with me they'll not be able to pinpoint where Axiom is. Chung has said he will give me another week until he files his report, after which they will check the location of the receiving device and then they will... act. It's not the only reason to leave, I'm a selfish martyr too, if I can get out of here... with this thing helping guide me, well, perhaps I can find her, perhaps I'll find Evelyn. You should see it, it has this map inside it, a map of the whole world!'

Teddy was not sharing in his friend's excitement. 'I don't want you to have to do this alone, but I can't go with you. Perhaps if the kids weren't here I could convince Monika, but how would I even get Lil Ted outta the Jurisdiction of the Corruptible? And Grace – well, let's just say Grace sees herself more as J3 guard than she does J17 sparky, and to be honest I worry that each day she also sees herself more as just another Resident, a cog in the machine than she does a Smithers.' Teddy looked dejected and sad and for a moment Bevan knew the troubles his old friend had been having with his eldest. There was a good chance that in this moment Teddy had completely forgotten about the Window, the emails, Bevan's escape plan, and Mourdorant's brave vision of a new future, and likely just felt a pang of guilt that he had somehow failed in fully integrating his adopted daughter into their family. He let out a long sigh, shook his head to clear it and asked, 'How do you think I can help?'

Bevan raised his glass and took a long sip. Staring ahead he said, 'I won't be alone out there, don't worry mate – but the less you know about that the better, believe me!' He took another long sip of his drink, 'But in answer to your question – how can you help? Well, I'll need some things to make a distraction... and... I'm sorry, but I need to talk to Grace.'

Chapter 18

Grizzly and Bevan left the Drifter's Haven to wolf whistles and jeers from their table of colleagues, but Bevan barely heard it. He was more focused on setting into motion actions that once begun could not be undone – and which would only be stopped with one (or worse he feared, *both*) of them dead. It was a plan with just a slim chance of success. It was late and most of Axiom were in their homes, already in bed or preparing for a good night's rest. A hush had descended over the city and the two J17 sparkies spoke in lowered voices.

'You don't need to do this, Teddy,' Bevan said as they emerged back out into the eternal grey and cold. 'I only need your help with the last bit. Only with Grace.'

'I know that, but what kind of friend would I be if I left you to potentially face the firing squad alone?' Teddy replied with a grin. Eternally cheery, that was Teddy Smithers. 'Plus how do you intend to get hold of what you need without my privileged access rights, hmm?'

'Just gimme the code to the storage unit and I'll go alone.'

'Nope, it'll be far less conspicuous if we just saunter up and I, a recognised man with access, just pop in to pick up some supplies.'

Bevan couldn't argue with the suggestion – it made the most sense and provided the best chance for success – but whether he liked it or not, or indeed whether Teddy knew it or not, his best friend was becoming more and more involved in this plan and he feared for him when the investigations began. *If* they were successful. 'OK, well, let's get going, we only have the rest of today and tomorrow before training for the expedition to the ice recommences.'

They skirted around the side of Drifter's, passed through a short corridor between it and the premium–grade sausage shop neighbouring it and hugged one of the Farm's perimeter fences in a straight line on a direct route to their training complex. Bevan absent–mindedly gazed out across the paddocks, still all lit in a faint orange glow. From each deathly quiet shed there was a steady stream of steam rising from the cracks in the ceiling, from the body heat and breath of those sleeping inside. From above, on each watchtower and along the walkways, there was the intermittent puff of breath from patrolling guards, too. They'd both be back here tomorrow Bevan thought. They had work to do on the fences – scheduled *and* unscheduled.

They journeyed the rest of the way in silence and as they approached the manned gate a spotlight clunked on and they were drowned in bright light. They both raised an arm to shield their eyes but it didn't really help. A shout from the guards on duty challenged them: 'State your name, Jurisdiction and business.'

'Teddy Smithers, 17, supplies required.'

The pause that followed made Bevan want to turn and run. Any moment now he was certain the game was up, two single shots would ring out over Axiom and two would–be–troublemakers from J17 would lie dead in the road.

As if sensing his worry Teddy gently gripped Bevan's forearm. 'Hold your shit together, man.' He sounded almost annoyed and Bevan supposed he didn't blame him. He'd accepted this whole plan might get him killed; Teddy was after all just doing him a favour.

'And Bevan Hughes, 17, stand-in carthorse for whatever supplies the big man needs,' he eventually called back. A moment later the light clicked off and the same voice called out for them to proceed.

'Bugger me, Grizzly, what the hell you need gear for at this time of the night? I know you've a wife at home you could be boinking. Damn, it's what I'd be doing… if I had a wife… and no shift… and if I was still young enough to boink anything aside from my left hand and even that usually gets too tired to finish before we give up!' The guard on duty was one Bevan had seen talking with Teddy before, when they'd met at the end of expedition training sessions. He seemed to be the most pleasant J1 you'd ever happen to meet.

'Precisely why I need this stuff now and do not need to get up early to come and get it. She's a minx in the morning, old timer! Kenneth, this is Bevan, a damn good friend of mine, the best! Bev, this is Kenneth. Don't ya be fooled by the J1 uniform – it isn't, in this rare case, the sure sign for an arsehole! Like I say, old man, we just need to grab a few things ready for our shift tomorrow and we'll be outta your hair… what's left of it!'

Kenneth laughed. 'Watch ya mouth, Teddy Bear. I do believe I'm well within my rights to have you thrown in the Farm for such bad-mouthing of a J1! Though I'm pretty sure that'd make me an arsehole, and I've spent a long time defying the general consensus, and they'd probably just throw my old arse in there too. Hurry up then – I'm gonna visit the little boys' room, by the time I've tucked my old saggy bits back into my boxers I expect you two to be long gone.'

'Hearing you loud and clear. Thanks, Ken – a little too much imagery, but thanks. We'll be in and out, promise.'

Kenneth was already hobbling his way over to the mobile toilet booth as he raised his hands above his head and thrust the index finger of his left hand through the circle of his thumb and index finger of his right, 'In and out tomorrow morning too, young Bear.' He hooted a little laugh as he walked away.

No sooner had the door to the toilet closed than Teddy's smile dropped. 'Let's get what we need and get gone,' he said with focused seriousness. No more than five minutes later they were on their way, the two packages they needed gently chinking against one another in the rucksack on Bevan's back.

When he returned home he very carefully placed the rucksack and the Window inside his secret inner wall cupboard. He stood at his sink and ran a cup of water which he gulped down in just four greedy swallows – the poli had thickened his head and he needed it clear. Clearer than it had ever been. He moved to sit at the end of his bed, which sagged and creaked under his weight which, with all that he now carried metaphorically on his shoulders, felt ten times his actual physical size. Sitting there and staring ahead, not looking at anything in particular, he slowly twisted his wedding ring around his finger.

'Perhaps I'll find you on the way,' he said out loud with a flicker of a sad smile, and for the first time since Evelyn was taken he wasn't so sure that he would see her again. This all felt even bigger than his selfish pursuit of love.

The next morning Bevan reported for shift as expected, as planned. He made his way as he usually would, meeting Teddy midway up his street, and they journeyed to the Farm to clock in as they always would (though only they knew that to do so in silence was a complete change of routine). The electric fences were still tripping out; they were expected and hurried through clocking-in protocol to get to work. They had to inspect cabling across a cross–section of fencing, and the circuit breakers of the substation at another nearest the main gate. It was not uncommon for the sparkies to switch between teams throughout the day and Bevan did just that, spending the morning out on the cross-section and the afternoon at the substation. It was his team and he signed both jobs off. He was the last to leave each area having completed a thorough test inspection himself, alone. Before he knew it, shift was over and it was time to head home. Thompson, Liv, Summerville and the others ribbed them both all day long and once shift finished they all headed to the Drifter's once again. They were openly and vocally disappointed that Bevan and Teddy weren't going to join them so that they might continue their banter.

As Teddy and Bevan walked home together the usual grey twilight they had always known felt more oppressive than ever. It wasn't until they reached the point at which they would go their separate ways that one of them spoke.

'Job done, eh?' Teddy said sounding a little detached.

'Job done,' Bevan agreed. He turned to face his lifelong friend, 'There may not be time tomorrow, I'm pretty sure it'll all happen quickly and I want you to know that... that... ' Bevan stuttered, a lump forming in his throat, '... that I love you Teddy, you've been a better friend to me than I ever have you.'

'Nonsense!' Teddy said with a wan smile. 'It's the way it's always been and I wouldn't have it any other way. We are the way we are because we are the way we are! You have hare-brained ideas, rope me in and we both get in trouble,' he said with a chuckle.

'Yea, I guess, but this one could be really different – you know, the kinda different where the trouble gets you killed!'

'That's as maybe, but if what those messages say is true, we are all dead anyway if you don't leave. So the way I see it, if you also get to find a better life, save a young boy and maybe, just maybe find Evelyn, then it's a good idea and one that I wholeheartedly back!'

Bevan reached up and clapped a hand upon his friend's broad shoulder. 'If I find this Efran guy, if things work out as I so hope they do,

I'll send word somehow, find a way for you to get out to find us...
somehow. OK?'

'I dunno, you know me, this place ain't so bad... but you know
what? Your idea still sounds good to me. Like I said, you'll have the
idea and I'll be sure to follow! I'll keep an eye on my mailbox.' He
pulled Bevan in close and they embraced in the street. None of the
usual macho backslapping but the full sincere embrace of two friends
who felt they might well have just spoken their last meaningful words
to one another. 'See you at the gate in the morning,' Teddy said as
he broke away and strode for home, an arm coming up to wipe the
tears from his eyes. He took a few steps before clapping a hand against
his forehead. and swivelled back around on the spot and trotted back.
He placed one huge hand on Bevan's shoulder and leant in close. 'I
damn nearly forgot to say – I asked around about this "Filakes" thing!
It's a Feral word and rumour has it that it has something to do with
a gang of them that specialise in people smuggling. Sounds like people aren't just hard currency in Axiom. Be careful out there, man.'
Teddy's hand came up from Bevan's and gently tapped him twice on
the cheek, and with that he turned and left. As he turned the corner
he left Bevan standing in the cold under the glow of an oil lamp, feeling the immensity of what tomorrow would bring.

That night he dreamt a dream from which he woke covered in
sweat despite the cold. In the dream, he had been in a field of purple
flowers – violets, he thought. They all swayed in a gentle breeze and
the sun lit the world around him and warmed his face and shoulders.
Purple spread in all directions as far as he could see. Purple. Violet.
And red. One red speck ahead of him. A deep red rose that stood
proud in this sea of purple violets. The summer breeze did not affect
it; it stood firm and strong and motionless. He made his way towards
it just as it in turn appeared to be moving towards him; the both
of them, he and the rose, slid silently through the field towards one
another. As he did so, though, the violets all around him began to
change and the sun dimmed and died; the breeze, so pleasant before,
built into a gale that began to uproot and fling the purple flowers
away. Those whose roots were deep clung onto the dirt, but they
were changing. They were no longer stems with leaves and petals but

stems with faces, children's faces. A young girl's, the saddest face he had ever seen. Her eyes were vacant, empty, emotionless. Yet even as he thought he could no longer look upon the saddest girl he'd ever seen, her face began to change and she was a boy. The boy? Benedict? It wasn't clear. Or was it still the girl? All the while he continued to slide towards the rose and it towards him. And now the flower children were dead. All of them blue-white in the face, their eyes empty sockets, their hair flying away in the wind, their sickly skin pallid, near translucent, now peeling away from skulls which stood atop dead stems, smiling sadder smiles even than the saddest girl he had just seen. He could not bear to look at them and now he was within touching distance of the rose. Its colour was vibrant, more intense than the ripest cherry and deeper than the thickest blood. It thrummed with a heartbeat of its own and he leant forward to touch its velvet petals. No sooner had his fingertips made the slightest contact than he shot awake as two incomplete sentences from two different voices echoed through his mind competing to be heard.

The first he did not know and it said '... hope to convince her... there is another... '

The second he knew, thought of every day. It was her, Evelyn and she said '... along the way... to the finish... ' Aside from 'Filakes', which she always uttered prior to changing form and disappearing, it was the first time she had ever spoken to him in his dreams. It felt like this could be another little sign that he should push forward with his plan, that getting out of Axiom in search of her would not be a fruitless journey.

A tentative knock at the door roused him from his bleary-eyed confusion. 'Shit, the boy!' he blurted out aloud, snapping out of his dreariness. Bevan leapt from his bed, wiped the sweat from his brow and raced across the room, pulling a hooded sweatshirt on over his head. He swung open his front door, but all that greeted him was the empty street, just dirty puddles of mud and snow slush. As he stood there, he chastised himself for being so foolish to trust in a boy and especially a boy who could barely hold a conversation. One crumb of macabre comfort he found in the knowledge that he need not worry about Stricken killing him on the expedition now. After all if, as he suspected, Benedict had blurted out what he knew, he would be rounded up and either Farmed or promptly executed before the end of the day. Most likely Farmed, he surmised, since decent electricians were relatively easy to come by whereas good quality meat was not.

He half-turned, ready to close the door and await the guards from J1 to come and collect him, when he heard, 'I'm very poorly, yes!' Benedict began snorting with laughter, his head peering around the door frame. He stood barely ten inches away, grinning from ear to ear. 'Knock, knock, yes, earlier than the work alarm, yes.'

'Good lad.' Bevan stepped aside and extended an arm welcoming him in, more relieved than he had ever known. 'Come on. Let's get going, I was afraid you were not going to show up!'

'I want to see that gadget now, yes!'

'Not right now, but soon OK? I just need to grab a few things then we can get a move on. Now pull your hood up – if we are stopped I do the talking, you very much do *no* talking, OK?'

'OK Bev, yes.'

He moved to the secret cupboard and slid it open. Behind him Benedict squealed with surprise and delight. It was a treasure trove to anyone in Axiom, but to Benedict it was simply awe–inspiring – a sneaky, secret cupboard full of so many exciting gadgets!

Grabbing up his backpack Bevan neatly filled it with the following:

- Two bottles of water
- Dry cured meat strips X 12
- Hard crust loaves of bread X 2
- A pack of 6 sausages
- The mini–pickaxe
- A lighter
- The halogen lamp
- 4 extra pairs of socks
- 2 additional jumpers
- Sleeping bag
- His father's pistol and X 12 bullets
- The Click he had taken from the addicts in J15
- The Window and its power cable.

It didn't feel a lot, and he'd certainly like to have had more food to take, but they would have to make do. There was only so much he could carry and they had to leave to meet Teddy at the gate.

He bent down and spoke to the boy. 'Now, you stay with me at all times, yeah – no matter what happens you stay with me. Always with me.' It wasn't a question...

'Yes, with you, yes' ... and Benedict knew it.

Bevan hoped that Teddy had been able to convince headstrong Grace to (momentarily at least) switch allegiances from wannabe J1 to her family and friends and get the main gate open. It only needed to be ajar just long enough for one nondescript J17 sparky and a young, timid–looking boy with his hood pulled up to slip quietly away.

As Bevan and Benedict battled their way hastily through the wind and light snowfall – one wearing a hat with his scarf wrapped around the lower half of his face, the other hooded, both with their heads bowed – they appeared to be just two average citizens off to beat the morning rush ahead of the shift alarm.

Suddenly two loud explosive thuds were heard in the distance. They instinctively broke into a jog. It had come sooner than Bevan had expected, but perhaps that didn't matter; the gate was not far.

When the third blast came a few moments later, however, they full-on ran. Something had gone wrong.

Chapter 19

Rosalyn woke with a start, leaping out of her bunk and looking around her as others in the shed were stunned out of their slumber too. Two loud blasts in quick succession had been shortly followed by a third, even louder, explosion. They sounded close.

She ignored the pain in her ribs from the sudden energetic movement. Usually the first thing Rosie would notice upon waking would be the gag-inducing smell of her surroundings. The half frozen shit that was not solid enough to lose its smell but too thick to get through the small drainage system, mixed with the ammonia from all the urine that had pooled in the corners of the shed. That vile aroma would be closely followed by the sounds of those around her moving into position to be let out for the day. This morning, though, she could hear and smell fire and smoke, and register faintly the angry buzzing of severed live electrical lines and the shouts and yells of rebellion, J1 guard panic and combat – gunfire and screams.

It was as if, as a collective, the whole herd held its breath waiting for the hatches above them to open and bullets to rain down upon them. The silence inside their shed was suddenly broken. It was a balding woman with a handful of teeth who wore the tatty remains of what would once have been a very fetching dress by Axiom standards. She would often whisper warnings of guards approaching or other activity from her vantage point on a top-tier bunk. It was positioned against the wall that looked out over the rest of the Farm and a knot in the wood had fallen loose; she would delicately remove it and peer out into the gloom whenever opportunity allowed. 'They're panicking! No-one is in control of nothing! It's a bloody revolution, break the doors, climb up and out those hatches! Now's the time for leaving with all the others, they're fleeing like rats up a drain pipe! The fences are all blown to shit!' she cawed down at them all, a toothless excited grin spread across her face.

Their momentary hesitation was well and truly broken and everyone burst into action, desperate for a chance for freedom or at the very least some retribution against their captors. Several of the larger members of the herd charged the doors which rattled against their hinges and cross-bar. A few more rams and there was the sound of splintering wood as the top hinge of the left–hand door broke away from the frame of the shed. They were nearly out. Some of the younger, more nimble individuals had already scaled the bunks and were hammering at the ceiling hatches. One or two had come loose, and they were scurrying up out of them like angry ants flooding from a nest. The old and the infirm among them waited in the centre of the shed, calling out encouragement to those who were making their escapes, and to those in front of them who in a few more minutes would break the door enough that they might all get out.

Rosie, though, had shuffled back when the rush had begun, had climbed up into a second–tier bunk and was watching it all unfold. Weighing up her options. Assessing her best chance for success. All the while she kept her eye on the herd's lead animal. Even though he was one of the most physically able amongst them, he was standing at the front of the elderly and weak mob barking instructions to those who were attempting to smash their way through the shed doors, 'One last push, you animals, break those fucking doors down... *now!*'

His underlings duly obliged, and with a final crashing blow the left door broke apart. The bottom hinge gave way and the mob funnelled out through the gap like pus exploding from a squeezed zit, as the wooden door cracked across the middle and hung lopsided from the cross bolt that had bent out into an 'L' shape.

Rosie could hear the clattering of semi-automatic gunfire and those who were at the front of the escaping herd slumped down dead; another couple of shots were let off and a dead animal fell back in through the ceiling hatch, lifeless bloodied body clattering off and between the bunks on its way to the floor. With strength in numbers, though, they continued their frantic, desperate surge for freedom. Another single shot was followed by a distant scream of pain, after which no more bullets were sent their way.

She made her move; hopping down from the bunk she clustered in amongst some of the elderly as they shuffled their way to the exit: they'd act as human shields if a guard turned his attention on them again. In watching the dead man fall from the hatch she had lost sight of the leader – he was gone, likely charging across the paddock towards a gap in the fence, hoping he'd get the chance to kill a guard on the way. Her own plan was also two–stage. It also included murder, but first was the need to escape the Farm. She didn't give a thought to the hows or whys of the sabotage to the Farm's fences; she was just determined to make the most of this completely unexpected opportunity.

As she emerged into the early morning gloom she scanned the scene before her – taking it all in, making judgements, making decisions. The three blasts had done all the damage needed to ensure the vast majority of the Farm could escape. This was no accident. One had ripped apart the adjoining fence link between six paddocks, likely a charge set in the guard tower that straddled the intersection. Another had blown a smouldering hole of charred wood and twisted metal in the outer fence and taken out half of the substation that powered the electric fencing. She assumed it was in amongst the circuit breakers that the charge had been placed for maximum damage. The third appeared to be a happy accident: a sparking, flailing cable from the partially destroyed substation had seemingly leapt too close to the cesspit methane release valve, ignited the combustible gas and sent a flame back down the pipe to the shit bomb below. It had created a huge crater in the ground, and another section of outer fencing and a guard tower had crumbled down into it. In the remaining towers, guards were rallying, arming themselves and firing into the crowds of fleeing cattle.

The fools were rusty, Rosie thought, ill prepared and not ready for the unexpected. It was chaos. They didn't have the firepower or numbers to stop the vast majority of the Farm's herds escaping out into the general Resident populace. Many of these animals would have families and homes to return to and seek help from. Many, like herself, would be out for revenge against those that put them there, and others would make for J15 to hide, to be lifelong fugitives and scratch a life amongst the ruins.

This was going to be bad for all concerned in the Bastion. When the dust settled, they could expect, she estimated, some 1,800 escapees flooding into the Jurisdictions spreading stories of the Farms, of their hatred for those who imprisoned them and a definite desire for revenge.

Rosalyn sprang into action, bursting away from the crowd (which would no doubt become a bullet sponge) and haring across the open ground alone, head down and moving as fast as she could in the slush of recent snowmelt. She was a fast-moving, small target unnoticed by the armed men above her on the gangways and in the towers. She made her way to the crater that had been left by the exploding methane-filled cesspit. Skidding down its smooth blasted sides she landed in the bottom, knee deep in filth but hidden from view. She trudged through the muck to the other side, fell to her stomach, her ribs a fury of pain as she hit the dirt, and crawled up the other side to peer over the edge. Here she lay for a moment catching her breath and re-surveying the scene ahead of her.

Hundreds of animals were swarming towards and through the hole in the outer fencing. They had made it across the compound and through the rain of bullets fired in by the desperate guards. Off to her right a partially collapsed guard tower lay slumped against the main headquarters building of the Farm's guards. The top of the tower had part of its roof caved in, and midway up it had smashed through an upper window. Not far away on her left a group were kicking and stamping a guard to death – he looked, in truth, long dead but in their bloodlust they continued to punish the bruised and bloodied sack of skin-wrapped broken bones and pulped organs.

What Rosie was most interested in, though, was the pistol he must have dropped when the beating began. It lay unnoticed beyond the frenzied rabble and just a few feet from where she lay. It wasn't essential to what she needed to do... but it would help. It was worth the detour. She scanned all around again for dangers and saw none – the guards were all distracted and concentrating their efforts on the main escape route, and the angry cattle were still intent on pummelling a dead man. She shuffled up into a crouched position ready to spring out, snatch the weapon and then make her way up the collapsed tower, in through the window of the station to *find him* and to *kill him*.

Now! She leapt forward... no! something gripped at her ankle like a vice and she crashed back down to earth, her damaged ribs an agony that made her wince and yell in pain as stars danced across her vision.

She looked back over her shoulder to see the herd leader clutching at her leg. While she was distracted by the tantalising prospect of the pistol he had slid his way down the bank just as she had, stealthy as a snake and with venomous intent. Except he must have, Rosalyn realised with revulsion, actually slid into and under the contents of the cesspit, to approach her like a crocodile ready to snatch prey at a watering hole. His face was grinning up at her, bits of what he'd just swam through sliding from his face. His hideous face – the man's nose had been broken so many times it zig-zagged down his profile with two close-set, dark–rimmed eyes flanking it. His smile was wide and sinister and the beard he had grown did a poor job of hiding two scars, evidence of an injury that must have near enough removed his entire lower jaw when it happened originally. His usual combover was pushed to one side and stuck to his face, revealing his bald pitted crown covered with flaking infected skin.

'I were coming for you that day, missy, the day your young buck got blatted, you always seemed to me to be the real threat, eh, the one I needed to make an example of,' he snarled. 'I were gonna slide this nasty little slice between ya ribs, pop a lung or tickle ya heart veins p'raps,' he continued as his other arm came out from under the ooze he was half submerged in and waved the steel shank. 'Shame ya buck got his head popped and sent everyone running. It might have been less of a struggle for you to bleed out in the paddock than this.' She couldn't believe he didn't vomit but he placed the knife between his own teeth and grabbed at her leg with his other arm and began to heave her back down the slope into the slop with him. 'It'll be more fun to see ya drown in shit than your own blood though, I reckon,' he finished with a maniacal look.

As she slid towards him her torso bumped and bounced over rocks and debris and her ribs seared with pain. She felt her legs reach the slurry and the cold liquid ran up her calves, her thighs; it seeped into her trousers and underwear and now it was coming up over her midriff and approaching her chest. Her assailant released her ankle and leaped forward directly on top of her. She had a moment to hold her breath and close her eyes and then she was completely under. He was as strong and as slippery as a python. It felt like he was writhing and touching her all over in his efforts to keep her from getting back to the clean air above. Rosalyn's arms flailed and her punches felt useless as they were slowed by the viscosity of the liquid all around her. Her lungs burned to exhale to make room for a big fresh hit of air. Yet still he beat down on her, grabbed and pushed. She felt his hands slide over her breasts and come to rest open–palmed on her stomach as he tried to push her deeper down. They pushed, but they did not grip and in this instant Rosalyn, against all natural urges to get to the surface, thrust herself down and away from his hands. Her bum hit the bottom of the pit and her legs tucked into a seating position, and in a flash she was standing up – her legs straightening and her whole body propelling her head upwards towards the air she craved, the air she *needed*.

As she burst free she gasped for air, one hand wiping clear her eyes while she swung the other before her, hoping to keep him at bay. The air rushing into her lungs filled her with rejuvenated fight, and as she took a step back her vision cleared and there he stood before her, dodging her blind swipes and preparing to spring at her again. This time she was ready for him though – she had that advantage. But this time he held the knife in his hand – his advantage was better.

Her wits were about her again now, though, and in truth it was not a fair fight at all. She was a trained elite member of J1, marked for a move into the Shrouded by her superiors, and he was just a thug from any one of the other Jurisdictions, a brawler with a knife he didn't really know how to use. He was all wild swings and slashes that over pitched his balance and used up energy. Rosie danced away from him with ease, pitched up onto the sloped edge of the crater to gain some height advantage, kicked the knife from his grasp and then leapt towards him, bringing her elbow down into his collarbone. There was a snap as it gave way and he crumpled to his knees.

He was a pitiful thing really; unsightly to begin with, he was now up to his waist in shit and piss, yowling in pain and clutching at his broken collarbone. He was begging for his life, but Rosalyn Torres was now on autopilot. A killing machine. She strode around behind him, placed a hand either side of his pig head, twisted and snapped his neck. Her would-be-killer fell instantly silent and dropped face-first into a murky grave. She retrieved the crude blade which was still clasped in his hand and scurried up and out of the crater. Fortunately nothing above them had changed. The dead man was still being beaten (by a slightly smaller group) and guards were still in disarray trying to shoot the hordes of escaping cattle. Rosie bent and snatched up the pistol and began her ascent of the fallen tower to access the main station. Revenge was well and truly on her mind.

Chapter 20

Bevan ran as fast as he could and Benedict followed hot on his heels. They were trying to make their way across Axiom to the main gate – it was the only way in or out and they needed to get out. Needed to get out fast – things were beginning to unravel.

The original plan had, in principle, been pretty straightforward. Teddy had helped Bevan secure all the elements he needed to make up a couple of simple homemade IEDs (the detail for how to do so had been provided by Chung via email on the Window). While on shift Bevan had planted the devices along fencing sections in the Farms. Timers were set and they were to detonate and cause a distraction only. While J1 and J3 forces were focused on the Farms they would make their way to the gate where Grace Smithers should be briefed to let them through. The third explosion was unexpected and unplanned. Bevan couldn't even hazard a guess at what it could have been but it must have been a chain reaction from his two initial bombs. There should have been no loss of life, and nothing so major that cattle should be able to completely escape J13, certainly not to the extent of the chaos raging around them.

There were cattle everywhere. They were charging through the streets. Some were desperate to escape; some were intent on causing damage. All were angry; all were determined to never go back to the Farms. They were breaking into homes and other buildings looking for things to steal, weapons to wield, places to hide. Many of the escapees were simply in frenzy. A form of bloodlust, euphoria brought about by freedom and the thrill of destruction.

Bevan glanced over his shoulder and was both pleased and relieved that Benedict was still in tow. He wanted to check he was OK, though, and so veered off and stood in a doorway and ushered the boy to him.

'Are you all OK, little man?'

To his utter surprise Benedict answered with a grin, 'Yes, thanks Bevan, yes. Lots of bang, bang, banging noise like fireworks on a graduation day, yes.'

Bevan smiled back, he couldn't help it. Despite the anarchy all around them there they suddenly stood beaming at one another, Benedict in his own little world excited by the events and Bevan simply in awe of the boy's heart-warming innocence.

The moment was interrupted as the door behind Bevan suddenly swung open, bashing into his back. He stumbled forward and managed to hold his footing by pushing past Benedict, who almost switched places with him and ended up almost completely obscured by the now open door. Bevan marvelled at the sheer luck of this, his wonderment at this fortune completely overtaking the fear he really should have been feeling, as standing before him was General Stricken.

'*Hughes?* What the fuck are you doing out here?'

'I, er…' He fought for something to say that would placate a man that only ever needed the slightest of reasons to kill at the best of times, and found himself wanting. Wit and cunning abandoned him and all he could do was stutter and stare over the General's shoulder at Benedict. The boy was literally cowering in the corner created by open door and wall. He had pulled up his hood and yanked the drawstring in tight, obscuring his face a bit. He was visibly shaking.

Stricken let out a yell of frustration and annoyance, brought up one huge hand, placed it over Bevan's face, shoved him to one side and marched off, 'Project WIND or not, any other time, Hughes, and I'd shoot a hole through your stomach. Get back to your shithole house in your shithole Jurisdiction. I'm preoccupied now but I'll think up a punishment for you later.' With this threat left hanging, he strode away and around a corner out of sight.

Bevan bent forward onto his knees, held back an urge to vomit and slowed his breathing. Then he remembered the boy.

He was still there but was down on his haunches, rocking gently and still shaking.

'Hey, Ben. Hey, it's Bevan, we are OK, he's gone.'

'He's going to, going to get me, yes,' Benedict's voice came out muffled from beneath his hood.

'No, no it's OK, he's gone. He didn't even know you were there. I sent him on his way, didn't I?'

Benedict looked up. 'No, he just left. Yes. You didn't say anything, silly. No.' He placed all his fingers inside his hood and spread them out, widening it and revealing more of his face. 'But we have to go, yes. Yes, we have to go right now. He has a punishment for you, Bev. Yes.' With that he hopped up and ran off in the direction of the gate. Bevan only shook his head and promptly followed.

Former J1 sniper, mother and most recently J13 cattle herd member Rosalyn Torres was motivated and determined and *very* dangerous. She had scaled the fallen guard tower with relative ease, its mangled sides a perfect ladder to ascend to the upper–floor window of the guard station.

She couldn't be sure if he would be here but it seemed like her best bet. Rumour had it that only about ten per cent of his time was spent actually formulating plans and delivering orders, the majority being split between the bars of J1, the poli brewery and the Farm – whoring, drinking his face red, and feeding his fat gut on the freshest cuts of meat.

She stood in a deserted corridor in a pile of broken glass which crunched as she swivelled on the spot and surveyed up and down. The building was dark: all the lights had blown as the power from the damaged substation had surged then died. She could hear the fires crackling outside in the compound behind her and the shouts and shots of the ongoing riot. It sounded to her like most of those who had been inside the station when the first blast ripped through the morning air were now either outside trying to handle the situation, on the ground floor trying to radio through for backup, or firing from the windows. Above her, she knew, were the canteen and the sleeping quarters for those swapping over shifts at the break of dawn and late at night. If he was here he'd not dirty his hands, he'd be stuffing his face, sleeping through it all or hiding. She would head up.

To the left was a dead end with just two doors on either side, both of which were closed and windowless. To the right was a similar set-up, but the corridor stretched away slightly further, ending in a door upon which a sign showed a stick man descending some stairs. She slid the blade she'd taken from the now–deceased herd leader into the back of her waistband, tore a strip of material torn from the sleeve of her shirt, and tied her loose, matted hair into a pony tail. She picked the pistol up from the windowsill and edged cautiously towards the stairwell.

Her footsteps echoed off the cracked, ageing linoleum floor and it felt as though they were loud enough to be heard from the other side of the city. She held her breath then let it out slowly, calming her beating heart. She passed a door to her left. Another two to her right. And froze. A sound from the next door up on her left. Dropping to one knee, she raised the pistol and waited with a smile on her face. The sound had been that of a toilet flushing and surely only *he* would feel the need to go and empty his bowels so calmly during a crisis.

The handle to the latrine door turned, the door swung open with a crash against the wall, and out he waddled, still tucking his shirt into his trousers – and accidentally his underpants too, the slob. As he pulled up his zipper, he turned to shut the door and saw her crouching there, not a few feet away, pistol levelled at him with a smile on her face so cold he visibly shivered to see it. He shivered despite the sweat that broke out across his forehead.

'Feeling better, Captain Benitez? Relieved? I know I am,' she said.

He sniffed and swallowed, but this time it wasn't just his phlegm. Rosalyn was delighted to see it was also tears and it was fear. 'Torres?' He paused and she could see the devious little cogs of his mind turning as he tried to work out the best possible way to attempt to wheedle his way out of the situation. He dragged his sleeve across his forehead. 'I was under the impression I'd just seen the last of you as I flushed that toilet! I did think that steak was a little chewy and not the succulent one I was assured I'd be getting!'

It didn't matter what he said, Rosalyn was hell–bent on killing him regardless but she was a little surprised he went down the antagonistic route. 'It's a pity your last ever meal was a disappointing one, Captain. Never mind, you'll be dead soon so you wont have long to dwell on it. Now turn, slowly and open the stairwell door behind you.'

'You've nowhere to go, Torres. Kill me and you're really no better off.'

'You see, Captain, that's where you are wrong. I will be so much better off knowing that you are dead and you can't kill any more innocent little girls! Now turn and do as I say.'

He turned slowly and placed a chubby hand on the handle of the door, 'You know, after seeing your spawn so terrified and the anguish you've suffered since, it did give me bit of a hard–on. I've put in a request with the powers that be to head up a new team with a proposal for the execution of illegal vermin children as opposed to Farming them.' He let out a disappointed sigh. 'Seems that'll be knocked back, though, now that we appear to have just lost a lot of good stock here today.'

He was calm. His words cut through her like the edge of a piece of paper across a thumb – they didn't cut deep, but they stung. The memory of Violet in her final moments flashed across her memory and tears sprung forth in her eyes. Her training was kicking in too, though, and despite the cruel cutting words he levelled at her a voice in the back of her head was asking, *Why is he so damn calm?*

Benitez drew the handle down, the latch engaged with a click and he held it there, 'You know,' he said, 'I've always been one to have second helpings!' With that he swung the door open and pitched to the left to expose the two guards who stood in the doorway with their weapons drawn as he himself moved to draw his own from its holster on his fat hip.

The corridor erupted with the confined thunder of small arms fire. Benitez's bodyguards got off three shots apiece while the Captain, with palms slick from nervous sweat, fumbled with the Desert Eagle that then snagged on his trouser pocket. One of their bullets found their mark and Rosie grimaced in pain as it tore through her flimsy shirt and the muscle along the right side of her abdomen just below her breast. She felt the warm release of blood that flowed out and down her thigh. All at the same time though, Rosalyn had herself pulled the trigger three times. All were true, all had a purpose.

The first left a small hole between the eyes of one guard who stumbled backwards, over the handrail to the stairs, his lifeless body tumbling down to the ground floor, clattering off other levels as he plummeted. The second bullet smashed through the left knee of the other guard, who collapsed to the floor, clutching his shattered joint and yelling curses. The third hit the gun, which Benitez had finally managed to dislodge and was raising to aim at her; it spun from his grasp, snapping his trigger finger with the force.

Rosalyn stood from her crouched position and brought a hand down to investigate the wound; it wasn't deep and the bullet had only passed through muscle and come out clean, no broken bone or debris that she could feel. It hurt. A lot. With time, though, it would heal just fine. She walked over to the two left alive and kicked away their weapons. 'Benitez, give this man a hand – I'd suggest your unbroken one. He'll need your help getting up the stairs.' Whimpering like a dog that knows it's going to be kicked, he bent down and slung the guard's arm over his shoulder and stood back up, supporting the other man's weight. 'Now climb!' Rosalyn instructed.

Kicking and cajoling them, Rosalyn had Benitez and the injured guard shuffle and hobble their way up the seventeen steps to the top floor of the station and out into the former canteen area. It was deserted. Ahead of them the open kitchen still had pots and pans bubbling away on the stove, and a frying pan was on the verge of bursting into flames as the unattended oil smoked and spat. Most tables still had half-eaten meals on trays upon them and chairs had been flung away as their occupants threw down their cutlery and dashed from the room. Over on their right-hand side there was a pile of broken concrete, bent, twisted chairs, a flattened table and shattered human limbs. When the ceiling had unexpectedly collapsed under the impact and weight of the falling tower, it seemed it had caught a group of Farm guards at breakfast. It looked like a game of oversized Jenga that had gone wrong and come crashing down on its participants, who had all lost in spectacular fashion.

'Sit. Stay.' Rosie addressed the snivelling man with the destroyed kneecap, and pointed at a chair that had been spun away from a table but remained upright. He slumped into it, delighted not to be putting any pressure on his ruined leg. 'You –' she thrust the barrel of her gun into Benitez's back between his shoulder blades and pushed him downwards, '– onto your front.' He complied without protestation and she heard his knees and back crack as he bent over, crouched and lay down. With the Captain now lying face down on the floor at the feet of the injured guard, Rosalyn strode across the canteen to the pile of rubble and crushed men. She stood there for a moment, scanning over the carnage, looking for something specific for the job. Having found what she was looking for, she grasped it with one hand, heaved it up to her body and wrapped her other hand (which still held her pistol) around it and walked back over to finish what she'd come for.

'Hold this,' she ordered the man in the chair. Without waiting for him to agree she dropped it into his lap and he clumsily kept a hold of it while shouting out in agony as his knee involuntarily jolted to adjust his balance in the chair. From the floor came the snivelling she knew would eventually and inevitably come.

'Please, please, wait! You don't have to do this. Just leave, escape like all the others here, find your way out. I can even help you on your way. I could –'

'You really do not get it, do you? As long as you are dead first, I don't care if I never leave this room!'

'Pleeeaaassee,' he wailed, and his saliva bubbled on his lips and ran down his chin; his eyes were wide with terror like a horse caught in a burning stable. Tears ran down his cheeks and pooled on his top lip, mixing with the snot that had dribbled from his nose in his panicked state.

'Stand up,' she instructed the man in the chair. He slowly struggled to raise himself, his good leg shuddering slightly as it took his weight upon it. In his trembling arms he still held the square–foot slab of broken concrete she had placed in his lap. Rosie stood there before the two of them, Benitez desperately writhing on the floor and his bodyguard standing over him shaking like a leaf from pain, strain and fear.

She spoke to Benitez but her voice was sad and distant, 'You killed me that day in that farmhouse on the hill. I died when you forced that terrible choice upon me and I pulled that trigger. You took *everything* from me. My poor sweet girl… ' Her bottom lip trembled and her eyes filled with tears. A vacant expression spread across her face and her raised gun arm fell limply to her side. Shaking her head imperceptibly she began a slow walk away from the two of them towards the door through which they had entered the canteen.

'I loved her more than anything in the world, more than anything or anyone I'd ever known, more than I thought was possible, more than I care even for myself! She was my sole purpose, my only reason for being… ' She stood in the doorway now and across the room the two men remained just as she had left them, though both had let out a small sigh of relief as she daydreamed away from them. Her tone changed then though, and she stared back at them, directly into Captain Benitez's tiny beady little eyes, 'and *you* took that away from me!' The gun she was holding came up so fast it was a blur, the man holding the concrete would not have even heard it fire. The bullet entered through his left eye, his arms went slack and the slab of concrete came down with a sickening crunch on Benitez's head.

Violet's impact on Rosalyn's life was permanent; her life and her demise held such contrasting emotions and memories. Her fleeting existence had forever changed Rosie. She felt both revulsion and sadness at what she had just done, to kill a man in such a calculated and brutal manner. In a time before she had her daughter, she knew that she would not have felt a thing – before Violet she was just a cold killing machine – but now she was more emotional, she retained all those deadly skills but a sense of being a mother affected all her actions and decisions.

She left the room and the grisly scene behind. Things were quietening down outside and she knew she did not have long before escaping the confines of the Farm would no longer be such an easy thing. Across from the canteen there was an office. She kicked the door wide open and entered with her weapon raised but the room was empty. She found what she was looking for: tucked in the umbrella slot of a metal coat stand next to the large desk before her was the Cold Bringer. She snatched it up, her hands perfectly fitting its grip; the familiar steel against her palms made her feel alive. She checked its barrel, firing mechanism and sight, and once satisfied all was OK, slung it over her shoulder and made for the city gate to leave. It was, she knew, only manned at this time of day by a young girl who wanted to be a guard but was anything but, and wouldn't pose a problem to get by. Incredibly, she mused, it was the simplest escape route – straight out the front door.

Chapter 21

Axiom was in chaos. Rosie estimated that perhaps 4,000, maybe 5,000 individuals had escaped the Farm. Nearly all of them had previously had homes and families and friends before they were Farmed and those loved ones had remained angry, bitter and vengeful. The hornet's nest had been thoroughly stirred up. None who had made it out of J13 could imagine being nor allow themselves to be taken back to the Farms, and they were now battling to maintain their recently found freedom. In many cases they were choosing to die fighting rather than return. The crack and pop of burning and flames and bullets being fired was all around and in the distance, near and far, she could hear the violence and rebellion taking place.

She moved fast, keeping low and as discreet as possible. This was not her fight anymore but she knew that they would come for her once (and it was only a matter of time) the J1 and Shrouded brought the populace back to order. There would be nowhere to hide; she had killed a high ranking member of the authority. Her case would be escalated and there was absolutely no way that General Stricken would be as sloppy as Benitez. *He* would be relentless and ruthless, he would love the chase, the hunt and he would love the thrill of the capture and kill.

Leaving the city was the only option. There would be a way to survive out there. Or so she hoped. There was water and there was food, that was a certainty – snow and ice meant water and she had seen animals, so she would not starve. Company was something she had never craved and the big empty alone did not faze her. Everything else she needed to survive she could fashion, find, adapt and develop in time. Most important at this stage, though, was distance. The plan rapidly formulating in her head began with opening up as much of it as possible between her and Axiom.

All around her the Jurisdictions were fracturing apart as Residents broke down barriers and fences and smashed through buildings, their anger, violence and destruction blurring the ancient lines of division.

Some were fighting one another – she witnessed a J9 man scuffling with two J11s over a plundered coat; a group of former J13s hell bent on ousting a family of J5s from their home with fist and fire. Mostly though, J1s were being targeted. They were for the most part outnumbered and when cornered and captured were in some cases literally being ripped apart. However, if there was one thing that could redress the numerical advantage, it was a machine gun, and in the situations where a guard was able to hold some high ground or shoot efficiently and effectively, the uprising of the masses was being quelled.

Rosalyn cut through a ramshackle building as a shortcut and emerged on a windswept street, an impassable row of burning houses directly in front of her. Looking left, the entire street was blocked off by a mob of furious, riot–maddened and emboldened J13 escapees. They carried primitive weapons – clubs, slingshots, spears of wood and steel and the odd handgun. They were gesticulating, yelling and taunting... her! No, not her, she realised as she glanced over her shoulder to the other end of the street. Here there stood just two of the Shrouded.

They both stood stone–still, their black and red uniforms doing their job of making them seem like evil demons against the white of the snowfall. One was a giant of a man – she felt he must have been well over seven feet tall. Strapped to his back was a vast broadsword, the handle and cross-guard of which were adding 'horns' to the demonic look. In his hands he carried an old MG42, a weapon that should only typically be fired using a tripod or mounted to a vehicle. The monster's partner was a man of unassuming stature; instead his apparent confidence was what Rosalyn found most unnerving. He stood in the shadow of the man beside him, arms folded across his chest, one hand lightly caressing the tip of a belt of throwing knives strapped across him. A cruel smile was spread across his taut face and he slowly blinked to reveal his tattooed eyelids.

Suddenly a molotov cocktail fizzed over Rosalyn's head and exploded not far from the two Shrouded. The fools, she thought before swiftly ducking back in to the building from which she had emerged, reminding herself again that this was not her fight. She knew that all those who had stood baying on her left would be slaughtered by the two demons who had been standing on her right.

Skirting back across the previous street she looped back on herself and found a crossing to the neighbouring Jurisdiction with little commotion. It felt like things were calming down already and so she knew her window of opportunity to escape the city was closing fast. The great wall of the city loomed up before her, a steel and concrete tidal wave. She scanned the top of the wall ahead from left to right. It was unmanned. Directly ahead the great impassable barrier split and she could see the gloomy grey sky beyond it. Below this gap and obscured by a clutch of small dwellings, she knew, stood the gate to Axiom. She dashed across the open expanse of the street and planted her back against the wall of the nearest of the buildings in front of her. Shimmying across the wall she peered around the corner to get a view of the gate to check security levels. It was, as she had hoped and suspected, lightly guarded. Just one single guard, a young woman – and even better, she observed, not even a full J1. Her J17 tattoo indicated she must be one of the few Residents who aspired to J1 status. Despite the skills which would have been engrained in her during this young woman's 'education' in the Jurisdiction of the Corruptible she had found a way to engineer work above, beyond and out of scope of her predestined occupation. She would have to be both brave and foolish, Rosie surmised.

The J17 woman with a fancy for authority and an automatic weapon stood before the gate which was sealed shut behind her. Her assault rifle was raised and aimed at three men, (though one might be a young boy, Rosie thought) who appeared to be remonstrating with her. Rosalyn shifted a little closer and squatted down behind a water butt stood at the corner of the building to listen to the argument taking place, curious at to how this might pan out. The wannabe would surely kill them – after all nothing guaranteed a promotion like putting a stop to a group of potential escapees. But it seemed she was showing some hesitation. Rosalyn's plan had always been to leave the gate wide open when leaving, in the hope others would follow. They'd muddy, confuse and scuff the trail Stricken would attempt to use to track her. So, she considered, would it be best if she saved these three and in doing so ensured at least three more bodies made it beyond the wall?

'Put the gun down, Grace.' The biggest of the three men spoke with authority befitting his size.

'No chance. I should shoot these two and you. I'm in control in this situation, not you! I'm the guard on this gate and you... them... you're all just... traitors!' The girl – Grace the big man had called her – was rattled, lacking control and discipline. She was too emotional. Rosie could see and hear that she was already bordering on hysterical.

'Look, just let my friends leave. No–one need ever know, we'll never even mention it again. It'll be as if it never happened, eh?'

'No! No, I'll know and then *he* will know, he sees your lies in an instant, how will I even explain why the gate has been opened? Wait, why am I even worrying about that? It makes no difference because you're all staying right there, not moving, not saying a word until my fellow J1s arrive and throw you all in the Farms!'

'Your "fellow J1s"?' The big man's tone carried a note of disapproval. 'You're not one of them. You're just a confused girl who should have had a more attentive father to keep you from this madness!' He raised his voice but not in anger – he was pleading as he stepped towards her.

'Stop! Don't move! I mean it!' She thrust the weapon's muzzle forward, reminding them of the steel authority she held in her hands.

'Grace, please... ' The other man now. '... Please, just let us walk out of here. We must leave – if we stay they'll kill him.' He pointed at the smallest of the three of them and from this angle now Rosie saw that he was just a boy, a terrified one by the looks of him. He looked too old to be doing so, but he held onto the sleeve of the man beside him and he was shuffling nervously from foot to foot. His eyes were darting back and forth, scared to make eye contact but even more scared of all that was going on around him. He flinched at the raised voices.

'Shut up! I don't care, they'll kill me if I let you go! I mean I can't let you go anyway, it's my duty to stop you! You always think you are such a smooth talker – well, talk again and I'll shoot the boy myself. I mean it, dammit!'

Seeing this scared boy brought back the terrible image she had seen of Violet right before she had done what she had to do, and she would not let it happen to another child. She leapt from her hiding place and was across the vacant space between them in a flash. Grace had barely registered the blur of movement from out of the corner of her eye before Rosalyn was less than four foot away from her. She tried to swing around and aim the rifle at her assailant. It was too late. Rosie ducked as Grace fired two wayward rounds into the earth and sky and before Grace knew it the highly trained and experienced former (real) J1 had disarmed her, driven a boot into the back of her knee sending her sprawling, and now stood over her with her own rifle pressed painfully against her temple.

'Wait! No, don't shoot, please don't shoot, please!' the big man pleaded, hastily stepping forward and defensively raising his arms.

'What do you care for the life of a J1 wannabe like this? She'll give us up in a second, and Stricken and all his merry men will be after us in a flash! Something as simple as knowing the exact exit we took will go a long way to helping them tracking our escape route quicker!'

'She won't, she won't say a word. I'm not leaving. I'll stay. I'll keep your secret safe!'

'You don't understand the nature of it then. She is not loyal to you, she is loyal to the system and the city. She needs to be made to forget she has seen us.'

'Us? We don't even know you! For all we know, and judging by the way you just disarmed Grace, you are one of them too! Why would we trust you?' the other man spoke and as Rosalyn glanced at him so the young boy stepped back behind him peering out at her, still clasping the man's jacket like an adolescent.

'Yes. Us. If you managed to get yourselves cornered and held at gunpoint by this amateur you won't last five minutes beyond the wall with Shrouded on your arse! I'll not see another child die –' she absently waved a hand, gesturing to the younger boy '– and since you appear to be leaving too it's probably best I keep an eye on you now, isn't it!' Rosalyn flicked the safety off the rifle, the tiny click deafening in the tension of the situation. 'Close your eyes and cover your ears, boy.'

The big man broke in again, frantic, 'You cant! Please, she's my daughter, my little girl!'

Rosie looked into the face of the big man. Tears ran down his cheeks and his eyes were frantic with worry, his hands now clasped together in a prayer to a long forgotten deity to save the day. She looked down at the girl – yes she was just a girl really, just cowering, more tears, more terror. She was also unmistakably related to the big guy. Once again the vision of Violet swam before her eyes, blurred from the tears she now realised she was shedding. How could she do this to a parent? To a child? Her emotions were taking over again, wiping away all that training in an instant.

The weapon slid from her grasp and clattered to the ground. She stumbled a few steps back, her shoulders sagged and she brought her hands up to her face and wept into them. The big man knelt down and took his daughter in his arms, pulled her close and through his own tears of relief whispered to her that she was OK, that he had her safe. Grace, though, was not listening. With her sobbing, consoling father embracing her, his face buried in her neck and stroking her hair he wasn't able to see her break her hold upon him and reach out for the fallen assault rifle. She pushed him away and sprung to her feet, raising the weapon and levelling it at Rosalyn. Grace's voice was ragged and choked with tears. 'I cannot let you through this gate. I'm sorry Dad, Bevan, I can't, they would kill me, then chase you and kill you too shortly afterwards. Just turn around and go, and we'll never speak of this again.'

Rosie did not even peek out from between her fingers, she felt like right now, if she were to be shot it would be justified. She had got her vengeance on Benitez. Perhaps the girl was right and it was time for this dog to be put down.

'Please Grace, please just let us through, me and the boy *have* to leave. If we stay we are definitely dead; if we can just leave the city then we *may* have a chance!' Bevan pleaded.

Grace turned to him, her face emotionless stone, the deep–seated desire to be recognised as a J1 burning in her eyes again, 'Yes, you're right. Stay here and you will definitely die… because I will shoot you for the fugitive scum you are! So turn around and leave and you may live, but you are not coming through this gate!'

'But... ' He felt his chance to escape slipping by. 'But it's the only way out... ' he murmured. His shoulders sagging and his head bowed, he felt a defeated man. The slim glimmer of hope he had allowed to take hold in his mind had grown hungrily over the last few days like a tiny ember in a bundle of dry grass and now it was well and truly extinguished by a bucket of despair.

They stood there in the shadow of the wall which loomed high before them. The only gate, guarded by a girl with a gun, a girl who he had once upon a time bounced upon his knee and whose hair he had playfully ruffled. The wall, the girl and the gun were now a truly impenetrable barrier to their flight from Axiom. The sounds of the Farm breakout which had been their perfectly executed distraction was now dying down to just the odd intermittent shouts, screams and gun fire. Order was being restored and soon a patrol would be along to check the city's perimeter, starting with its weak point – the gate. Their situation was bleak and a mood had descended more gloomy than the murky combination of the usual morning half-light and shadow in which they stood. At Bevan's side, Benedict began to whimper and when Bevan reached out an arm to comfort him he flinched and shoved it away. He wasn't a smart boy but Bevan could tell from his manner that even he realised that he'd surely rubber–stamped their already signed death warrants to the front of the execution queue.

He tried one last time but even as he spoke the words and heard them he knew they were weak and knew it was hopeless: 'Grace... please... it's the only way... '

She stared back at him, an eerie coolness about her but always that fire burning in her eyes. Yet then when it truly began to feel completely hopeless and the gloom felt like it was getting completely dark a glimmer of hope shone out and shocked Bevan to the core. He had not registered it at the time – he was too intent on attempting to talk Grace into opening the gate – but Rosalyn's tears had stopped and a true killer's poise had returned to her demeanour as she spoke. The shock came not from her change from despair to stoic defiance; it was because what he heard, her words, were ones he had heard before.

'You cannot hope to convince her. But there is another way... if you will trust me,' she said. They were some of the words that had been spoken by the unknown voice which had come to him in his dream the night before. The voice that had been mixed in with that of his lost wife Evelyn. One of the two voices that had melted the dream and shook him awake and back to reality.

Chapter 22

Bevan turned to the source of the voice; he turned to Rosalyn Torres knowing immediately that his premonition had provided them with the clue to the real way forward and he would not miss this window of opportunity. 'Lead the way,' he said. He glanced across at his life-long friend Teddy Smithers and knowing that this was no time for sentiment simply said, 'Miss ya till I see ya, buddy!' and with Benedict's hand held within his own set off at a jog, with Rosie leading the way. As they ducked and weaved their way through the turmoil of the rapidly fading rebellion, Bevan promised himself that when – it had to be when, he had to believe they would make it – that when they reached their destination, if he could, he would send word to Teddy. He would work out a means of escape and make sure his friend and his family could follow the way to find him.

Glancing back over his shoulder he saw that Grace had allowed them to flee. She was held in her father's embrace, one hand tight against his back, his jacket balled into her fist holding him close, the other down at her side still holding her weapon. Bevan felt in his heart that they would be OK; whether Teddy chose to leave some day or not he and his family would always be OK. Very soon J1 reinforcements would certainly arrive as Grace had warned, but they would just find a caring father comforting his daughter in the midst of the biggest riot in living memory. More importantly though, they would find the gate sealed and the perimeter secure. Grace would likely never get her reassignment to full J1 status but she would also never stop trying. Bevan felt both admiration and pity.

Running along at his side, Benedict suddenly spoke, and despite the pace was barely breaking a sweat while Bevan felt himself rapidly running out of puff. 'Where are we going Bev? You said we would go through the big gate, yes. But the big gate is back that way, yes, not this way, no!' To the boy's credit and Bevan's relief he didn't resist or check his stride, and they continued to run along trailing the woman ahead of them.

'I know, but the gate was locked, wasn't it, so we need to go a different way. We'll follow our new friend here and she will help us find a way out, OK?'

'Not my friend, no… she is scary, yes!' A statement, not a question.

'Don't be scared, little man, she is taking us somewhere safe. We can trust her, I know we can.' A pain was building in his side and Bevan hoped it was just a stitch and not a niggling doubt about the statement of trust he has just made. 'When we get a chance to stop and rest we can speak with her, you can make friends, eh?'

A pause and a slight check in his stride told Bevan that Benedict was not so sure about this idea and he answered with a question, 'Do you like her Bev, yes?'

'I think I do, Ben. I *think* I do.'

Up ahead of them Rosie had come to a stop at the corner of a building with a smouldering roof. She was peering around and down the adjacent road, on the other side of which stood a row of completely dilapidated homes of rusty tin, corrugated iron panels and wooden fragments. It appeared completely uninhabited, but Bevan knew where they were and he knew at least one resident of this long forgotten street. This was the street Vulture lived on.

'Where are you taking us'? Bevan asked, bent forward leaning on his thighs and breathing heavily. Behind him, head bowed, shuffling from foot to foot, was Benedict.

'You'll see. Just keep quiet, I'm trying to think! I need to work out a way beyond that row of old houses. We need a way into J15.'

'Well then, you're in luck,' Bevan said, standing upright with a grin while wiping sweat from his brow, 'I know a way in – but I also know that J15 is a dead zone, full of ruin, rubble and Click addicts. The one thing that remains intact in there is the City wall. We need to get out of the city, not leave one mess for another… unless… '

'Unless I know something you don't – which I do!' Rosie cut in and Bevan's grin faded. 'So if you know how to get in there, then hurry up and lead the way. We'll indulge in the chit-chat later!' She stepped to one side and extended her arm in an 'after you' gesture.

Bevan cleared his throat to retort but thought better of it and instead leant out into the road himself, checked it was all clear, and with a quick call for Ben to follow him he shot across the street and up along to the house of Vulture. The other two swiftly followed his lead. The three of them stood in the shallow alcove entrance to Vulture's house.

Bevan tapped lightly on the closed front door and spoke in a harsh whisper full of urgency. 'Vulture, open up man, it's Bev.' No response. 'Vulture, it's bloody important... please. It's Bevan, I need your help!' The house remained quiet as a crypt.

Rosalyn shoved him to the side and in one smooth motion drew her pistol and kicked open the door. 'Chit-chat,' she tutted as she did so.

The door splintered and flew open on its hinges, crashing into the wall and sending up a cloud of dust and a small shower of loose plaster from the ceiling. She trained her sights down the empty corridor. The first doorway was doorless and from within there came no sound. There was a strong smell of mould and the dim half-light of Axiom coming through the partially covered front window, but that was it. The second door was open and a faint glow oozed out into the hallway. The third door was shut tight with a row of four bolts that were all padlocked.

Rosalyn took a single step into the dust and trash-strewn corridor and turned to Bevan with a look that asked the question: *Which room?* He held up two fingers. She advanced with pace and purpose and only a cursory glance into the first room. The man and the boy remained in the doorway.

Bevan had no love for Vulture but he truly hoped he would not be foolish enough to lie in ambush and attack. He felt certain this new 'friend' of theirs was a whole different level of dangerous. It certainly would not make the case for convincing Benedict to trust her any easier if she was to demonstrate that now.

She moved into the second room, the sidearm held out before her, and disappeared from sight. Bevan held his breath and Benedict, uncomfortable in the tension, let out a little whimper. They heard no sounds of a struggle. They heard no sounds at all; she was as silent as a cat stalking an unsuspecting mouse. After what seemed to Bevan to be an impossibly long time to search what he knew was a small room, Rosalyn re-emerged, her gun still in one hand, but in the other now a set of keys which she twirled once around her index finger then gripped in a fist. She moved towards door number three and Bevan moved inside the house, pulling Benedict in with him and closing the front door behind them which crunched and jammed back into its splintered frame.

By the time they reached the end of the hallway, Rosalyn had undone the padlocks and stood holding the bolt ready to slide it open and advance. 'What am I going to find in here?' she asked without any effort to quieten her voice.

Bevan answered with a wince at the volume of her question and whispered back, 'No man can lock himself in a room like this. Vulture must have fled when everything kicked off, so I'd say it'll be just what we need – a back door into J15.'

'Good. Stand back… then follow.' She slid open the bolt and eased the door open with a creak, moved to kneel on one knee and swept her gun across the empty room. A room which as far as Rosalyn Torres was concerned only had one doorway and she was standing in it. 'Are you sure this is the right house? There is no way that –'

'I'm positive,' Bevan said, and marched over to the heavy wardrobe and swung the door open revealing the J15 access hole inside. 'After you, I insist,' he said, perhaps a little too smugly, for the look she shot him promptly wiped the smile from his face.

'If this "Vulture" lives in this pigsty I'm not sure I want to meet him, but it appears he is a resourceful creature! You can tell me about him when we are miles away from here,' Rosalyn said as she passed Bevan and stooped to enter the wardrobe.

After some encouragement, Benedict crawled through the hole after her, with Bevan bringing up the rear and closing the wardrobe door behind them. They stood in the gloom and Rosalyn tilted her head. *Follow me,* the gesture said. Bevan found Ben had taken to clutching at his sleeve again and they set off jogging behind her once more.

As they moved through the dead streets of the crumbling Jurisdiction the Coldbringer clattered lightly against two ammunition clips strapped across Rosalyn's back; this, their footsteps and breathing were the only sounds. They stuck to the main roads, not bothering to journey out of sight. Bevan assumed Click addicts were not considered much of a threat to an armed former J1. They passed by the old staff master's house that Bevan had almost fallen through when with Vulture and the small double row of staff lodgings which it overlooked. Past this point, it was factory after factory of varying sizes and levels of disrepair and collapse. Some barely a recognisable shell of a building, others whose only sign of decay were some smashed windows. And rust. So much rust. Any scratch taken here would surely be swiftly followed by tetanus. It gave the buildings an orange tinge and a darker shade ran from the rooftops and down the sides from years of snowmelt, Bevan felt it was like the whole Jurisdiction was weeping for its once productive and valuable status – or perhaps it was just bleeding to death.

As Bevan was considering this they skirted a corner and were confronted by a huge pile of rubble sloping up before them to its peak, some ten foot high. It completely blocked the road before them, piled high from the walls of one building on the left–hand side of the street right across to the one on the right.

'We are going over here,' Rosalyn said. 'Take your time – it looks pretty settled but one loose rock can soon become a hundred, and a hundred falling rocks will happily shatter a leg... or a skull.' With that foreboding assessment of the task ahead she turned and began to scale the obstacle before them.

'Feel OK with this climb, little man?' Bevan asked Benedict.

To his surprise the boy answered promptly and in the affirmative, 'Yes, I'm a good climber, yes. I like climbing, yes!' he said with a grin and began his own swift ascent, scuttling up the treacherous pile as effectively as a spider on a brick wall. Bevan allowed himself a smile at this and followed in an altogether more cautious and calculated manner. By the time he had reached the top the other two were waiting for him at the bottom on the other side. They stood apart, her with her hands on her hips looking impatient and he looking up at first with a look of concern which was replaced with that of relief when he saw Bevan crest the summit of rubble. Bevan skittered down twice as fast as he had ascended and no sooner as his feet had reached solid, level ground than Rosalyn had beckoned them on again.

As they moved down this street with its flanking high–rise factories,

Bevan came to recall precisely where they were and began to construct an idea, an inkling of just where they might be heading. Sure enough, less than two minutes later the three fugitives of Axiom stood on the sinkhole in which Bevan had found the charging cable for the Window. They travelled down into the gloom in the same order as they had scaled the rubble pile and once more Bevan was impressed with the boy's dexterity and fearless approach.

As they made their way across the bottom of the underground cavern and skirted around the great tangle of wires, cables and leads, Bevan spoke, his voice echoing throughout. 'There's a tunnel through the wooden door isn't there, a tunnel to the outside?'

'So you've been here before? So was it your haste or stupidity that made you attempt the main gate?' Rosalyn replied.

'I didn't know what lay beyond that wooden door until just now. Which of the two were your excuse for the bad choice of the main gate as escape route option one?'

'Hmm, touché,' she said with a wry smile. 'I thought it would be quicker for a start, and had you guys not been there bickering I would have just kil–' she glanced at Benedict, who had now pulled up his hood and trudged uneasily alongside Bevan, '– erm, easily got through the defences. In hindsight, this may well prove a better route since only a select few were aware it was here and they are no longer capable of being aware of anything. So why were you down here if it wasn't to get beyond the wall?' she asked.

'Well now, that's the part of things I know that you don't, and I'll be sure to bring you up to speed when, as you asked, we are well beyond the city's perimeter – part of the chit-chat you promised,' Bevan answered, with a sideways glance and wink.

Rosie appeared outwardly satisfied by his answer, though Bevan suscpected she was probably also a bit irritated by his cheeky response. She changed tack to discuss the next steps of getting to the point of the journey where he would spill the beans. 'Beyond the door and the tunnel we could be spotted by watchers on the wall – there is some exposed land between it and the Barrier. We'll have to move fast and quiet, but once we are inside that old forest we will be covered sight and sound. Then if we strike out on a relatively straight path westward, not a few hours from here there is a field of crops, in the centre of which there is an old crumbling farmhouse where we could rest up and work out our next move. It's a place I would sooner not return to unless… well, which direction does your unknown purpose take you?'

'You are in luck, since we need to go east.'

'East it is, then', Rosie replied looking oddly relieved. Then her training must have kicked in and overruled any emotions she had been feeling. 'On second thoughts we will go west a little way, but I'll explain as we go, we can't stand here wittering like old women at the Merchants' Quarter. We will stick close to the wall and track it around to the opposite side before branching out. Perhaps there we will find we have a route with more cover.'

'Sounds like a plan,' Bevan said, though he felt a little marginalised already – this was his escape plan and they were heading in the opposite direction to that which he had originally set in his mind. He wasn't really certain if it did sound like a plan at all but rather a hope and a chance – but, since there was no turning back and no alternative way forward, they would go ahead anyway.

She pulled open the creaking old wooden door and, in the dark of the underground cave, the outside gloom that flooded in seemed positively startling in its brightness. Of course it was not though, it was a half–light, and the three of them passed from the dark into the grey, feeling half hopeful they'd see tomorrow.

Epilogue

Transcript excerpt from the crisis meeting of the Solacity leadership committee, 17 April 2038

In attendance:

Co-chair – Cynthia Bloom (CB), owner and CEO ST Corp.

Co-chair – Zhangrong Shi Wan (ZSW), PRC Holdings board member and managing director YZ Ltd.

Secretary – Brent LeShay (BL), managing director ST Corp.

Biyu Chang (BC), technical director YZ Ltd.

Steve Chipperman (SC)

Dingxiang Xu (DX)

Mary Cleethorpe (MC) – transcribe.

Apologies:

Claire Holby (CH)

CB: Steve, I'm sorry but that is completely out of the question, now more than ever our thoughts and efforts must be entirely concentrated internally...

SC: So you are proposing we just sit here in this bubble and ignore the rest of the world?

CB: The rest of the world? There won't be anything left by the end of the week! You must see that?

SC: *We can't just turn our backs! We could make a difference, we could help so many!*

ZSW: *We will help! But in our own way, on our own terms and in a way that does not compromise all that we have achieved here, not to mention the safety of our people, our families!*

BL: *Shit, Chipperman listen to yourself. Fuck 'em all! We foresaw this and we moved to secure a future, whilst they scrabbled around all looking to get one up on each other, and for what? It's been our careful planning, some expense – Christ, some obscene expense! – and by some crazy stroke of luck we find ourselves in the perfect position. I ain't waving no charity flag, fuck 'em, we keep quiet, we shut up shop and wait...*

DX: *I'd have been more eloquent I'm sure, but I completely agree. We went out of our way to do all this under the radar. If we cannot help everyone we shouldn't help at all – would you be the one to pick and choose who we let in and those we send away?*

SC: *I can't believe I'm hearing this! We are sat here staring at the end of the world and you are all talking about putting an end to any form of humanity that there might be left!*

BC: *Steve, please calm down. What would you have us do? Think about it: we open our gates, offer help just once and countless sick, wounded, desperate and needy people will turn up. We'd be overrun...*

SC: *I can't just ignore all of what's going on out there, they are all dying, guys!*

BL: *Quit snivelling, do you wanna fucking die too, is that it? Shit, I know it's like the end of the world and stuff, but grow some balls man, this is the time of hard decisions you spineless...*

CB: *Gentlemen, please, this is a meeting, remain professional! Out there things may be falling apart but here civility will endure! It would appear the committee has reached a majority decision. We shall continue as we had planned before the tragic occurrences of the last three days. Solacity remains a secret and a haven for our specially selected and invited population.*

ZSW: Good then, it is decided... does anyone else have any other business?

CB: I do not, thank you.

BL: Nope, me neither.

DX: I'm done.

BC: Nothing more from me.

CB: Steve do you have any AOB to raise?... I'll take that as a no. Then we are done. Let's wrap this... Claire? What is it? What's happened?

CH:It's all gone!

CB: What? What has?

CH: Everything... everything is gone... ST Corp... all our friends and colleagues back home... not just California, most of the States! Before all communications went down, they were saying... they were saying on the radio, telling us all that it was the end! They were talking about thirty–eight confirmed atomic bomb attacks!

CB: What? How? Who? What happened? Our friends in China? any word from them?

CH: I'm sorry everyone – Zhangrong, Biyu, Dingxiang – it's not just the U.S... this is widespread... and... and before confirming they were cutting all funding to our project, the Government of the People's Republic of China were also systematically bombarded with nuclear airstrikes! ... it's despera-tion, it's every man, every human being for themselves! No–one knows who struck first but once one was launched it was a domino effect!

[General hubbub in the meeting.]

CB: Order! Order! I will make up a list of all those and only those that will receive invitations to join us on behalf for ST Corp. We will arrange for private transfers to us here in Solacity. We will do this immediately.

ZSW: I shall do the same for our interests.

BL: Well I'll be goddamned! You see, Chipperman, this is it, we are the world now, we are a superpower! The Superpower!

DX: Mr LeShay is right! Don't you all see? Now literally no–one knows we are here, we must take advantage of this fact! We must accelerate three vital components of our research – synthetic botany, advanced solar collection and weaponry…'

To be continued…

Acknowledgements

My gratitude to Sally Ives and Rowan Thompson, for their invaluable efforts in reading and critiquing early iterations – you gave me the confidence to continue and the insight to improve; to Les Ives for your everlasting, unwavering support throughout my life – this publishing dream has been no different, thank you; to Unbound, without which it may never have happened – thanks for taking a punt on me; and to all those who pledged to support the Axiom crowdfunding campaign online. Words cannot express how grateful I am for the opportunity.